"A deftly crafted contemporary romance novel by an author with a genuine flair for originality and a narrative storytelling style that presents alternating perspectives of Marin and Brad, "Starfish" by Lisa Becker will prove to be an immediate and enduringly popular addition to community library collections."

Midwest Book Review

"The romance is sweet and passionate, providing all the emotions and happenings of a forbidden romance as Brad and Marin's relationship starts off as friendship and grows into something more and the chemistry between the hero and heroine sizzles with lots of heat from every page."

InD'Tale Magazine

"Simply a fun, beautiful, sizzling and adventurous book!!"

Guide to Romance Novels

"IF you are a fan of smiling. IF you are a fan of happiness. IF you are a fan of romance with no cheating, no games, no pretense, no general douchebaggery, well then go ahead and read STARFISH by Lisa Becker. You will be entertained. Your heart will thank you."

Escape in a Book

"Starfish has heart, and the writing is so well done. An enjoyable rockstar romance from start to finish!"

Oh So Many Feels

"This book has all the feels. Made me laugh, made me cry, made me want to tour with Kings Quarters."

Of Texts and Books

"Not your typical rock star romance with interesting dynamics and relationships between all the characters."

Fun Under the Covers

“Ahhh another beautiful novel by the exceptional writer Lisa Becker. I can't seem to get enough of her books.”

Books Writing and More

“I read this all in one night because it was such a witty and heartfelt story that was making me smile. I couldn't put it down!”

Book Book Owl

“Starfish was my first Lisa Becker book, but it sure as hell won’t be my last. I absolutely LOVED everything about this story!”

KSquaredReads

“Starfish is an easy page-turner, filled with heartfelt emotions, clever humor and rockin’ romantic fun. Readers will find themselves fans of the band, the characters and of course the book, too!”

Belles and Rebelles

“This read was the best! If you love anything music related for books, grab this read up”

Novel Grounds

“Starfish is an amazing, fun, hot story that will keep you turning the pages until the very end! Lisa has created another delightful, engrossing tale that will sweep you off your feet.”

The Book Bag

“With a slow burn lusty romance, hot rock stars, funny practical jokes, and just enough drama to keep you going, you’ll fly through this book.”

Roses are Read

“You can’t help falling in love with the characters in Starfish. I think this is Lisa Becker’s best book yet and I loved reading about a rockband on the road.”

Girl with Pen

Praise for Links

"Witty, heartfelt, and emotionally satisfying. Everything I want in a second-chance romance! Once I picked it up, I couldn't put it down!"

New York Times best-selling author Rachel Van Dyken

"A second-chance romance at its finest . . . sweet, alluring, fun, sexy, and romantic. This story is definitely on my top faves list for the year."

Sassy Book Lovers

"Simply put, *Links* will make you fall in love."

The Book Blvd

"I adored this book start to finish . . . The writing was stellar with witty banter, clever humor, and smirk-a-minute teasing exchanges. Lisa Becker is a comedic genius and my new favorite author."

Books & Bindings

"WOW!!! Now I remember why I love Lisa Becker's writing style and stories so much! This is another one to add to the shelves, my friends. You are going to fall head over heels for Charlotte and Garrett's story."

Pretty Little Book Reviews

"This book has a good dose of comedy, especially with the secondary characters. It's funny, sweet, romantic, and will show you that people can change when the time is right."

The Bookery Review

"If you're looking for a perfect summer read, this is one you should pick up."

Lisa Loves Literature

"*Links* by Lisa Becker is the perfect summer read . . . light and quick."

Devilishly Delicious Book Reviews

"Becker has spun a wonderful story about second-chance romance that will have you smiling and wishing this was a series."

So Many Reads Review

"*Links* is a relatively quick and light read. I loved some of the comedic moments and the t-shirts that Charlotte wears with quirky sayings. If there was a sequel or spin-off to this book I would not hesitate to read it."

Much Loved Books

"*Links* is a fun, delightful story that I devoured on my vacation. It is the perfect getaway book that leaves you with a good feeling."

The Book Bag

"One of the best romantic chases I have read."

Donna Huber, Girl Who Reads

"A quick, light, and fun read. Seriously, this book can be devoured in one sitting. The characters and quick-wit banter make you breeze through the pages, all the while laughing and shaking your head at their antics."

Cozy Books and Coffee

"I loved this story. It's light, fun, sexy, and smart."

Two Book Pushers

"This was a feel-good read, one that had me smiling from ear to ear and one that left me with the warm and fuzzies."

The Romance Cover

"All the snark delivered with heart, all the friendship and love to spare truly made this an enjoyable read."

Satisfaction for Insatiable Readers

"If you are looking for a witty, snarky, and cute romantic comedy, then you have definitely come to the right place with *Links*."

Comfy Reading Blog

Praise for Clutch

"I thought the comparison to men and handbags was so genius! Becker really knows how to write to her audience, and this clever novel had me giggling throughout."

Chick Lit Plus

"LOVED. The perfect blend of sassy, smart, and stylish!"

Amazon Bestsellers Liz Fenton & Lisa Steinke

"*Clutch* is a bit like *Sex and the City* meets *Fifty Shades of Grey* sprinkled with a bit of *Bridget Jones's Diary*. It is a fun and lighthearted read and highly enjoyable."

By the Letter Book Reviews

"I loved every minute reading this book!"

Girls with Books

"Fun, witty, and sure to have you laughing and shaking your head!"

Pages Abound

"Becker always delivers a fun, feisty novel that I typically read in just two or three nights. I loved every chapter."

Marika Flatt, PR by the Book

"Do yourself a favor read *Clutch*; I promise you this story will put a smile on your face, and at times, it will melt your heart."

The Kindle Book Review

"She creates characters and stories that are realistic, engaging, and full of charisma."

Radiant Reviews

"*Clutch* was such a fun and lighthearted story. It easily kept me engaged and entertained as Caroline and Mike's opposite approach to dating is full of dramatic and hilarious twists and turns."

Jersey Girl Book Reviews

"The writing is simple yet smart and detailed . . . If you are looking for a sweet and sexy romance, then *Clutch* is for you."

Reading Diva

"*Clutch* is a quick and entertaining read about a woman looking for her one true love. I had so much fun reading Caroline's love adventure. Never a dull moment."

Bookingly Yours

"*Clutch* is a light, fluffy read which is a must-read if you're on the lookout for a cute, short chick lit to devour in one sitting!"

Ruzaika, The Regal Critiques

"Grab a bottle of Caroline's favorite wine, Chardonnay, and sit back and enjoy this fun dating tale!"

One Book at a Time

"As with the Click series, Becker writes good characters, with great, witty dialogue."

Pure Textuality

"This book is absolutely hilarious."

Pretty Little Book Reviews

"I adored everything about this book—the plot, characters, humor, and witty banter. The writing style was crisp, engaging, highly enjoyable, consistently entertaining, and lushly descriptive. I think I have a girl crush . . ."

Books and Bindings

"*Clutch* is a wonderful, entertaining look at the dating world, and I can guarantee that you will start thinking about what category of bag the guys you meet would fall into after reading this book. What fun."

The Book Bag

Also by Lisa Becker

Starfish: A Rock Star Romance

Dear Future Self: A Starfish Novella

Links

Clutch: A Novel

The Click Trilogy
Click: An Online Love Story
Double Click
Right Click

THE SUBWAY GIRL

LISA BECKER

"You don't find love, it finds you.
It's got a little bit to do with destiny,
fate, and what's written in the stars."

Anais Nin

PROLOGUE

Those catlike green eyes. That long, silky brown hair, flowing over her right shoulder from underneath a pink beanie. A radiant smile of straight, gleaming white teeth, lined up perfectly, sinking into a juicy magenta lip.

Ryan Carlson looked up after offering his seat to an elderly passenger and knew his life had changed forever. Leaning against a pole several feet in front of him on the crowded 1 train to Times Square stood the most exquisite woman he had ever seen. And, for just a brief beat, she was looking right at him, too.

In a moment, as quick and powerful as a strike of lightning, he knew he *had* to meet her. *Yeah, right, approach a total stranger on the subway.* He had no doubt he'd come off looking like a weirdo or a stalker, as there was certainly no shortage of those in New York City. He knew he was neither. Just a regular guy, a decent guy, looking for the right girl.

He took a moment to study her further. There was no engagement ring or wedding band on her finger, although she did wear a wide silver thumb ring. She was dressed in a pair of black workout pants, a gray sweater and that pink beanie.

She probably had a boyfriend. One look at her, and it was hard for him to imagine someone wasn't already lucky enough to be with her. He'd been on the receiving end of betrayal and wouldn't put someone else through that kind of hell. Men probably approached her all the time. But maybe she was single.

His mouth went dry as he tried to think of what he would say. He honestly didn't know. It wasn't like this situation had come up before. All he knew was he was determined to meet her. Maybe it was his fate to meet her. *Yes. It's fate.* He was convinced of it.

His heart raced as he took a deep, calming breath. With sweaty palms, he grabbed the pole next to him and pushed forward while he considered his next move. As he got closer to the woman, he could hear her singing to herself under her breath, and her charming accent caused his stomach to clench in the most amazing way.

"Fifty-Ninth Street–Columbus Circle," the conductor droned over the loudspeaker as the subway car rattled and whistled. The lights flickered, and when they came back on, the woman was no longer clinging to her pole. With rising panic, Ryan surveyed the car. She had managed to move toward the door just as the train pulled into the station. Ryan tried to keep an eye on the pink hat as passengers pushed to get off.

A large man with a bad comb over, dressed in a tattered brown suit and scuffed shoes, blocked Ryan's way. Not wanting to be rude, Ryan gently shifted the shabby businessman aside. "Excuse me, getting off," he muttered.

Ryan stepped off the train and stood on the subway platform, two exits before his intended stop, stretching onto his toes to look left and right, seeking out the pink beanie. He jumped up a few times, trying to see over the hordes of people exiting and entering the train.

"Watch it, asshole," a woman carrying two reusable shopping bags said as she pushed her way past him.

"Pardon me, ma'am," he responded. With each passing second, his mystery girl was getting farther and farther away.

Knowing he had a fifty-fifty chance, Ryan turned left and traversed the packed underground tunnel, seeking her out. He walked back and forth, peering up and down staircases and escalators to no avail.

She was gone.

ONE

THREE WEEKS LATER

Angie Prince examined Ryan as he raised his hand to his brow, shielding himself from the bright light, while a sound engineer strapped a microphone battery to the back of his belt.

Ryan was dressed in a pair of stonewashed jeans, suede sneakers and a fitted gray button-down shirt. Simple. Casual. Comfortable. He was a good-looking guy, in a classic, boy-next-door way. Light brown hair, a little long and wavy on top, framed an oval face with caramel-colored eyes, an unassuming nose, high cheekbones and full lips. In her background research, Angie had found he was an All-American baseball star in high school. He was tall, broad—but not overly built—and athletic. Yeah, the camera was going to love him.

"I'm not crazy, you know. Or a stalker. I'm really just a normal guy," Ryan called out, interrupting her inspection of him as the lights dimmed and he noticed her looking his way.

"Don't worry. We'll make sure you come across just as earnest as you are," Angie assured him. She walked to him and patted his shoulder, impressed with the solid build underneath his shirt.

She turned away and trotted over to Harlan Jacobson, the barrel-built camera operator, whose tight-fitting t-shirt barely covered his overrunning belly.

"Is this aw-shucks, good-guy, country-bumpkin crap for real?" She snorted. "You should have heard him talking earlier about true love and fate," she added with a roll of her eyes.

"Our audience is going to eat this shit up. It's brilliant, Ange," said Harlan, pulling up his dark chinos from the back, which fell right back down to their position low on his hips.

"I know. Ryan is my ticket out of this tabloid hellhole." Angie balled her hands into fists.

"I don't know why you're always complaining. You're a shareholder. When the website goes network, you're gonna be rich."

"Well, yeah, when Barry convinced me to invest in the company two years ago, he gave me a stake in future ad revenues and a payout if he ever sells the show to television," she explained. "But before that, when he first hired me for this job, he said I would get the chance to do serious news stories, not this crap."

"Trusting Barry was your first mistake," Harlan said, shaking his head.

"And my second?" asked Angie, her hands perched on her hips.

"Getting the investment buy-in money from your mom."

Angie sighed, her shoulders sagging in acknowledgment that Harlan was right. *Why did I let my mom mortgage the house so I could take on this risk?*

"Well, this is it," she said with uncharacteristic enthusiasm. "This series is going to be a huge hit, Barry's going to get his deal, I'm going to get my money back, Mom is going to keep her house, and I can finally quit this shit job," she said with conviction.

"Oh yeah. Sounds foolproof. Nothing could go wrong there." Harlan looked down his nose at her. Angie stuck her tongue out at him, as Barry Osler, their boss, walked over.

Barry wore a black Zegna suit with a sharp purple tie and crisp black shirt. With his slicked-back hair and dark hooded eyes, he looked like a Mafia boss ready to call a hit. When his tongue darted out of his mouth to lick his thin, dry lips, he took on a lizard-like quality, and not in that "cute GEICO Gecko with the Cockney accent" way. No, he looked like a creepy, slimy reptile.

"How is our superstar doing?" Barry asked.

"Oh, I'm fine, thank you." Angie lifted one shoulder in an attempt at humor.

"I was talking about Ryan there," he said, "but *you* will be my superstar if you succeed here. I have a meeting with the network later today, and I don't need to remind you that a home run here and we're certain to take *Celebrity Monger* to the next level."

Angie didn't need reminding. Her future was wrapped up in her ability to succeed right here, right now, with this story. If she could help Barry get a network deal for their web program, her personal windfall from the sale would be enough to pay off her mom's mortgage and provide a cushion for her to quit her job and find a better one.

"Listen, I was thinking we could–" began Angie.

Barry cut her off. "I need you to make sure Ryan signs the release form giving us unfettered rights to all the footage we shoot. He must also sign the exclusivity agreement. When this thing gets big, and believe me, it will, I don't want him running off to *TMZ* or the *Today* show. I want all eyeballs on *Celebrity Monger*." He thrust a clipboard at her.

"Yeah. I got it. But listen, Barry, I was thinking we could do a more hard-hitting piece about love, technology and–"

"How many times do I have to tell you?" he barked. "Our audience doesn't give a rat's ass about hard-hitting, unless it's the latest scoop on a steroid-ravaged athlete hitting his girlfriend. Just stick to what works and get him to sign."

Angie nodded and bit her tongue, something she only did with Barry. With everyone else, she spoke her mind, argued her point, engaged in confrontation. Barry's phone rang and he moved aside to answer it.

She turned to Harlan. "I went to Columbia School of Journalism for this? I only took this gig to pay the bills until I could be a serious journalist. Three years later and I'm still peddling this junk." She watched Barry, still on the phone, as his eyes lit up like those of a child offered an oversized novelty lollipop.

"So, quit already," Harlan said with a shrug.

"You know I can't." It was easy for Harlan to say that. His future and his mom's home weren't wrapped up in the success of this show.

"I understand, Angie. I do. Despite needing the money, you also have principles and lofty aspirations. Lucky for me, I don't." He chuckled. "Cash is king. The way I see it, I've got a job that pays me handsomely and gets me access to some of the hottest spots in town where celebrities hang out," he said, grinning.

"And I love you for it." She tapped his arm, warmed by his honesty and humor.

"I've never heard you utter the word *love* before," said Harlan, giving her a sideways glance.

That's because love isn't real, she wanted to say. But she knew he was teasing her. Angie stuck her tongue out at him again, as Barry hung up his phone and returned to them.

"That was one of my contacts at the Bellamy Hotel. Some teenage sitcom star just checked in to a room with a known prostitute. This is gold. I need to get going," he said with a devilish smile. He turned to Angie. "Go get him to sign." He tapped his foot impatiently.

Angie looked over to find Ryan engaged in a friendly conversation with the woman who was applying a thin layer of powder to his face. He smiled at the makeup artist and said something that made her giggle. Ryan gave a small shrug and an impish grin. The makeup artist shook her head and giggled again. Ryan's charm was going to come across perfectly on the screen. Angie gave herself a mental high five for scoring this winning opportunity.

Ryan looked up from the conversation about the childhood incident that led to the little scar under his chin to see Angie walking toward him.

She was tiny. She couldn't have been more than five foot one and had a small build. Ryan thought of that *Star Wars* Yoda quote about the folly of judging someone for their size and chuckled to himself. He definitely wouldn't make that mistake with Angie. She might be small, but he imagined that when she got fired up and poked a finger in your chest to make a point, you knew she meant business.

When she'd first approached him about taking his Subway Girl search to the *Celebrity Monger* website, he'd initially balked. She talked about fame and notoriety, page views and daily rankings. She was passionate and fiery. But it was when she explained that the added exposure on the national platform would increase the likelihood the Subway Girl would recognize herself—that's when she hooked him.

He guessed a lot of guys disregarded how spirited Angie could be because they were blinded by not just her size, but her adorableness. She looked like the Kewpie doll his little sister had when they were kids. Big, wide eyes with long eyelashes, a small upturned nose, round cheeks, and heart-shaped lips.

"So, Ryan, we're just about ready to get started. I think your story is beautiful, and I promise to do it justice and help you find the Subway Girl. Before we begin, I need to get your signature on those two documents your attorney reviewed last week." She handed him a clipboard. "First, this is the release form, which gives us permission to use any of the footage we shoot. Please initial each page and sign and date the last one."

Ryan took the clipboard from her hand and smiled. "No problem. Just promise to only shoot my good side," he joked. Although, as with most jokes, there was some element of truth in it. He hoped he wouldn't come across as a weirdo and they could find his mystery woman quickly. His stomach churned at the thought of another public humiliation. He shuffled through the sheets of paper, initialing where indicated, and signed and dated the bottom page before handing the clipboard back to Angie.

"And this one is the exclusivity agreement. This basically says that you won't do interviews about the Subway Girl with any other news outlets or websites." She attached the second document to the clipboard and handed it back to Ryan with the pen.

"So we're in this together?" he asked as he signed.

"Absolutely. Finding the Subway Girl is my top priority," she said with conviction.

"Well, I was surprised when you came calling, so I can't imagine anyone else jumping on board. If this helps me find her, though, I'm in."

"Okay, then. Thanks. Be right back, and we'll get started," said Angie. She walked the papers over to Barry. As Ryan watched her retreating form, he felt hopeful. And for the first time since Angie had come calling about all this, his stomach settled. This was where he was supposed to be. *This crazy idea just might work out after all.*

Barry took the clipboard, glanced through to ensure the signatures and dates were complete, and then kissed Angie on the forehead. Despite her best efforts to hide it, Angie shuddered.

"Well done," he said, licking his lips, his eyes gleaming. He walked out of the studio, no doubt on his way to manipulate the next big tabloid story.

Angie turned to Harlan. "All right. Let's get this romantic shitshow started." She plastered a phony smile on her face, while Harlan shook his head and laughed quietly.

"Some guy, somewhere, really did a number on you," he said.

Angie gave him a playful sneer and walked over to Ryan. "Let's begin. I'm going to ask you some questions, and you just look at me and answer them as best you can. Sound good?"

"Okay. Ready," Ryan said, but by the way he shifted in his seat, Angie could tell he was nervous. She turned to Harlan and indicated they were ready to start rolling. Harlan turned on his camera and gave Angie a thumbs-up.

"So, Ryan," said Angie. "Tell me a bit about yourself."

After a deep breath, Ryan looked toward the camera and said, "My name is Ryan Carlson, and I'm a web designer in New York. I'm originally from a small town in Iowa and moved to Manhattan about three years ago." He paused and looked back at Angie. "How was that?"

"That was a great start," she lied. "Just ignore the camera, though." Angie worried he wouldn't be comfortable enough to do the interview and she wouldn't get the footage she needed to cut the piece.

"Okay. Should we do that again?"

"Sure. I'll ask the same question. Your response was perfect. Just look into my eyes and talk to me, like you and I are having a friendly conversation," she advised. "Just like the first time we met and you shared your story with me." They tried again, and this time Ryan relaxed, looking into Angie's eyes. As he spoke, she noticed sincerity in them. He didn't seem like the type of guy who was just interested in some fleeting internet fame.

No, he seemed *genuinely* interested in the Subway Girl. That honesty and authenticity was something Angie hadn't expected when she first approached him. She initially figured he was some sad-sack loser/stalker, unable to get a date and fixated on this poor girl. She didn't expect him to be good looking. Or polite. Or sincere. Or what she could only describe as kind. Yet he was all those things, and she just knew the public was going to eat this romance up, even if she didn't agree that love—*real* love—was possible.

"Ryan, you had what you consider a life-changing subway ride a few weeks ago. Can you tell me about that?"

"I was riding the subway from a client meeting back to the office when I saw . . . her." His smile brightened. "I'd never seen anyone so beautiful in my life. And she had a *Playbill* for *Wicked* tucked into her bag. I had just seen that show the day before and thought it had to be some sort of sign."

His eyes glazed over a bit. "But it was more than that. Even though we only made eye contact for a brief moment, it felt like she saw me. Really saw *me*. And despite being strangers, it felt like we'd shared a thousand memories. That probably doesn't make any sense, but that's what happened." He shrugged as if he couldn't explain it better. "I just knew I had to meet her. Before I could muster the courage, the train pulled into the station and she was gone."

"What was going through your mind when you saw her?"

"It's hard to explain. I just knew I had to get to know her. I know that makes me sound crazy or like a stalker. I can assure you I'm neither of those. I'm just a guy who really believes in fate," he said with another genuine yet playful shrug.

"That's really beautiful." Angie mustered all the sweetness possible while thinking, *What a rube*. "From what I understand, you did something rather unusual to try and find her. Can you tell us about that?"

"Being a web designer, I turned to the medium I know best. I created a website called TheSubwayGirl.com and included all the information I could remember about her. I sent the link out to my friends in the city in the hopes they could help me identify her or she would hear about this and recognize herself."

"Can you describe her for us?"

"She is a beautiful brunette with striking green eyes. She was listening to a bright pink iPod Nano and reading a paperback booklet. She had on a pink beanie. It was March ninth around three o'clock in the afternoon. She was riding the 1 and got off at Fifty-Ninth Street–Columbus Circle. Oh, and she had the most charming British accent."

"Well, she certainly sounds like something special," said Angie, smiling up at him, as sincerely as she could. "I'm confident we can help you find her." *I need to find her,* she thought.

"The good news is that it led me to you." His face brightened.

"To me?" Angie asked, a bit flustered. She wasn't sure why that rattled her, but it did.

"You and *Celebrity Monger*," Ryan explained. "I'm hoping the legitimacy of this is going to convince her to contact me." Angie stifled a laugh as she glanced back at Harlan with an incredulous look. She couldn't believe Ryan thought *Celebrity Monger* was legit. Harlan winked at her.

"How was that?" she called.

"As Barry would say, 'Gold! Pure gold!'" Harlan said. "Angie, let's have you over here and record a kicker for us." He motioned for Angie to move to a lit space within the studio to record a closing sound bite for the segment.

Angie looked directly into the camera. "*Celebrity Monger* has set up a special link where the Subway Girl can send a video to Ryan. We all hope to hear from you."

Harlan gave Angie another thumbs-up, and she removed her microphone and returned to Ryan.

"That was great, Ryan. We'll cut the piece together and have it up tomorrow. Hopefully she will see the story and reach out to us. I'll call you with an update."

"Thank you so much, Angie. I'm grateful for all your help." Ryan smiled.

"Sure thing," she replied, brushing him off. She wasn't used to people being so genuinely appreciative. Uncertain how to respond and confused by the foreign fluttering in her belly, she swallowed hard and plastered on a fake grin.

"You're my Ambassador of Quan."

Angie stared at him blankly.

"You know," Ryan said. "From *Jerry Maguire* . . . the movie."

"Of course. Yeah. *Jerry Maguire*," replied Angie, faking it. "All right, then. I'll be in touch." She walked away toward Harlan. A production assistant guided Ryan out through the studio door while Angie shook her body in mock disgust. "I feel like I need to take a shower."

"Aw, don't say that. He seems like a sweet kid," said Harlan.

"Exactly. Sweet." Angie tried to keep the sneer from her tone. So sweet he was giving her a cavity, which reminded her she needed to make an appointment to see the dentist about all the tooth pain she had been having. And go grocery shopping. And balance her checkbook. *Ugh! So much to do.* But this, this right here was the priority. This needed to happen. "But hey, when America falls for this romantic shit, all the better for me."

Across town, Barry unbuttoned his high-end men's jacket, making him more comfortable as he gestured in front of the large TV mounted on the conference room wall.

"Here you can see our weekly traffic has increased at a consistent rate, outpacing our competitors like *TMZ* and *Dlisted* who also inhabit this space." He gestured to a colorful GIF of a chart, which repeatedly showed the growth of *Celebrity Monger* over other tabloid sites.

"What do you think accounts for your success over theirs?" asked one of the television executives, a generic-looking suit, indistinguishable from his colleagues in the room.

"I think it's important to note that our competitors have seen a sizable increase in traffic, too. We just happen to do it better than them." He clicked a handheld remote and advanced the presentation to the next animated slide. "In fact, our ad revenue has also grown exponent–"

"But what sets *you* apart? Why you and not *TMZ*?" the executive interrupted.

"Two reasons," began Barry. "First, we have the most comprehensive and exclusive network of busboys, bellhops, personal assistants, valets, concierges and limo drivers out there right now. When any type of celebrity scandal happens–from crimes against spouses to crimes against fashion–we are the first to break the news."

"Those numbers are fluid," said another suit, with skepticism. Other suits nodded in agreement. "In order to get the green light, we'd need to demonstrate the viability of a television show based on your site."

The first network executive, who seemed most intrigued with Barry's proposal, called out, "You said two reasons. What's the second?"

"I think you'll be pleased with another original exclusive we are starting tomorrow called the Subway Girl, which chronicles a man's search for the dream girl he saw and subsequently lost on a crowded subway."

"Is this a scripted show?" asked a suit.

"No. This is a real guy, looking for a real girl, and we've locked in an exclusive with him. It's going to drive page views and online engagement beyond other exclusive series we've done before."

"As you know, that's the bottom line for us," said an executive. "Ratings drive revenue." Several of the other executives looked at each other and made low chatter. "Let us take a look at your proposal in more detail, and we'll be in touch about setting up a meeting with JP."

Barry reached over and shook hands with each of the suits. "Excellent. Let me just say this deal will be a win-win for all. Our audience will get all the news they want, our network of informants will get handsomely rewarded, and your investors will get a great ROI as our ad revenues skyrocket."

As he walked out the door, Barry's initial confidence faltered. Before this meeting, he'd believed the website's current rate of growth—both in general terms and in relation to the competition—would be enough to secure a meeting with the head of the network. It was now clear that aggressive growth would be needed to push these execs over the edge toward deciding in his favor. *Angie better deliver.*

TWO

Angie dropped her keys into a small bowl next to the front door as she walked into the Brooklyn apartment she shared with her bestie, Josie. While the commute home was longer than her previous walk to the Manhattan apartment she'd shared with her ex, this place was worth it. It boasted two bedrooms with walk-in closets, a living room with enough space for a couch *and* a love seat, a kitchen allowing more than one person to stand inside it at a time, and someone who always had her back. To Angie, it was a respite from the hectic, crap-filled world outside.

After changing out of her work clothes, she flopped onto the couch. She rubbed her neck and let out a loud exhale, feeling the effects of a long day on the job and dealing with Barry. She chuckled to herself, recalling her interaction with Ryan. What was the deal with that guy? She'd never met anyone so seemingly honest and sincere. There had to be something else going on there. But at this point in her "career"–if she could call it that–she wasn't worried about finding out. Whether he turned out to be a sweet, lovesick farm boy or a psychopath, it was all fine with her. Either way it meant ratings, and ratings were her ticket out.

While she scrolled through her favorite Thai restaurant's online menu and debated between pad thai and panang curry, Josie busted through the door.

"Yes!" Josie pumped her fist in the air. "You're home."

"I'm home," Angie agreed.

"Get up and get changed." Josie leaned over and kissed the top of Angie's head. "We're going out."

"I've already taken my bra off. That's the international sign for 'not going back out tonight,'" Angie replied, grinning at Josie and batting her eyelashes. Josie pulled Angie off the couch and dragged her down the hall toward her bedroom.

"It's supposed to be the international sign for 'touch my boobs,'" Josie fired back. Angie chuckled. Josie lifted her scrub top over her head and sniffed her armpits. Angie cringed and Josie swatted at her playfully.

"Well, clearly I'm not speaking the sex language, and that's not just because I'm in for the night."

Josie grabbed a white peasant blouse, which looked beautiful against her dark skin, and shrugged it on before pulling her hair out of its ponytail and shaking it out with her hands.

"And who's fault is that?" Josie pulled down her scrub pants and tossed them into the laundry hamper, grabbing a pair of skinny jeans at the same time.

"Based on how low that blouse goes, looks like I will be in for the night . . . all alone." Angie wiggled her eyebrows up and down.

"Come on. I only want to have a drink or two. This isn't about guys. This is about me," begged Josie. "It was a crazy week at the hospital."

Angie groaned.

"Please. I just want to let off a little steam, and then I promise we'll be back here, on the couch, TV remote in hand."

"Ugh. My bra is off," Angie whined. Despite her protests, she was heading to her bedroom to change into some going-out clothes.

"You don't even need a bra," Josie shouted down the hall.

Angie walked back to Josie's doorway. "Thanks for the reminder. You know, you're not endearing yourself to me right now." Angie wagged a finger at Josie in jest. Josie swatted the finger away.

"What I mean is you have a gorgeous petite figure. I would kill to be able to wear a backless shirt like you can. My girls would be hanging down to my knees."

Angie let out a howl of laughter while Josie pushed her out of the doorway toward her bedroom.

Twenty minutes later, Josie and Angie found themselves at Malone's, the local bar a few blocks from their Brooklyn apartment.

"So, how was work?" Josie asked.

"Oh, you know." Angie sipped her gin and tonic. "Same shit. Different day."

"Wow! That's some serious constipation you've got there."

"Good thing I have a nurse around," Angie said. "What about you? What was so awful about today?"

"First, there was this really good-looking guy who brought his buddy into the ER with severe abdominal pain. I'm taking his statement about what his buddy had eaten, where he had been when the pain started, and he's totally flirting with me. And then he pulls his hand from his pocket and the glare from his shiny wedding ring practically blinds me."

"Ugh! I hate that." *More infidelity. Shocker.*

"Yeah. Nothing worse than spotting an amazing-looking guy and then he stands up to kiss his wife," Josie groaned.

"Worse, he stands up and is smoking a cigarette." Angie waved her hand in front of her face and scrunched up her nose in disgust, like she could smell the smoke right there.

"Agreed. And I'm not just saying that as a healthcare provider."

"Ooh. Even worse. He stands up and he's wearing cut-off denim shorts," Angie said.

"Ding-ding-ding! That's your winner."

"So aside from the flirty married guy, what else happened?"

"This first-year resident yelled at *me*," Josie scoffed. "*Me*. Like it was *my* fault that *he* couldn't put in a PICC line."

"Did you say 'pick-up line'?" An athletically built guy with short brown hair and a smug, lopsided smile leaned on the bar next to Josie. He wore a fitted gray t-shirt with an outline of Superman in Clark Kent glasses and a "Super Hipster" slogan. "I wouldn't yell at you for sharing one of those."

Angie rolled her eyes at the cheesiness. Josie, as usual, seemed less offended by the cheese and smiled brightly at him.

"Is that your attempt at a pick-up line?" Josie said.

"I'm not about attempts. I'm about completions," he replied with a smirk. *Ugh! This guy is a Neanderthal.*

Although Josie was getting her flirt on, Angie knew the guy wasn't getting lucky tonight. First, Josie had promised to return to the apartment with her, and Josie was a woman of her word. And second, she knew from experience when Josie was directing sincerity in a guy's direction and *this* . . . this just wasn't going to happen.

It didn't stop Josie from engaging in some friendly conversation while she polished off her cocktail. So over the next twenty minutes, Josie and Super Hipster shared their favorite pick-up lines and joked about funny dating experiences. Meanwhile, Angie—ever the wing woman—made small talk with the guy's buddy.

Once Angie saw Josie's glass was empty, save for a small sliver of ice that had yet to melt, she tilted her head toward the door, indicating it was time to go.

Super Hipster clearly noticed Angie's interest in calling it a night. He leaned in and whispered in Josie's ear. Josie tilted her head and gave him a sympathetic smile.

"Sorry. That's not why we came out tonight. But thank you," she said.

Josie was so sweet. Even when she was turning you down, she did it in such a nice way. But Super Hipster didn't like Josie's rejection, softened as it was.

"Fuck, you're such a tease," he said while shaking his head. "Maybe she's a lesbian." He smirked, turning to his friend and tapping him on the chest with the back of his hand. Josie, with a disgusted look on her face, was about to respond when Angie stepped in front of her and stared the guy down. He looked down at Angie's tiny frame with a "what are you going to do about it?" expression.

"There are a lot of reasons a woman wouldn't want to go home with a guy, and they have nothing to do with being a tease or her sexual orientation," Angie said, pointing a finger at him.

"Oh yeah." He chuckled. "And I suppose you're going to enlighten me, Tinkerbell." *Tinkerbell. Oh, hell no.*

Super Hipster looked at his friend, and the two guys laughed. Angie thought back to a meme she recently saw about not being fragile like a flower but being fragile like a bomb. Little did Super Hipster know, but she was about to go off.

"I'm quite certain I could rattle off ten reasons right here. Care to place a wager on it?"

Super Hipster looked at her as if he couldn't believe this tiny little thing was planning to rip him a new one. "Sure. Loser pays the winner's tab."

"Deal!" She thrust her hand out for a shake. Once they had agreed, she gave him a friendly grin and batted her eyelashes before climbing up onto a barstool. "Attention, everyone!" Several people around her took notice and quieted down their conversations. "Attention!" she repeated, garnering a larger audience. "This . . ." She shuddered. "This *Neanderthal* here thinks the only reason a woman wouldn't want to go home with him is because she's a tease or a lesbian. I'm here to offer him some other possibilities."

Super Hipster's shoulders turned in and his look of confidence faltered. She smiled inwardly. He'd clearly underestimated her.

"So here goes. One, she has her period." Angie raised one finger in the air. Several of the guys that comprised her audience looked uncomfortable, while a few of the women nodded in agreement. "Two, she has a yeast infection." Those uncomfortable-looking guys were looking even more pained; the women let out small giggles.

"Three. Maybe she prefers that the guy at least *knows her name*," Angie sneered at Super Hipster, indicating her disdain for asking Josie to go home with him before he even asked her name. He rolled his eyes and shook his head, though his subtle shift from one foot to the other didn't go unnoticed by Angie. She could tell she was getting to him.

"Four. She has a dog at home that needs to be walked. Number five, she has an early-morning yoga class."

"C'mon," Super Hipster scoffed. Angie gestured to the ladies who were gathered around, and they all nodded in agreement. Angie gave Super Hipster a knowing smile.

"Number six." She pressed her hands together in prayer and looked heavenward. "She's gotten the calling from God and is leaving for the convent tomorrow." The crowd laughed along.

"If she's joining a nunnery, she should go out with him." a floppy-haired blond dude shouted out. "You know, go out with a bang."

"No," chimed in Josie. She turned to Super Hipster. "Surely she would only be disappointed."

"Ooooh," the growing crowd responded.

"Maybe she's just afraid I'll ruin her for all other men," Super Hipster retorted.

"Sure." Angie shrugged. "Why not?" She rolled her eyes. "We'll make that number seven. Thanks for the help, by the way." Super Hipster tipped an imaginary hat to her and then gestured for her to continue. He seemed less uncomfortable and more amused with each explanation.

"Reason number eight, she just thinks you're a prick, and reason number nine, she figures you only *think* with your prick. Finally, number ten, maybe she doesn't want to go home with you because she's just afraid you *have a tiny prick*." The crowd erupted into cheers, both the men and the women congratulating her on an epic takedown. Super Hipster and his buddy bowed down to Angie as Josie helped her from the barstool. "And bonus, number eleven," Angie said, leaning into him. "She doesn't need a reason. She doesn't owe you anything."

"Damn," Super Hipster muttered. "You just tore me a new one, Tinkerbell."

Angie smirked. She called out to the crowd of twenty or so bar patrons who had been enjoying the show, "Next round on me." She turned to the bartender and waved her hand toward the group that had been listening. "Put the next round on my tab . . . and then give my tab to him." She pointed to Super Hipster, who lowered his head and shook it back and forth before acknowledging to the bartender that he would pay the bill.

"So, if I wanted to take *you* home with me"—he pointed to Angie—"I guess I need to ask your name. Unless you prefer to be called Tinkerbell?" he said in amusement.

"Why don't you stick with Tinkerbell, because I'm not going home with you. You will never be calling out my name. And I would have no doubt rocked your world."

Super Hipster shook his head and exhaled sharply through his nose, as if admitting defeat. "Well played," he conceded. "Well played."

Angie curtsied, then looped her arm through Josie's. She turned to the crowd, who were enjoying their free drinks and chattering about her performance.

"Good night. Don't forget to tip your waitress," Angie called out. A smattering of applause followed her and Josie out the door. The two giggled all the way back to their apartment.

THREE

Frankie Lee, dressed in an Ella Moss sheath dress and Tory Burch platform shoes, strode into the Bloomingdale's employee breakroom and surveyed her surroundings. Human resources posters touting workplace safety, OSHA standards and time-off policies covered the walls, while fashion magazines from *Lucky* to *Vogue* littered the tables.

Two of her co-workers sat on cushioned folding chairs around a table. Corrine, a full-figured woman, was eating a salad from a takeout container. She was the leader in store commissions due to the big personality that matched the big curves. Devoted clients and new customers alike flocked to her for fashion advice.

Sitting next to her, in stark contrast, was Donna, who was built like a fourteen-year-old boy. The other salespeople nicknamed her "The Human Hanger" because everything looked good on her. She knew it, too.

Frankie internally sneered as Donna methodically reviewed each page of a fashion magazine—including the ads—and placed

Post-it notes on items of interest, which would no doubt look perfect on her.

Also in the room was Maria, a curly-haired pixie with a heart of gold. If there was a flyer on the bulletin board asking for donations to a charity or offering a reward for a lost pet, chances were Maria posted it. Her eyes were trained on her cell phone, earbuds in her ears, as she sat on a tan couch against the breakroom wall. Frankie was certain Maria hadn't even noticed she'd walked in.

"Noelle is such a bitch. She's making me work new inventory this weekend," complained Frankie, looking in the full-length mirror affixed to one of the walls. She tilted her head side to side, examining the application of her eye shadow.

"That's what you get for flirting with her husband," said Corrine sassily.

Then she shouldn't let a tall, dark and yummy man like that walk around the women's department unattended.

"At least you'll get to see all the new Vince Camutos before they hit the floor," said Donna. "Maybe you'll find one that suits you."

Of course, she brought up the Camutos. She knows I can't pull off those silhouettes.

Before Frankie could think of a snappy response, Maria pulled the earbuds out of her ears and sighed.

"What's it this time, Maria? More returning soldiers surprising their kids at school?" asked Corrine.

"No. It's this romantic story about this guy who sees a girl on a crowded subway and now he's trying to find her," Maria replied with another dreamy sigh.

"So . . . a stalker," said Frankie. Donna laughed as Corrine gave Maria a sympathetic look.

"No, he's this really sweet romantic. He just fell for her, and before he had the courage to talk to her, she got off the subway, and he's desperate to find her."

"Sounds like a future serial killer to me," said Frankie, shaking her head. She walked over to the refrigerator and pulled out a takeout food container. She popped it in the microwave, and while it heated up she scrolled through messages on her phone.

"I'll be the judge," said Donna, grabbing Maria's phone. Her eyes grew wide, and she got a mischievous smile on her face. "Hey, Frankie," she called. "Isn't this your ex-boyfriend?"

Frankie walked over and looked at Maria's phone. "Gimme that." She moved her finger along the screen to start the video over and watched as some reporter interviewed Ryan about his Subway Girl search.

"That is him, isn't it?" cackled Donna.

"He's famous," remarked Corrine, impressed.

"Famously lame," said Frankie. "One clip on *Celebrity Monger* doesn't make you famous." *What the hell?* Frankie considered Ryan and his never-ending quest for true love. What a sap. Sure, she had loved him once, when they were in high school. But once she got to New York and her eyes were opened to the world, she knew he was too small-town, too simple for her. She should have been happy for him. Happy that he was finding someone else, but why would he be so public about it and embarrass her like this?

"You should know," said Donna. "Sounds like you're jealous."

"Of what?" Frankie said defensively. "That some other poor girl is the object of his affection?" *He used to be all moony-eyed like that over me.*

"No, that his move is getting him more play on *Celebrity Monger* than your fling with that baller."

I really hate her, Frankie thought. Since when did Ryan even know anything about celebrities, and why would he be involved with *Celebrity Monger*?

"I don't care about stuff like that." Frankie suppressed the desire to snort . . . or protest too much . . . or just slap Donna across the face.

"Since when?" Donna asked skeptically.

"That's your ex? He's so cute," interrupted Maria, giving yet another sigh. "I wish a guy like that would see me on the subway and track me down."

"What about Simon?" Corrine asked, referring to Maria's on-again, off-again beau.

"Oh, he just calls when he wants a blow job."

"Don't they all," said Frankie with a shake of her head, happy to have the subject changed.

A stone's throw from Bloomingdale's, Ryan, Luke and Diego stared at an oversized computer monitor in one of the minimal but functional offices of their graphic design shop in midtown Manhattan. Luke used manicured fingers to sweep his shaggy blond hair to the side. He was in dire need of a trim and kept swiping the hair out of his eyes while he studied the screen. Ryan had no idea why a guy who was so well groomed would let so much time pass between haircuts.

Ryan and Luke had started their own graphic design business three years ago when Ryan moved to New York but was struggling to land a job. After their chance encounter in the elevator on Ryan's way to an ad agency interview, he and Luke struck up a friendship and business venture.

"Dude, just get your hair cut already. I'm getting tired of watching you push that shit off your face," said Ryan.

"I can take care of that for you." Diego ran his hands over his buzzcut. Diego Sandoval had joined Ryan and Luke a year ago to handle billing and financials as the company grew. "Got the clippers at home and could bring 'em in," he offered.

"Trust you with my gorgeous locks?" Luke gestured to his hair as he walked back to his desk. "I don't think so, asswipe. If your cut is any indication of your hairstyling talent, I'll pass."

"You wish you could pull off this look," said Diego, preening.

"The only buzz I want is after a few cold beers at a bar full of hot women," said Luke.

Ryan leaned over for a fist bump. "All right, then. Make an appointment at that fancy man-salon you go to. It's becoming an annoying distraction." He edged back to his desk to review the Mendoza project.

"I'm growing it out," Luke explained with a shrug. "GQ says long and shaggy is the next big look."

"God forbid you're not at the height of fashion," said Diego, swiveling in his chair to look back at his computer.

"Can't disappoint my fans," Luke quipped. "Not everyone wants to look like they're reporting for duty."

"I'll have you know the ladies love this."

"Since when do you know any ladies?"

Diego scowled but otherwise ignored Luke's jab. "Feel this," he said, sliding on his office chair across the wood floor and pushing his head toward Luke. Luke playfully slapped his cheek, turning Diego's head away. Diego leaned over to Ryan, who ran his palm over the short hairs.

"Yeah," Ryan admitted. "That actually feels nice."

Luke laughed. "When did you get so in touch with your feminine side?"

"You're asking *me* about my feminine side? You're the one with a manicurist on speed dial," Ryan said. Diego reached his hand out for a high five. "Anyway, I'm secure enough in my masculinity to touch a guy's head and comment on how his hair feels."

"Yeah, you're all man," conceded Luke, "and believe me, the ladies are going to eat that shit up." He gestured to Diego's monitor, where Ryan's *Celebrity Monger* interview had just played. "Oh, he's so sweet. Oh, he's so romantic," he said in a high-pitched, mock-female voice, clasping his hands over his shoulder, batting his eyelashes and raising his remarkably well-groomed eyebrows up and down. Returning to his normal tone, he said, "Ladies are going to be waiting in line."

Ryan scowled. "I just want to meet her." He glanced back over at Diego's computer terminal. He couldn't shake the feeling that fate was at work here. That something about this was meant to be. Without that pull of the unexplainable, there was zero chance he would have been undertaking this crazy search. He just hoped his family and friends back home didn't get wind of it. His breakup with Frankie had been a source of embarrassment for him back in his small hometown. Everyone had assumed they were meant to be, including Ryan. He didn't want to endure public humiliation again.

As if he could read Ryan's mind, Luke asked with a disapproving look, "You think she's the one and not that cheater, Frankie?"

"Hey, she may not be perfect, but she's still—" Ryan rushed out.

"A heartless wench?"

"She's still the first girl I ever loved," said Ryan wistfully. "If that makes me sound like a chick, so be it." He shrugged. It wouldn't be the first time the guys razzed him for wearing his heart on his sleeve. He was used to their good-natured ribbing and gave as good as he got. "Not all of us want to be a three G-er."

"Three G-er?" asked Diego.

"You know. Like Luke here," Ryan said. "Get in. Get off. Get out." Diego laughed out loud.

"Speaking of three G-ing, want to hit Bar None tonight? It's ladies' night," said Luke.

"Yeah, a cold beer sounds good." Ryan could use a drink now that this whole thing had launched into the stratosphere. "If I'm going to get out of here in time, I've got to get the Mendoza site finished, and you guys need to get those graphics and invoices done ASAP. But first, I've got to take a leak." Ryan walked back into his office to find Luke holding his phone and crooning into it seductively.

"Angie Prince, huh? You're that gorgeous reporter from *Celebrity Monger.* I just saw you on the web. I'm Luke, Ryan's boss." Ryan shook his head, grabbed the phone from Luke's ear and punched him in the arm.

"Gimme that," he said to Luke with a scowl. "Hey Angie. It's Ryan. What's up?"

"Hi. Listen, we've already gotten some hits on the link we set up for the Subway Girl. Can you come down tomorrow morning and we'll look through them?"

"*Some* hits? Huh." Ryan wondered why there would be more than one response. "Well, sure. I can be there. What time?" He would have to skip Bar None and put in some extra hours so he could steal away tomorrow.

"How about nine-thirty? Harlan will meet us there and set up the room so we can record the viewing session."

"You're going to record me watching videos?" He was confused as to how him watching a video would itself make for good video.

"Our viewers will want to see your reaction when the Subway Girl contacts you," she explained. Ryan considered her response, which made sense. He might like to have his reaction to her for posterity himself.

"Okay. Yeah. Sure. See you tomorrow." He turned his attention back to his bank of computer monitors. "No can do on Bar None tonight," he called over to Luke and Diego. "Have fun without me."

"We always do," deadpanned Luke.

"Asshole," muttered Ryan on a laugh.

FOUR

Ryan walked up to the receptionist at *Celebrity Monger*, butterflies swarming in his belly. He was nervous and anxious at the thought of meeting the girl from that subway car nearly a month ago. The girl that some crazy force was pulling him toward.

"Hi," he said to the receptionist, Gina, whose head was down, browsing a celebrity gossip magazine. She glanced up with what appeared to be an annoyed look on her face at being interrupted. But when her gaze landed on Ryan's smile, she smiled in return and tucked a strand of hair behind her ear.

"I'm Ryan—"

"Oh, I know who you are," she breathed out, licking her bottom lip and re-tucking the hairs.

"Oh," Ryan said in surprise. He shook his head and chuckled at his naïveté. Of course she knew who he was. She worked here. He wasn't certain he would get used to people recognizing him or being invested in his story.

"So . . ." She twirled a chunk of hair around her finger, tilted her head back and forth and smiled.

"So . . . could you let Angie know I'm here?"

"Angie, yeah, right," she repeated. She lifted her phone and dialed Angie's extension. "Ryan is here," she said before turning back to Ryan, who rocked back on his heels and smiled uncomfortably.

"Thanks."

"Sure. Anything. I mean anytime," she corrected.

Uncomfortable with the receptionist's attempt at flirtation, Ryan turned away and gazed around the lobby. He pretended to examine the pictures on the walls, which showed the site's owner with various celebrities. After a few minutes of avoiding eye contact with Gina, he was relieved to see Angie rushing through the doorway leading to the lobby.

"Ryan, come on back," she called to him. Ryan was glad to escape the awkwardness and followed Angie down a nondescript hallway.

"How's it going today?" he asked, giving Angie a warm smile.

"Fine," she said, cutting off any attempt at small talk. "Ready to see if the Subway Girl has made contact?"

"No time like the present." Ryan again gave Angie a smile. It was a genuine smile too. He was feeling optimistic. It had been months since he had felt the comfort and familiarity of a relationship. To some people, that kind of stability might sound boring. To Ryan, it was the foundation of intimacy and passion, satisfaction and connection–things he wanted in his life. He could sense he was on his way to making those things a reality once again.

"Super." Angie led him into a windowless room with a desk, computer, oversized monitor and two chairs. Along the back wall was a slightly stained but clean enough gray couch.

Harlan sat on the couch, scrolling through emails. He looked up and gave a quick "hey," then went back to his phone. Next to Harlan was a recording set-up. Angie gestured for Ryan to take a seat at one of the office chairs in front of the computer terminal.

"After you," he said, holding his hand out. Angie sat down and let out a little huff.

Angie logged in to a computer, and the three of them waited in silence for the site to load. Ryan took a deep breath and exhaled sharply. It was hard to believe that in a matter of moments, he could be face to screen with the woman who'd been running through his mind for weeks. The woman who could be his future. He was *hoping* would be his future.

"Damn!" muttered Angie. Ryan looked at the frozen computer screen. She tapped some keys to no avail. She hit the escape key several times, but nothing happened. With a groan, she turned to Ryan and shrugged. She picked up the phone and dialed for help.

Angie and Ryan waited in silence for IT support to arrive. An awkward silence as far as Ryan was concerned, but thankfully not as bad as what he'd endured with the receptionist.

A man with pasty white skin, thinning hair and what could only be described as a porn-star mustache walked in and ushered Angie out of her seat. He sat down and tapped away on the keyboard. Ryan's head swirled as he watched lines of code scroll down the screen. He was a web designer and knew programming, but this level of system failure was a lot to take in.

"Well, here's your problem. More than a hundred and fifty responses. The system wasn't set up to handle that kind of traffic," explained the IT guy.

"A hundred and fifty?" The disbelief in Angie's voice was unmistakable.

"More than a hundred and fifty," the IT guy corrected her.

"Shit," Ryan said under his breath. How could there be a hundred and fifty responses to his video plea?

"I'll need to reboot the computer, set up an overflow cache network and reload everything." The IT guy shooed them away with his hand.

"How long will that take?" asked Angie. It wasn't hard to miss the frustration in her voice.

"Give me an hour," he said matter-of-factly.

"Thanks." Turning to Ryan, she asked, "So, you drink coffee?"

"With the thought of looking through a hundred and fifty—"

"More than a hundred and fifty," the IT guy corrected him.

"*More* than a hundred and fifty responses," Ryan acknowledged, turning to Angie, tilting his head and bugging his eyes out, "I might need something a bit stronger," he joked.

"It's five o'clock somewhere," he and Angie said at the same time, before looking at each other and laughing.

Man, her laugh. For some reason, he didn't want her to stop. It was so infectious, he didn't want to stop either. And the way she tossed back her head without a hint of self-consciousness, just pure joy at their shared humor, spurred him on further.

Interrupting Ryan's unexpected response to Angie's laugh, Harlan waved them off, making it clear he wasn't interested in joining them. Angie gestured for Ryan to walk ahead of her, but he shook his head, indicating for her to go first. He followed her down the hall and outside of the building.

Once out on the street, Angie said, "I know the perfect spot, this way." They walked in silence for a block or so. All the while, Ryan scanned the crowd as was now a habit, hoping to spot his mystery girl in the pink hat.

After a few blocks, they reached the St. Regis, one of the city's oldest and most prestigious hotels. They passed through an airy, grand, lobby with marble counters and gilded walls. It was clear Angie knew her way around by the way she walked through a hallway to an old-fashioned bar.

Ryan leaned his head back and took in his surroundings, impressed with the grandeur of it all. He let out a little whistle.

Angie gestured for him to grab a stool as she sat down. "Birthplace of the Bloody Mary," she informed him.

"Really?" replied Ryan with interest.

"Yup. Invented right here in 1934." The bartender, a tall man with graying temples, wearing a formal uniform of red vest, crisp white shirt and black slacks, walked over and placed napkins down in front of both Ryan and Angie. "Two Bloody Marys, please." She looked to Ryan to confirm he would like one. He nodded. The bartender smiled and walked away to prepare their drinks.

"So, that seems like something a native New Yorker would know. Are you originally from here?" Ryan asked.

"Born and raised. I even went to journalism school here in the city."

"Cool. As you likely know, I went to college in Iowa where I majored in film studies."

Making no effort to hide her teasing, Angie said, "Iowa? Really? You mean you're not a big-city boy?"

Ryan responded, with an equal amount of sarcasm, "I can see that surprises you."

"Well . . ." Angie smirked.

"Let's just say it wasn't my choice to move out here. I would have been content to stay in Iowa. But my girlfriend, Frances–she goes by Frankie now–and I graduated from college and she couldn't wait to get out of Iowa and to the big city, the biggest city. She's kind of always wanted to be famous."

"But Frankie didn't go to Hollywood?" Angie blurted out and then grimaced. "Sorry. Bad joke."

"Relax." Ryan winked, hoping she'd pick up on his musical reference. "I thought that was funny."

"Well, I guess that relationship didn't work out or else you wouldn't be here with me," she said. It most definitely didn't work out, he considered confessing, but decided to keep things less complicated.

"She got caught up in a crowd of fashionistas who were all obsessed with celebrities and the club scene," he said, hoping that explanation would pacify Angie's interest.

"So, you two just drifted apart?" Angie sat stone-faced, patiently waiting for a response. As the seconds passed, Ryan felt more and more compelled to fill the void of silence.

"More like she drifted into the bed of an NBA player."

"No!" said Angie, putting her hand up to her mouth.

"Yeah. Kinda sucked." Ryan sighed deeply and scrubbed his hand over his jaw.

"How did that happen?" Her eyebrows rose up on her forehead.

Ryan prepared to recount the story he'd only told twice before–to Luke and to Diego. He didn't know what had actually happened, as he hadn't been there. But the story had become cemented in his mind as being truth–gleaned from what Frankie had told him, what he read about online and what he had heard from her vapid friends.

"Frankie and three of her friends were in some hip nightclub when Jason Stark walked in. Apparently, Frankie was impressed because he used to date one of the Kardashians. He bought them some drinks and then asked her back to his place." He looked back up to see what looked like sympathy in Angie's eyes. *Fuck.* That, right there. That look in Angie's eyes was why he hated recounting this story. His stomach churned thinking about his friends and family knowing of her public infidelity. He knew they pitied him.

"Wow. That's . . ." Angie appeared speechless.

"Yeah." He completed her thought without having to say more than a simple word. "Supposedly, she told him she just needed to make a quick phone call."

"She broke up with you over the phone?" she said with a gasp.

"Yup. I found out the next morning she was with Jason because my buddy Diego is obsessed with the tabloids and saw a picture of her leaving the club with him that night. I learned more of the details days later."

"That's awful. I'm so sorry. How long ago did that happen?"

"Yeah. It came as quite a blow. It was eight months ago. I thought we were really meant to be together. In fact, I thought she would come back and tell me it was all a mistake and we'd reconcile."

"Would you have been able to forgive her?" There was a flicker of challenge in Angie's eyes, but Ryan chose to ignore it. Yeah, Frankie had screwed up by screwing that guy. She was callous and selfish.

But he also knew she was funny and tender. His heart filled with warmth thinking about Friday-night football games and county fairs, summers by the creek and long walks through the cornfields with hands and lips seeking each other in urgency.

How she made him homemade soup whenever he was sick and dropped love notes in his locker at school. He knew that girl was still somewhere in that couture-covered body. It wasn't all bad. It was pretty damn great until . . .

"Honestly, I think I could forgive her for anything. She was my first love."

"And yet you're certain now that you're meant to be with the Subway Girl?" Angie probed. Ryan could tell she was trying to reconcile these two seemingly competing statements of his.

"I'm certain I was meant to *meet* the Subway Girl," he clarified, trying to make sense of what was propelling him to find her. "I know it probably doesn't make sense, but I just know fate is at work here."

"Well, good for you for being willing to try again," she said, smirking. Ryan sensed there was a story there.

"What about you? I'd be surprised if you didn't have a boyfriend."

Angie shook her head and rolled her eyes. "No, I haven't been very lucky in the love department."

"What happened?"

"I had a serious boyfriend in college. Harrison," she explained. "He was studying business to become a broker on

Wall Street. He could be very charming. And we were both in love . . . with him."

"I'm sorry to hear that. I can tell there's someone out there for you. You're meant to find a great love. You just need to give in to fate." He smiled at her because he really believed it.

"Thanks, but I'm just going to focus on my career," she retorted, a bit too defensively.

Ryan sensed she wanted to change the subject. "How long have you been a reporter for *Celebrity Monger?*"

"I've been there for three years, but I'm just waiting for my break to become a serious journalist," she said. "No offense," she spluttered.

"It's cool. To be honest, I hadn't even heard of *Celebrity Monger* until you called, and Diego told me you were legit. So, no offense to you either." He tossed her a little wink.

"None taken. And I'm not sure I would categorize us as legit," she said, feigning horror. "I just . . ."

"What?"

"I just imagined I would be writing transformative pieces that would have an impact on people and policies and . . ." Angie said wistfully, letting down her guard for a moment, which he sensed was uncommon for her.

"Well, you're having an impact on me," he said encouragingly.

"Thanks." She smiled, and he hoped she was absorbing the fact she really was having a positive effect on his life. "So, can I ask you a personal question?"

"More personal than you helping me find the possible future mother of my children?" he mocked.

Angie laughed. "What is it about you and fate?"

Nodding his head, Ryan replied, "My parents met in kindergarten in the same little town where I grew up. My dad walked up to her the first day and said, 'I'm going to marry you.' My mom looked back at him and said, 'Okay.' They were married at seventeen, and in all the years they've been married, they've never spent a night apart. They are completely in love with one another. If it was anyone other than my parents, it wouldn't be so disgusting." He gave a joking grimace.

Angie choked out a laugh. "I can see that."

"That's what I grew up with, and that's what I want. Someone you can't bear the thought of spending a night away from." He shrugged. "What about your parents?"

"My parents?" huffed Angie. "I think they only spent one night *together*. I was raised by my single mom, and we never talk much about my dad."

"I'm sorry." Sorry that she didn't have a father figure in her life. Sorry that she didn't grow up with a daily example of a loving relationship. Sorry that she seemed to think love wasn't in the cards for her.

"Yeah, me too." By the way Angie averted her eyes and looked at her watch, he could tell she didn't want to talk about it further. "Well, we better get back. I'm sure IT's solved our computer problem by now." Angie gulped down the remainder of her Bloody Mary, and they walked out.

When she and Ryan returned to *Celebrity Monger*, Angie found their screening room empty but the computer monitor cued up to view the *more-than*-a-hundred-and-fifty videos.

"Why would there be so many submissions?" Ryan asked.

"I'm hopeful she's one of them," Angie reassured him.

"Me too, but why would there be more than one? Why so many?" he continued to question.

"You've got to understand, Ryan. Not everyone is like you. There are a lot of people who just want the fame and attention that comes with being featured on TV or online," she explained. *Thank goodness there are,* she thought, *or I might be out of a job.* Ryan nodded.

For the next three hours, Angie and Ryan watched video submissions from women who weren't the Subway Girl but were willing to play the role. Much to their disappointment, none were from the true subject.

"Well, that was a huge waste of time," said Ryan.

"You've got to give it some time," Angie said. "This is a good sign."

"How so?" Based on the way he scoffed his response, she could sense his skepticism.

"The more people who submit videos, the more attention the site and your story will get. With more attention comes the increased likelihood someone is going to solve this mystery." Never mind the fact that this level of engagement early on was just what Barry needed to drive the network deal.

"Yeah," he conceded. "I suppose you're right." After walking Ryan out and promising to call him tomorrow with an update, Angie returned to her office.

"Ugh," she groaned quietly. While she had been honest with Ryan that video submissions meant increased attention on the search, she had some niggling concerns this story may not be the slam dunk she needed.

She hoped the message boards would stoke the fire, so she logged in for the first time to see what people were saying.

> DrillTeamBabe: @maribel5 @everychance @gogo18 @ameliarb @karilb @ PicklesNTickles8 YOU HAVE TO CHECK THIS OUT! LOVE! LOVE! LOVE!

> > PicklesNTickles8: @DrillTeamBabe I will totally watch this show. What time is it on?

> > gogo18: @DrillTeamBabe OMG!!!!!!! This is my new obsession. I've watched this video over and over.

LuluLove: Is it wrong that I want to climb that man like a tree? FML he's hot.

> JulesDiamond: @LuluLove No way. He's HAWWWWTTTTT!

LadyBoy: Pussy!

> SaveIt4Later: @LadyBoy your screen name is LadyBoy and you're calling Ryan a Pussy?

> LadyBoy: @SaveIt4Later yeah well you can put your screen name to work and shut the fuck up.

GracieL: Does this mean Ryan is the new "Bachelor"?

RedRook: Tall? Check! Handsome? Check! Sweet? Check! Has a good job? Check! I think we just found the perfect man.

MCValdez: Total hoax. No guy is that romantic. Ladies, don't fall for the BS.

HoneyBoo: How much money do you think he getting paid?

HowUDoin5: That boy be lickable!!!

Zoinks2002: Looks like a fame-whore stalker to me.

EHChien: Don't be such a cynic. Why cant he just be a good guy looking for love

Lizardman69: @EHChien On the NY subway? No one looks for love on the subway. Stupid!

EHChien: @Lizardman69 That's sort of the point asshole. He didn't LOOK for it on the subway, that's just where it found him.

Load 178 more comments

FIVE

It had only been a few days, and the video submissions and message board comments continued to roll in. Most of the online chatter centered around public reaction to the sampling of videos Angie posted online.

> Adored66: @CallMeMaybe12: What the actual fuck? Did you see the video from the girl in the red sweater?!?

> > CallMeMaybe12: @Adored66 She can't be serious! Ryan said she was a brunette. These blondes are just trying to get attention.

> > TrustMeL: @Adored66 @CallMeMaybe12: Blondes do have more fun.

CallMeMaybe12: @TrustMeL @Adored66: Spoken like a f@*%ing blonde.

Adored66: @CallMeMaybe12 @TrustMeL: LOL!

PWWR: I'll put on a fake accent if Ryan will have me.

99Probs: Third video down? Is that Kendra?

TGIF888: To the red head with the big tits—yes please!

Garth4Ever: @TGIF888: Shwing!

SaintM: @Garth4Ever That is sooooo 80's

Load 1,320 more comments

After a fruitless review of more video submissions with Ryan, a trip to the dentist to discover she needed her wisdom teeth removed—which she had neither the time nor money to address—followed by a thirty-minute subway ride, Angie hopped off the train in Sunnyside, Queens, and walked three blocks to the modest two-bedroom house she grew up in. Kids doing Fortnite dances in the street reminded her of her childhood in this small community only miles from midtown.

Back in the 1920s, executives bought affordable houses here for their mistresses because it was cheap and close to the city. Angie used to imagine her dad—essentially a sperm donor—

was like one of those execs, squirreling away his lover and love child while he went to his legitimate kids' soccer games and school recitals. Her mom had done her best on her own, and for that Angie was grateful.

"Hey, Ma," she called as she strolled through the door to find her mom sitting on a threadbare recliner watching a game show.

"Shh," her mom responded, holding a hand up to silence Angie. "I've almost got it." Her mom studied the puzzle while the woman in a sequined gown revealed new letters. "Burt Reynolds Wrap." She turned back around to a grinning Angie.

"Good job, Ma," she said, leaning over to give her a side hug. Her mom shooed her away, instead standing up and enveloping Angie in a warm embrace.

"Hello, gorgeous girl," she said. "I didn't know you were coming by. I would have made some dinner." She walked toward the kitchen. "Let me put a plate together for you."

"It's okay, Ma." Angie reached out an arm to stop her. "I already ate."

"Oh, okay. So just came by to check on me, then?"

"Yeah. I wanted to drop off a check and talk about the mortgage." Angie reached into her purse and handed her mom a check. "I know it's not going to cover this month's payment in full, but I figured continuing to show the bank a good-faith effort could only help."

"Thanks, doll face," her mom said, taking the check and placing it on top of a folder sitting on the wooden table where Angie used to do her homework. "I'm going to meet with the bank manager Tuesday to discuss an extension."

"I can meet you there. You know, explain about the network deal and how close we are," Angie offered.

"Two o'clock. The branch on Havenhurst."

Tuesdays at two were weekly *Celebrity Monger* planning meetings, and there was no way Barry would let her miss it, not with the crucial network meeting coming up. Angie worried her lip between her teeth.

"Is there any way we can reschedule?"

"No. We're already cutting it close as it is. But it's okay," her mother assured her, placing a comforting hand on Angie's shoulder. "I can handle it on my own."

"Ma–"

"Ah-ah," her mom said. "I got this." Angie's stomach and jaw tightened. Last time her mom had "handled" something on her own, she'd let her own health insurance premium lapse and had to pay exorbitant out-of-pocket expenses for an urgent care visit for her sciatica.

"I think–"

"You're busy with work. I know what I'm doing."

I am busy with work, but not too busy to worry. She didn't trust that her mom was equipped to deal with this on her own. Angie's shoulders hunched forward under the weight of it, but right now, she didn't have another choice.

"So, have you talked to Harrison?" Angie's mom asked.

Distracted from the mortgage stress, Angie scoffed. *Ma fell for Harrison's charms hook, line and sinker.* Staying with him was never going to be worth the financial stability her mom always wanted for her.

"We've been over this, Ma," she sighed.

"But you were so in love."

Love doesn't mean sucking up to your girlfriend's mom while some random girl sucks you off in a nearly empty subway car.

"*Were* is the operative word." Angie scowled at her mother.

"You're a beautiful young woman. When are you going to make me a grandmother?"

"Jeez!" Angie said in exasperation. "I'm trying to be the strong, independent woman you raised." *Yeah, right.* Her mom had never encouraged her to be strong or independent. That was Angie's way of rebelling against her mom's insistence that finding a solid man to marry would make sure she was set for life.

"You are, doll face," her mom said. "I just want you to find someone to make you happy."

"Well, Harrison's not the answer."

"Then how about someone else?"

"Let's just get back to your show," Angie suggested. "I only have a little while before I need to head back to my place and get in a run."

"You running with Cousin Sabrina?"

"No. By myself," Angie huffed in annoyance.

"I don't understand the running. You start here. You end here. What's the point?"

Angie inhaled deeply, doing her best to hold her tongue. She scrubbed her hand over her face. Work, Harrison, mortgage–it was all too much. Angie and her mother moved to the couch and sat down, content to put answers in the form of questions for the next twenty minutes.

As Angie left, she asked her mom to keep her posted on efforts with the bank. On the train ride home, she tried not to let panic set in and instead focused her thoughts on how Ryan's search for love would be her salvation.

Back at home, Angie turned on her computer and changed into her workout gear. She was mentally exhausted from dealing with her mom and slogging through another round of videos directed at Ryan, and she hoped a run would help.

On one hand, she lamented the sad state of her career, which consisted of watching women try to dazzle Ryan with their charm, wit, cleavage or other assets. On the other hand, she recognized this search was her best shot at getting away from *Celebrity Monger* and taking her career to the next level–a legitimate journalistic level.

Then she recalled joking around with Ryan at the office today. There was something so easy about being around him. He was unlike any other guy she had met before. Comparing Ryan to other guys only made her think about her ex, which was a rabbit hole she didn't feel like going down tonight.

Instead, she logged in to her email account and was glancing down the list of new messages in her inbox, clicking on the junk mail she would trash, when her eyes landed on *it*. A response from the *New Yorker*. The subject read "Re: Prince, Angie Submission for Consideration." She took a deep breath and exhaled sharply, an "o" forming on her lips. As her eyes scanned the email, her shoulders slumped in defeat.

> *Thank you for your recent submission to the New Yorker. I regret that the New Yorker is unable to publish your article at this time. We receive many submissions each day and as such we must turn down many that might have potential. Remember that sometimes writers endure long terms of rejection before they find the winning combination for themselves. I wish you all the best in pursuit of your effort to be published in the New Yorker and invite you to submit another article in the future.*

She clicked the generic rejection email closed and transferred it into an email folder entitled "*The New Yorker*." She opened the folder and solemnly looked at a long series of email messages with the subject "Re: Prince, Angie Submission for Consideration." She closed the folder and rubbed her temples.

In school, her professors had told her how talented she was. That she would go far as a reporter. That she had good instincts for a story and solid writing skills. Had they been lying? Because out in the real world, all she was achieving was rejection.

Forgoing a run, she walked to the refrigerator and removed a roll of Pillsbury cookie dough. Spoon in hand, she took in small bites of comfort and stared at the wall, contemplating her future.

SIX

Ryan leaned back into the black leather office chair. His shoes were off and his feet—clad in a subtle pair of *Star Wars* socks—were propped up on the conference table.

"How many does this make now?" he asked wearily. He glanced over at Angie to see the janitor enter the room with his rolling cart of cleaning supplies. "Good evening, sir" said Ryan. The janitor nodded. Ryan stood up and moved aside so the man could get to the trash can under the desk.

"I think we're up to four hundred," Angie sighed. "Ugh!" She rolled her neck from side to side. "I'd rather watch anything than another video right now."

"Anything?" Ryan asked with a raised brow.

"Anything."

"Challenge accepted! Um . . . Watch your grandmother compose and send a text. Would you rather watch that?"

Angie smiled. "Yes. As painful as it would be, I would rather watch that."

"Hmm. What about seeing naked Abe Lincoln?"

She shook her head in amusement. "Where the heck did that come from?"

"I've been watching the Ken Burns Civil War documentary. I guess I've got Abe Lincoln on the brain."

"Got it. Okay, point of clarification. Is that naked Abe Lincoln now, when he's a rotting corpse, or naked Abe Lincoln back in the day?"

Ryan tilted his head and looked up, giving it serious thought. "Back in the day," he confirmed with a nod.

"Is he wearing the stovepipe hat?"

"Sure." He chuckled. "He can keep the hat on."

"Can he use it to cover his twig and berries?" She held her hands together in prayer.

"Nope. Everything is on display."

"That's a tough one," she said. "But I would rather see naked Abe Lincoln than watch another video. More popcorn?" Angie stood up and tossed a popcorn bag into the microwave. She turned back to Ryan, who stroked his chin in thought.

"Sure. Popcorn's good. How about run a 5k?" he asked.

"I would rather run a *marathon* than watch another video," she retorted with a mixture of defiance and humor.

"Bikini wax?" What prompted him to think of that, he wasn't sure. But now that he'd said it out loud, he was consumed with thoughts of Angie in a swimsuit. He had to admit it was a much better visual than naked Abe Lincoln.

"Cakewalk compared to this." The microwave timer dinged, and she removed the bag, opening it up to let the steam out.

"Wait in line at the DMV to get your driver's license renewed?"

"I don't have a license." She walked over to Harlan, sitting in the back of the room, and poured some popcorn into a bowl for him before returning to the seat next to Ryan. Angie placed the popcorn bag down in front of him and grabbed a handful for herself.

"How can you not have a driver's license?" It amazed him that this sophisticated city girl didn't know how to drive a car.

"Don't need one living in the city."

"Everyone needs a driver's license," he practically shrieked at her. "Back me up on this, Harlan." They both turned to the camera operator.

"A driver's license is a must," Harlan agreed.

She shrugged. "Okay. I'll look into it."

"I've got it," Ryan said in triumph. "Give up pasta forever. I know you would rather watch another video than do that." He nodded and gave her a knowing look.

"Yeah," she conceded. "You got me there."

"Yes!" Ryan grinned at her smugly and clicked the computer mouse to load another video before shoveling a handful of buttery popcorn into his mouth. A piece fell on the ground, and he reached to pick it up and place it in the now-empty trash can.

A voluptuous blonde appeared on the screen. Dressed in a low-cut tank top with heavy makeup, she was vamping it up for the camera. Angie watched Ryan's head rear back and his eyes bug out.

"Hi, Ryan," said the blonde vixen in a husky voice. "I think the subway girl you're looking for is me. While some women wouldn't be caught dead taking the underground train, I don't mind going down." Ryan's jaw dropped open, a few kernels of unchewed popcorn still in his mouth. Angie threw her head back with a riotous laugh.

"Oh my god! That is hilarious!" exclaimed Angie.

Ryan regained his composure. "I think we've found her," he said flatly.

Angie playfully slugged his arm. "You can't be serious," she scoffed. "You find that attractive?"

"Hey, I may be a romantic, but I can still appreciate a pretty face."

Angie shook her head in disbelief. She clicked to load the next video.

"Let's see the next one." She raised her eyebrow at him disapprovingly. The screen loaded to show an old woman who had to be at least seventy-five. Her voice was shaky from age.

"If you're looking for a mature woman, I think I could be your subway girl. Why don't you give me a call?" She smirked.

"Aha! The future Mrs. Carlson." Angie pointed her index finger in the air, as if it were a true eureka moment.

"I think she already *is* Mrs. Carlson. That looks remarkably like my grandmother," Ryan deadpanned. Angie leaned back her head and laughed again before clicking the mouse.

A young, chubby brunette said, "Blimey! Oh, 'i there, Ryan," in a horrible fake Cockney accent accompanied by off-screen giggles. "It's me. Yar Subway Girl. Call me. 'Nuff said, yeah?" She erupted into laughter.

Ryan looked down at his feet. "Is that what people think? That this is all some sort of a joke? That I'm a joke?" A lump caught in his throat at the thought of people mocking him and his belief in fate.

He understood. It wasn't the first time someone had made fun of his romantic tendencies. If he had a dollar for every time Luke or Diego razzed him, he'd . . . well, he'd have a lot of money. But he'd use all that money to buy rounds of beer for them, because they were his buddies.

This seemed different, though. This wasn't friends ribbing one another good-naturedly. This? This bordered on cruel and had him questioning whether this whole endeavor had been a colossal mistake, adding another layer of pain and embarrassment on top of his breakup with Frankie.

"There are a lot of stupid people who will use the anonymity of the web to do and say things they normally wouldn't. I don't think you're a joke," Angie soothed.

"I just thought . . ." He stood, looked out the window and ran his hand through his hair. "I just thought this was going to be my, you know, boom box moment."

"Boom box moment?" asked Angie.

"Yeah, you know. That classic moment when John Cusack waits outside Ione Sky's house and lifts up his boom box . . ." he explained. Angie continued to look at him blankly. ". . . playing 'In Your Eyes' by Peter Gabriel."

"You might as well be speaking a foreign language. I have no idea what you're talking about," she said with a hint of exasperation, clearly exhausted from watching dozens upon dozens of video submissions without a break.

"It's from the movie *Say Anything*. It's an '80s romance classic," he said. "You should definitely watch it."

"I will. But for now, we better keep watching these. We've got a girl to find."

Buoyed by her resolve and encouragement, Ryan walked back to the desk and loaded the next video.

"Yeah, you're right." Though he wasn't entirely sure he would ever find that girl.

After a few more videos, less mocking in nature but still not from *her*, Ryan rubbed his eyes and got up. "I'm really starting to think that maybe this wasn't a good idea."

No! No, no, no! thought Angie. She'd come too far and too much was on the line for Ryan to back out now. Yes, she thought this whole story was a bunch of baloney. Fate? No such thing. True love? Not likely. What she did believe in wholeheartedly, though, was that a home run here needed to be delivered to Barry. Too much was riding on it.

She wasn't a great actress. And she feared he'd see right through her. See that she was using him and see that she wasn't sure this would be a success. She drew in a deep breath and thought about everything at stake.

"We'll find her," she said in an unwavering tone—an effort to convince Ryan and herself. She placed a reassuring hand on his shoulder and craned her neck so she could look up into his eyes.

"This isn't what I thought it was going to be. I think it's time to call it. I'll find her another way."

"No," Angie said. "This *will* work. It's just going to take some time."

"Maybe I should have my lawyer take a look at the agreement. There's got to be some way for me to get out of this," Ryan mumbled, more to himself than anything.

"Hey," Angie soothed. "Look at me." Ryan squeezed his eyes shut. When he opened them, Angie did her best to look sincere. "She's out there. We know she is."

"I know," he said. "I just didn't think it would . . ."

"Take this long? Be so hard?"

"Be so public," he said with a resigned sigh.

"So public?" She laughed and noticed his demeanor soften right away. "You created a website to search for her," she teased. She figured if she could get him to laugh at himself a little bit—at the absurdity of it all—that perhaps he wouldn't take it all so seriously and too much to heart. That he would agree to stay the course with her.

"Yeah, I guess that's pretty public."

"They don't call it the *worldwide* web for nothing." She winked and could see the tension lift from his shoulders. "Look. I know this isn't playing out as either of us had initially thought, but we'll find her."

"Okay," he replied with a small smile.

"Why don't we call it a night and regroup tomorrow?"

"Yeah. That's a good idea," he said. "Let me just run to the restroom." He walked out the door and down the hall.

Once she was assured Ryan was out of earshot, Angie let out a loud exhale and collapsed into a chair. "Well, that was close. I thought I might have lost him."

"Nice save, for now." Harlan stood from his chair to shut down the camera equipment that had been trained on Ryan in the hopes of capturing his response to finding the Subway Girl. "But seriously, you've never seen *Say Anything?*"

"No. Have you?" she asked with a scornful sneer to which she knew Harlan wouldn't take offense. She couldn't believe that *Harlan* of all people would have seen a romantic comedy.

'Well, yeah," he replied with an equal amount of scorn. "It's a classic."

SEVEN

Angie waved her hands underneath her arms, creating swift bursts of air. The organza sleeves didn't allow for a lot of air circulation, and her pits were working up a sweat.

It was Saturday night, and yeah, she was wearing organza. Not just organza, but *forest-green* organza. *The things I willingly do for my friends.* Thuy was a great friend, too. She had joined *Celebrity Monger* to work in advertising sales the year after Angie. When she didn't have Barry barking in her ear, she was quite good at getting things done.

It was while at a sales meeting with a real estate company that specialized in finding roommates for singles living in the city that Thuy met her husband of, so far, thirty minutes. Hence the green silk-and-organza dress that Angie was sporting. The six other bridesmaids had just finished helping Thuy bustle up her wedding gown so she could make her grand entrance into the hotel ballroom, arm in arm with her new husband.

Angie walked over to the sign-in table, leaning down to adjust the buckle on her three-inch-high gold-toned sandals—also a Thuy pick—which were digging into her ankles. She took a deep breath and scanned the array of seating cards in search of her name. She figured she was either sitting at the "work" table or the one designated for the hopelessly single. She wasn't quite certain which would be worse.

When she made her way over to table thirteen, several colleagues from the office were already seated. She sighed in relief knowing she would be surrounded by friends, even if she wasn't in the mood to talk shop. At least she wasn't with some depressing group moaning about how they'd never find anyone and drowning their sorrows in glasses of Chardonnay or tequila shots, courtesy of the open bar.

When she got closer, she saw an addition to her table—someone who didn't work at *Celebrity Monger* but had been spending a lot of time there.

"Hey there," she said, sitting down and bumping Ryan's shoulder while noticing how he filled out his navy-blue suit jacket.

"Hey, yourself," he responded, inspecting the sweetheart neckline of the overly flouncy dress Thuy had forced Angie to wear. She looked down, fluffed the tulle-lined skirt a few times and gave him an exaggerated grin. Judging by his smirk, she was guessing he could tell how she felt about the dress.

"Of course you were invited to the wedding," she said with a roll of her eyes, exhaling sharply through her nose. *Everyone loves Ryan.* He'd only known Thuy for a few weeks, yet here he was at her wedding.

As she thought more about it, it made perfect sense. No one at the office was immune to his considerable charms, except for Barry, and he wasn't known for being all warm and fuzzy. *And me,* she thought. *I'm immune to his charms.*

"And here I thought she only added me to the list for the toaster oven I got them at Bed Bath & Beyond," he quipped. Angie laughed out loud. Okay, so maybe she wasn't *completely* immune to his charms.

"Small appliances are really the only reason I would ever consider getting married." Angie tried to say it like a joke, but judging by Ryan's slight grimace, she knew it had fallen flat.

"Wow. You must *really* be cynical about love if you can't even be happy at a wedding."

"I'm kidding." She reached out and touched his arm. "Totally kidding." *I am kidding, right? I'm not completely heartless.* Okay, so she didn't think love was in the cards for her. And knowing that her father had left her mother and never looked back was hard. And all the infidelity she saw on *Celebrity Monger* didn't help. But she was hopeful that Thuy and her husband would be happy together. She *wanted* to be hopeful. And she hoped Ryan would find happiness with the Subway Girl. As she was about to protest further, a blur of green organza grabbed Angie's hand and lifted her out of her seat.

"Thuy's getting ready to toss the bouquet," Green Organza explained.

Angie groaned and sat back down. "Oh, I think I'll pass," she muttered.

"No, you have to go." Green Organza, whose name Angie couldn't remember no matter how hard she tried, pouted. "Have to," she said, jutting out her hip and placing a hand on it for emphasis. "It's tradition."

"Go on without me. I'll catch up with you in a minute." Angie plastered a fake smile on her face. The fellow bridesmaid asked about the marital status of the other women seated near Angie before bounding over to the next table to recruit more participants.

Angie's disinterest in the bouquet toss didn't go unnoticed by Ryan. "Not a fan of flying flowers?" he asked.

"I have nothing against flowers, flying or otherwise," she replied, lifting her bridesmaid's bouquet off the table and showing it to him. "I just think the bouquet toss tradition is barbaric. Herding all the single ladies onto the dance floor so everyone can mock their singleness," Angie said in disgust.

"I'm pretty sure the tradition started as a way for brides to pass their good fortune along to someone else."

"Why does being the next to get married equate to good fortune?" she huffed. Ryan was at a loss for words, so Angie continued with her tirade. "And you think anyone wants to hook up with the girl who caught the bouquet? The girl who *willingly* went out onto the dance floor and fought off the competition so she could be next in line to be married? The girl with marriage on her mind?"

Ryan could see the fire burning in Angie's eyes. He liked seeing her get all fired up about something. He also liked when he could defuse the tension with humor.

"So . . ." he started. "Hooking up at the wedding? Is that on your mind?" Okay, so that wasn't so much humor as a distraction. Ryan wasn't sure why he was asking her *that*. It wasn't like anything was going on between him and Angie.

"You offering?" She chuckled, her temper cooling.

"Perhaps." He quirked a brow at her. *Am I?*

"Believe me," she replied, "you'd have no trouble finding a willing participant." Ryan's cheeks warmed, and he felt a flip-flop sensation in his stomach. "There's a big double standard in that."

"What is *that* supposed to mean?" The flattery Ryan had been feeling was eclipsed by frustration. What was she getting at?

"I'm referring to the wedding-garter toss, where all the single guys vie for the thigh scrunchie in an effort to be the next to marry."

"Yeah, so?"

"Being a single guy who wants to get married is attractive. Women fall over themselves for shit like that."

"Not all women," he said pointedly.

"No." She laughed. "Not all women. But most. Being a single woman who wants to get married smacks of desperation. Being a single *guy* who wants to get married is like . . . hitting the dating mother lode."

Before Ryan could argue that a woman who wanted commitment, stability and enduring love was beyond desirable, Green Organza returned, imploring Angie to join her on the dance floor. Ryan reached over to grab Angie's hand. He looked up at the blur of puffy fabric and flashed her a dazzling smile.

"She's already spoken for."

Angie looked up at Green Organza with a grin.

"Aww. I didn't realize you were taken," the bridesmaid cooed. "You guys are so cute together."

"Thanks," Angie said in a saccharine voice, giving Ryan's hand a squeeze and letting out a deep, lovelorn sigh.

"Good luck to you, though," Angie told the blur, pointing at the dance floor. The bridesmaid smiled brightly and moved on.

As the photographer took photos of the bouquet and garter toss winners, the DJ invited everyone to the dance floor. A driving bassline thumped through the speakers.

"May I?" Ryan stood and extended his hand to Angie.

"Yes. Just give me a moment." She leaned over and unbuckled the high heels, likely so she could more comfortably enjoy dancing to "Uptown Funk" or "YMCA," which were no doubt on the playlist.

As they reached the dance floor, the DJ switched things up, moving from an upbeat dance number to the 1960s Dean Martin classic, "You're Nobody Till Somebody Loves You." While Frank crooned about finding someone to love, Ryan took Angie into his arms, her head resting underneath his chin.

Ryan missed this. Not holding Angie, per se. He had never done that before. Although he would admit that her small frame did feel good pressed against his body.

More than that, he missed this connection and intimacy with someone. He was glad Luke couldn't hear his inner monologue because he would no doubt give him shit for it. But it was true. He missed having someone to think about and to hold and to feel something for.

Sure, he'd had a few hookups since his breakup with Frankie. At first, being with someone else—someone new after having only been with his high school sweetheart—was exciting and fun and hot. But after a few random one-night stands—two of which he'd tried without success to turn into something more—he realized he was a relationship kind of guy.

"This is an awful song for a wedding," Angie said.

Ryan joined her in a laugh. "What about 'Every Breath You Take'? Stalker much?"

"Oh my god! You're so right. I never thought about that before."

"Every download of that song should come with a free restraining order." Ryan shook his head while Angie craned her neck to look up at him.

"Last year, I was at a wedding where the bride and groom danced to 'I Will Always Love You.' Of course, you will know that song because it was in a movie," she joked.

"It was indeed," he confirmed. "Most notably from the '92 film *The Bodyguard*. But why is that a bad wedding song?"

"She sings that if she stays, she'll only be in the way," said Angie, her eyes bugging out the entire time. Ryan chuckled. "It's a breakup song."

"I never thought about the lyrics before," he said with a snort. "Not to one-up you, but I'm gonna totally one-up you," he warned, as Angie continued to sway in his arms.

"Bring it."

"I was at a wedding a few years ago where the bride and groom danced to Madonna's 'Like a Virgin.'"

"You are shitting me?" she half laughed, half gasped.

"Hand to god." He let go of her hand and placed his over his heart. Missing the closeness with her, he grasped her hand again.

"I'm taking it that the bride was less than virginal?"

"I grew up in a small Midwestern town. As a teenager, there was nothing to do except drink beer in the cornfields and have sex." He swallowed hard. Thinking about sex, with Angie in his arms, was more arousing than it should have been, and he willed the bulge in his pants to soften.

"So, more appropriate if they had danced to 'She's Having My Baby'?" Angie offered.

Ryan burst into laughter. "More like they should have danced to 'Part-Time Lover' because turns out that's what the groom and maid of honor were to each other."

"Ouch! Maybe they should have started out with 'Separate Ways' by Journey?"

"More like 'Highway to Hell,'" Ryan fired back, in humor, though his voice was tinged with a hint of personal hurt.

"What about the 'Macarena'? I mean, really. This isn't your nephew's bar mitzvah," Angie said, and he figured she was trying to get the fun banter back on track. The muscles in Ryan's back relaxed, and he enjoyed a body-shaking laugh once again, grateful for Angie's ability to ease all of his tension. "And if you ever, I repeat ever, see me in a conga line to 'Hot Hot Hot,' just kill me and collect the life insurance."

EIGHT

Ryan was sitting next to Angie, groaning in frustration over having to endure yet more of these horrendous videos, when a text from his little sister popped up.

> FINLAY: *Were you going to tell me?*
>
> RYAN: *Tell you what?*
>
> FINLAY: *You're an Internet sensation!!! You're the new Bachelor!!!*
>
> RYAN: **Sigh**

Having already fueled the small-town gossip mill for weeks when he and Frankie split, Ryan had been hoping his friends and family in Iowa wouldn't hear about this, unless of course the Subway Girl really was "the one." Then he would happily take her home and introduce her around.

> RYAN: *Do mom and dad know?*

He looked up to see a woman with spiky blonde hair on the computer screen. He gave Angie a disapproving scowl and looked back down to his phone, while Angie watched the remainder of the video clip and made notes on a legal pad.

> FINLAY: *No. Mom's still using a flip phone and dial-up AOL and dad is elbow deep in vajajays.*

Ryan practically choked. Angie looked over at him with concern, but he brushed her off with a wave, letting her know he was okay.

> RYAN: *Jeez, Fin!*
>
> FINLAY: *What? Not my fault that dad is the most popular OB/GYN in town.*
>
> RYAN: *No need to be so graphic.*
>
> FINLAY: *You're complaining about ME being graphic?!? Have you seen the videos from these women who can't wait to take a ride on the Ryan Express?*

Little did she know Ryan had seen *all* the videos and had been sitting next to Angie for the last hour watching the latest batch. *Ugh! These videos! And these women.*

> RYAN: **Groan* I really don't need to hear my little sister talk about the "Ryan Express."*
>
> FINLAY: *LOL! I do love making you uncomfortable.*
>
> RYAN: *How did you find out?*
>
> FINLAY: *Edna at Hoffman's Diner.*
>
> RYAN: *Damn. Only a matter of time before mom hears.*
>
> FINLAY: *Yup. There's the telephone. The telegraph. And the tell Edna.*
>
> RYAN: *Maybe we'll have found her by then.*
>
> FINLAY: *So this is for real? Not some Internet hoax?*
>
> RYAN: *All real. At least for me.*
>
> FINLAY: *Oooookay. So . . . you really saw the girl, your heart swooned and now you're all over the web?*

It was more than a heart swoon. Something . . . inexplicable was pulling him toward this endeavor.

RYAN: Yup. Teamed up with Angie at CM and she's guiding the search.

Ryan glanced over at Angie, who was chuckling to herself while a dude professed his love for Ryan in a video plea. *Not only isn't he the Subway Girl, he's not even a girl!*

FINLAY: You do love the idea of love. I'll give you that.

RYAN: Am I crazy? Do I come off as crazy?

Ryan's stomach rolled. Even if the search turned out to be fruitless, he didn't want to be a laughingstock.

FINLAY: Yes, you're crazy! But no, you don't come off as crazy.

RYAN: As only a supportive pain-in-the-ass sister could say it.

FINLAY: Speaking of pains in the ass, how's Luke?

Ryan's folks and Finlay had been for a visit last year. It was like a bad family vacation movie from the '70s, complete with wayward subway rides, tacky tourist photos, foam Statue of Liberty crowns, and one puked-up Nathan's hot dog after a ride on the Coney Island Cyclone. Ryan had noted that Finlay, at age sixteen, seemed to take too much of an interest in his co-workers.

RYAN: *Too old for you!*

FINLAY: *Pshaw! I know that. He's ancient.*

RYAN: *Ancient? He's six months younger than me.*

FINLAY: *And your point?*

RYAN: *He's the same. Not sure he'll ever change.*

FINLAY: *What about Diego?*

RYAN: *Also too old for you.*

FINLAY: *Is not.*

RYAN: *Is too!*

FINLAY: *He's only 9 years older than me.*

RYAN: *ONLY 9? You're messing with me, right?*

FINLAY: *Sure.*

RYAN: *"Sure." That's your comeback? Hmmm. Not buying that.*

FINLAY: *Whatever. I don't like Diego. No.*

RYAN: *Wait a sec. You like Diego?*

FINLAY: *No!*

RYAN: *You totally like Diego!*

FINLAY: Do not!

RYAN: Yes you do. You love him.

FINLAY: Do not!

RYAN: Do too!!! You want a cheesy couple name with him like Finlo or Diegy.

FINLAY: You're that tabloid site's new boy toy and now you think you're all about the celebrity?

RYAN: Don't deflect. You love Diego!

FINLAY: DO NOT!!!!

RYAN: I'm going to tell him.

FINLAY: No!!! Do not!!! Do not!!! I will call that Angie lady and tell her embarrassing stories for her to share with the whole world.

Yeah, he definitely needed to keep Finlay away from Angie. She may have been eight years his junior, but Finlay knew how to spin a yarn (a skill she'd inherited from their mom) and knew just enough to make her dangerous.

RYAN: Okay. Okay. I yield. I won't tell Diego you love him . . . even though you totally do.

FINLAY: You're such a jerk.

RYAN: Yeah? And your point is?

FINLAY: Don't tempt me into calling Angie.

RYAN: She won't believe you. She loves me.

FINLAY: Really?!? Like love, loves you?

RYAN: No, ding dong. She just thinks I'm a boy scout.

FINLAY: Did you tell her you were an Eagle Scout?

RYAN: I'm sure she already knows. She's very big-city.

FINLAY: Like she whose name we dare not say?

To say there was no love lost between Finlay and Frankie would have been an understatement as wide as the Grand Canyon. Frankie had been the big sister Finlay had always wanted. The two of them would watch movies, go shopping, bake cookies, and paint their nails. Finlay even called Frankie, who went to college an hour away, to come pick her up from the nurse's office when she got her first period.

When Frankie and Ryan first broke up, Finlay had blamed him. What did you do to her, she'd challenged. Why would you drive her away? How are you going to fix it? Those were unsurprisingly all the questions Ryan had for himself.

When the reality started to emerge and Finlay learned the truth, she took it personally. So much so, Frankie told Ryan a few days after their breakup, that she had to block Finlay's number, as the threatening texts and calls were becoming too much.

Ryan got it. He really did. But if anyone had a right to be pissed, it was him. He just hadn't been able to muster the kind of wrath toward Frankie that Finlay had thought was warranted. And he still couldn't.

> *RYAN: Hey now. Don't need to go there. And Angie is nothing like Frankie.*
>
> *FINLAY: *shudder* What is Angie like? She looks so sweet. I want her nose!*
>
> *RYAN: Your nose is perfect and she's definitely not sweet. LOL! In fact, if she heard you say that, she'd throw down. She's fierce and opinionated and smart and funny and really talented.*
>
> *FINLAY: Wow! Sounds like YOU like HER. No, you LOVE HER!*

Love Angie? Yeah, right. He couldn't imagine her ever being interested in someone like him. Judging by the way she mocked his "saintliness," rolled her eyes at his movie references, argued with him about most everything? Yeah, she was most definitely not into him.

> *RYAN: Brat!*
>
> *FINLAY: Yup.*

Ryan looked up to inspect Angie as she scribbled notes on her note pad while advancing through videos he knew he didn't need to see.

RYAN: What happened with the election?

FINLAY: You are looking at the new president of the Howard High FFA chapter.

RYAN: YES! You must have used my slogan: A Vote for Finlay or Udder Nonsense

FINLAY: Hell no!

RYAN: That was genius!

FINLAY: It was cheesy.

RYAN: Cheesy? Look at you busting out the puns.

FINLAY: I didn't mean it like that, lame-o.

RYAN: You should have.

Ryan let out a howl of laughter and looked over to see Angie staring at him with a bemused expression on her face.

"You look like you're having a little bit too much fun over there. What gives?" Angie asked.

"I'm just texting with my sister, Finlay. She just won the election to be the president of her school's Future Farmers of America chapter."

"Is that seriously a real thing?" she said, raising an eyebrow.

"It is. She's like a crazy mad scientist who wants to solve world hunger by creating hybrid plants that can resist all kinds of pests."

"Wow! That sounds . . . actually . . . really amazing."

"Yeah, she's pretty remarkable. Oh, and she loves your nose."

"My nose?" She let out a chuckle.

"Yup. She said she wants it."

Angie instinctively moved her hand to her nose. "You Carlsons are weird." She shook her head.

"We are indeed." He held up his phone to indicate he was going to continue texting. "We were just sharing some farming puns."

FINLAY: *Do you know how exhausting you are?*

RYAN: *Beets me!*

FINLAY: **slaps her head in frustration**

RYAN: *C'mon. That was funny.*

FINLAY: *You think you're soooo amoooosing.*

RYAN: *YES! Now that's what I'm talking about.*

"Why can't the bankrupt farmer complain?" asked Angie.

"Huh?" Ryan looked over at her in confusion.

"Why can't the bankrupt farmer complain?" She nodded encouragingly.

"Umm, I don't know," he answered with suspicion in his voice. He wasn't really sure what she was talking about.

"Because he's got no beef," she said with a wide grin. Ryan stared at her dumbfounded. "Get it? He's got no beef."

A joke. Angie had just told a corny joke, and it was . . . hilarious. Ryan threw his head back and howled.

"That's a great one," he congratulated her. "Let me tell Finlay." He texted the joke to his sister and could almost hear her groaning all the way from Iowa.

FINLAY: On that incredibly ridiculous note, gotta get to class.

RYAN: Stay classy!

*FINLAY: *Eye roll**

RYAN: Love you Fin!

Ryan put his phone down and leaned back into his chair. He looked at Angie, a smile spreading across his face. Angie looked back at him suspiciously.

"What?" she asked, squinting at him as if assessing what was going on in his head. "Do I have something on my nose? The nose your sister apparently wants."

"No." He chuckled. "Nothing on your nose."

"Then why are you grinning at me like a loon?"

Ryan reflected on Angie's joke. When they first met, he wouldn't have guessed she had this playful side to her. Between sharing silly dances at Thuy's wedding a few days ago and hearing her spot-on pun, he was seeing a side to Angie that he really enjoyed.

"I'm just reflecting on your perfectly executed joke."

"Oh, well in that case, feel free to congratulate away. In fact, I would prefer yellow and orange streamers in my ticker tape parade and the statue erected in my honor cast in bronze instead of marble."

"So noted," Ryan said, all the while too focused on why hearing the word "erected" uttered from Angie's mouth was so inappropriately arousing.

NINE

The last batch of videos had been another bust as far as the Subway Girl was concerned but did provide Angie with some new hilarious submissions to post to *Celebrity Monger*. She and Ryan were planning to grab lunch, but he had to return a phone call first, so Angie took the opportunity to look at the balance in her checking account.

Huh? There seemed to be an excess of funds. Not that she was going to complain about having too much of her most scarce commodity—money. She wasn't crazy, after all. But it was odd and had her concerned that a mix-up with the bank was going to eat away at her second most scarce commodity—time.

Before she could ponder this further, Ryan returned, and they hit the streets. Angie watched Ryan scan the crowd, as usual.

"Looking for the pink beanie, huh?"

"Yup. Speaking of, what did the tie say to the hat?"

Angie prepared herself for some awful joke. Her only response was a raised brow.

"You go on a-head and I'll hang around." Ryan placed his hands under his chin and gave her an "Aren't I cute" look. *He is cute*, she thought. *Adorable*.

"I know, I know." He shook his head. "I'm the worst."

"I'm not saying anything." She grinned smugly.

"Not with your mouth," he retorted. "But your eyes say it all. Or more accurately, your eye-roll says it all." He chuckled.

In the relatively short time they had known each other, it had become a well-established fact that Angie was a champion eye-roller. If eye-rolling were an Olympic sport, she wouldn't be a gold medalist. No, she would be a paid professional with corporate sponsors, wearing one of those jackets covered in so many brand logos she wouldn't even qualify for amateur status. And now she was directing that perfected eye-roll at Ryan.

"Well, eyes are the windows to the soul. At least that's what you romantics always say." She was teasing him, but people really were eating all this "romantic" stuff up. All because of the man across from her. At that thought, a brilliant idea came to her. She should tape a series of segments with Ryan, showing him in his element—at work, with his friends, just being the all-around good guy that he was.

The woman might have already recognized herself as the Subway Girl but is fearful of coming forward. Showcasing Ryan as the genuine, kind, funny and amazing guy Angie knew him to be might help assuage any concerns.

It might also help to drive views of *Celebrity Monger*. The selection of submission videos she had posted—of women hoping to be Ryan's dream girl—were increasing traffic to the site daily, but not enough to satisfy Barry.

Yeah, we need more of Ryan. His warmth in the first video had definitely come across on camera. You only needed to watch the hundreds of video submissions to know that women responded to him. And it wasn't just his good looks. There was something special about him, enough that women were clamoring to be selected as his love interest.

Based on her three years of experience at *Celebrity Monger*, Angie put the celebrity tabloid/reality-show consumers into three categories: one, the naïve, information-hungry people who believed everything they saw; two, the hardened skeptics who thought everything was pure manipulation; and three, the realists seeking entertainment. They understood that reality TV, while rooted in reality, wasn't necessarily *all* real, but were drawn to the drama, comedy and sheer ridiculousness.

She was confident Ryan could win over all three groups. It was easy to believe Ryan was truly as earnest as he appeared. She'd never come across anyone—and she'd covered some of the biggest actors and actresses in the entertainment industry—who could pull off an act like that. It *had* to be real. And the more of him she could show the public, the more people would flock to watch his story unfold.

He's certainly won me over. Ryan had become not only an integral part of her career aspirations, but of her life in general. Whether they were sharing a meal, a laugh, an amusing anecdote about their friends, or a discussion about something of importance like the relevance of the electoral college in modern voting or how to address homelessness in the city, she always welcomed their time together.

When they reached the diner door, Ryan, ever the gentleman, held it open for her. Before she could step through, a group of three young women walked out. They chatted excitedly among themselves, and one muttered a "thanks" to Ryan for his politeness. Only when the second woman looked up and saw him did the others stop to take notice.

"Hi," she breathed, pulling her lower lip into her mouth and biting down, hard. Angie barely resisted rolling her eyes.

"Hi." Ryan smiled down at her as they both stood in the diner's doorway. The two other women whispered to one another and giggled. "Have a nice day."

"Yeah." The young woman licked her lips and ran her fingertips across the collar of her sweater. Ryan pushed through the doorway, placed a hand on Angie's lower back, and ushered her to an empty booth. Angie looked back and saw the three women standing outside the diner, talking animatedly then pointing to Ryan and sharing a huddled giggle. Oh yeah. She needed more Ryan. *Wait, what? I meant, we, meaning* Celebrity Monger, *need more Ryan.*

Angie opened her menu and studied the diner's options. Once she'd closed it, she looked up to see Ryan staring at her. It made her self-conscious, like he could sense what was going on in her brain and in her heart. That intensity was more than she was prepared to handle, so she went to her go-to and defused it with sarcasm.

"What?" She tilted her head to the side and looked at him skeptically. "Do I stereotypically have something on my face?"

"No." He laughed.

"Then what? You're staring at me."

"I was just thinking that I bet a lot of people misjudge you."

Angie snorted. "What does that mean?" Her tone was clearly affronted.

"Exactly that! You look very sweet and innocent. And your diminutive size doesn't help. But underneath it all, you're this fireball who just says what you think. It's awesome."

"I'm a New Yorker." She shrugged. "It's part of my DNA."

"I suppose that's something you can't learn. It's just who you are."

"Yup," she said with pride. "Just wish I could be like that with Barry," she added, with much less bravado in her voice.

"I know what you mean. He kind of scares me." Ryan recoiled in mock horror, but Angie could tell he wasn't completely joking.

"Yeah, well, I think it's just in your DNA to be a genuinely nice person."

"I wish I were a bit more like you."

"You just keep being you," she advised. *Because you're pretty awesome just the way you are.* "Speaking of, I was thinking that maybe the Subway Girl could be a bit nervous about coming forward because she doesn't know much about you. What if we did a few segments of you in your everyday life?"

"No. Absolutely not."

"Why not?"

"This is already too public. I don't want to put myself out there like that. And I definitely don't want to involve my family or friends."

"I really think it could help," she said. And even if it didn't help find the girl, Angie knew it would bolster interest in the search, and at the end of the day, she just needed to move the needle enough with views and likes and posts for Barry to get the network deal through. At this point, she didn't really care if they found the Subway Girl.

"That's a hard no, Ange."

She wanted to explain that there was *so* much depth to him. They just needed to find a way to showcase it. Before she could outline in more detail what she had in mind, a waitress with long dark hair pulled into a messy bun, wearing a pale-yellow apron, approached the table.

"Hi. Welcome to the Sunflower Diner. Can I start you off with something to drink?" she said unenthusiastically. Ryan gestured for Angie to order first.

"I'd like an iced tea. And a BLT, no mayo," she said. The waitress looked up at Angie and then turned to Ryan.

"And for you?" she droned.

"May I please have—"

"Hey," the waitress interrupted. "Wait a second. I know you. You're the Subway Guy, right?" She narrowed her eyes at Ryan and then turned to Angie. "Are you her?" she asked excitedly. "Are you the Subway Girl? I didn't realize they found you yet."

"You are correct, somewhat," Angie said. "This is Ryan." She gestured toward the man sitting across the booth from her. "He is indeed searching for the Subway Girl. But I'm not her." *No way would a man like this be looking for someone like me.*

"Oh." The waitress deflated. "So, is it not real? I mean, you're here with another woman," she said, turning to Ryan.

"Oh, it's real." He smiled. *Of course he thinks this is all real.*

"This is Angie Prince." He pointed at Angie. She plastered on a smile to cover up her cynical thoughts. "She's the reporter who's helping me track the Subway Girl down."

"Cool." The waitress's shoulders relaxed in relief. "I hope you find her. It's such an awesome love story."

"Thanks. I appreciate that." He nodded with a bit of pride. The waitress returned his smile, seemingly dazzled by Ryan's sincerity, and walked away.

"Uh, could I place my order?" Ryan called out after her.

"Oh, sorry." She turned back toward the table, shaking her head as if she were trying to come out of a daze. "Yeah, what can I get you?"

Over their casual lunch of sandwiches and fries, Ryan shared some of his favorite movies with Angie, who was surprised and impressed by his eclectic taste, from Italian foreign films to sci-fi B movies from the '60s. She loved the ease of their conversations, even if they were disagreeing, and how invested he seemed in listening and absorbing what she had to say. When the conversation turned to *her* passions, she reluctantly explained that she'd had numerous submissions and subsequent rejections from the *New Yorker.*

"Can I read one?" Ryan asked.

"Oh, I don't think so," she scoffed.

"Why not? You were hoping they would be published, right?"

"Well, that is true, but obviously the editors at the *New Yorker* didn't think they were good enough for public viewing."

"Nonsense. Just because they didn't publish them, doesn't mean they aren't good. Seriously, I want to take a look."

"Really?" She scrunched up her nose in a rare display of insecurity.

"Yes, really."

"Okay," she said reluctantly. "I'll email you a few of them when I get back to the office."

"I'll take this whenever you're ready," the waitress said, putting the bill down on the table along with a large slice of chocolate cake. "And this," she said as she pointed to the treat, "is on me. Good luck."

"Wow. Thanks," said Ryan, flashing his most winning smile at the waitress before turning it to Angie. He gestured for her to help herself. Angie picked up a knife and sliced through the cake, using the knife's edge to pull one of the pieces closer to her. Ryan eyed his piece of the cake with suspicion.

"That doesn't look like half." His brow furrowed as he looked at her with disapproval.

"It's just the way the knife went through it." Angie shrugged, lifting a bite to her mouth.

He quirked an eyebrow. "Just how the knife only went through a *third* of it?"

Angie chuckled and cut off a chunk of cake from her slice and pushed it toward Ryan. He tossed her a wink while grabbing his fork.

After he wrapped up his work for the night, hours after Luke and Diego had gone home, Ryan hopped on the subway back to his place. As usual, he began his train ride scouring through the passengers for the Subway Girl, hoping to see her once again. As he looked for the pink beanie and green eyes or kept an ear out for the sound of her British accent, he thought about Angie and how lucky he was to have her by his side for this journey. How he enjoyed their time together, their debates and discussions, their talk about movies and culture and society.

He popped his earbuds into his ears, placed his computer on his lap and opened up one of the articles Angie had sent to him. Reading through the various samples she provided, he was beyond impressed. In fact, he was so engrossed, he missed his stop and had to double back.

She had a sophisticated but not overly complicated writing style and covered some pretty heavy subjects. And while a few of her topics could have fallen into the category of fluff pieces, she skillfully incorporated statistics and interview quotes to give them needed weight. He pulled out his cell phone to send her a text.

RYAN: *Not amazing enough for the New Yorker? Really?!? What do they know about writing anyway?*

ANGIE: *You're not just saying that, are you? You don't have to spare my feelings. They have rejected them ALL.*

RYAN: *I would never lie to you. Excellent articles. Your passion and fire are evident.*

ANGIE: *You mean my NY attitude?*

RYAN: *Yup! Especially the one about NYC places. So obvious you love the city. Like a walking I ♥ NY t-shirt. LOL!*

ANGIE: *Who needs a t-shirt when I have the logo tattooed on my . . .*

RYAN: *Yes . . .*

Ryan swallowed hard at the prospect of cool ink adorning Angie's tight little body. It wasn't the first time he'd thought about her in that way. He was a guy after all, and she was pretty, smart, and oh-so-spirited.

ANGIE: *Ha! I couldn't think of something that wouldn't be even remotely inappropriate.*

RYAN: *I'm hard to offend.*

ANGIE: *Good to know.*

The idea of being hard to offend—and just *hard* thinking about Angie having a tattoo—caused Ryan to shift on the plastic subway seat. *Refocus.*

RYAN: *The one thing on your list I haven't experienced is a schooner sail in the city.*

ANGIE: *Super fun. We should definitely go this summer.*

RYAN: *This summer for sure.*

This summer? He liked the idea that he would still be hanging out with Angie this summer. He liked the idea of hanging out with Angie anytime.

TEN

Ryan hit send on an email, leaned back in his chair, crossed his hands behind his neck and let out a loud exhale. He felt a wave of satisfaction and relief at having finished the next round of edits on a client project on time. He'd been spending more and more time with Angie, and it wasn't just time reviewing submissions to the Subway Girl search link. He found himself sharing a meal or coffee with her more often than he ate alone. A few hours wouldn't go by without one of them texting an article or funny meme or random thought to one another.

On more than one occasion, he'd snapped himself out of a computer-coding daze realizing he was thinking about her. *Angie.* If he had to go through this search with anyone, he was glad she was by his side. She was so funny and spirited and so damn optimistic about this search. *Not that I'm not an optimist. I couldn't believe in a "one true love" if I weren't.*

Yet, whenever he felt discouraged, that maybe this whole Subway Girl search was a fool's errand, she would remind him it would all be worth it in the end. For someone who seemed so cynical about her own prospects for love, she was convinced that his efforts wouldn't be in vain. She made him feel hopeful and positive, and that must be the reason why he'd grown so comfortable with her, always looking forward to their time together.

That had to be it, right? Otherwise, what was he still doing searching for this mystery girl? He took a glance at the *Celebrity Monger* message boards, scouring subject lines from "Get a Life" to "Skanks R Us," and sagged into his chair.

He reached into his back pocket for his phone to call home for his weekly check-in with Mom and Dad, but it wasn't there. He stood up and patted down the pockets in the front and back of his pants. He picked up a stack of paper on his desk to look underneath.

"Damn," he muttered.

"What's wrong?" asked Luke, sliding his chair across the room.

"I can't find my phone," Ryan responded, shaking his head.

"Just call it." He reached for his own cell phone.

"I put it on silent while I was at Angie's office earlier," Ryan replied with a scowl. He could kick himself.

"If you like it, then you should have put a ring on it," said Luke with a humorous glint in his eyes. Diego, who had been across the open office space working on some invoicing, quickly and silently slid his chair across the room and gave Luke a high five, before just as quickly and just as silently sliding back and resuming his work.

Ryan searched online for the *Celebrity Monger* phone number and picked up his office phone. "Hi. It's Ryan Carlson. Is Angie there?"

"Could have just used 'find your phone,'" Luke whispered. Ryan smirked and gave him the finger.

"Hey, Angie. Glad you're still at the office. Hope I didn't interrupt anything."

"Just writing," she replied.

"Making any progress?"

"I've written fifteen hundred words today," she said.

"Fifteen hundred? Wow. I don't think I even *know* that many words."

"Well, some of them do repeat—like 'the' and 'and,'" she lobbed back.

"Excellent." He wondered if she could hear him smiling. "Anyway, I'm sorry to disturb, but I think I left my phone there." He could hear her moving around and shuffling papers on her desk.

"Yup. I have it right here."

He sighed with relief. "At least it's not lost."

"I'll be here for a while if you want to come by and get it."

"Yeah, I can swing by in a little—"

Luke motioned for Ryan to hand the phone over to him.

"Gimme the phone," Luke commanded. Ryan reluctantly complied, unsure of what Luke was going to say.

"Angie. I'm Ryan's buddy Luke. You need to come out with us tonight." Ryan shook his head, imagining Angie's response.

"Come on," Luke implored. "Take a break. We'll meet you at Malone's on Greenpoint Avenue at eight. I would pick you up, but my license got suspended for driving all the ladies crazy."

Ryan would have bet big money that Angie was rolling her eyes right about now. He would have also bet money that Angie would shoot Luke down.

"And bring a hot girlfriend with you, okay?" Luke continued. Before Ryan could even hear Angie's garbled voice on the other end of the line, Luke said, "Breathe for yes. Lick your elbow for no."

A moment later, Luke handed the phone back, patting Ryan on the shoulder and giving a quick affirming nod.

"I'm sorry about that. So, so sorry," Ryan said to Angie in half jest, half apology. "He'll likely say flirty, inappropriate things, but underneath it all, he's a good guy."

"It's okay," Angie said with a chuckle. "I live a few blocks from Malone's, and I'm sure my roommate will be up for grabbing a drink. She gets a kick out of that flirty humor. It will be good to have a laugh. I'll see you there and bring your phone." *Her laugh.*

"See you soon." Ryan hung up the phone and gave Luke a playful slug in the arm, all the while happy to know he would be spending time with Angie tonight.

A little after eight o'clock, Angie and Josie strode into Malone's. It wasn't too crowded for a Friday evening. Patrons lined the bar one or two deep, but there were a few empty tables and booths here and there.

In one of the booths was where Angie spotted Ryan, sitting with two other guys, one of whom she assumed was his pal Luke. When Luke had initially invited her, Angie's first response was to politely decline. Politely, of course, because Ryan's impeccable manners were beginning to rub off on her. That thought caused a ghost of a smile to cross her lips. After hearing Luke's beyond-cheesy lines, her second thought was also to decline. Her track record with guys like that wasn't so hot. But after a few moments of consideration, she knew she would have to go. She was eager to meet Ryan's friends, having heard so much about them. As they approached the table, Ryan caught her eye and waved.

"He's much hotter in person," whispered Josie.

"I guess," replied Angie with a shrug. If she was being honest with Josie and herself, she would have said, "Hell yeah, he's hot." Empirically, Ryan was a good-looking guy. When you added in his charming personality, sincere generosity and kindness, he was downright amazing. She even enjoyed the incessant movie quoting, although she would never admit it to him.

Angie only hoped that if they did find the Subway Girl, she would be worthy of such a great guy. It would kill her to see Ryan get hurt.

"Angie, I would recognize you anywhere," said the blond walking toward her in a baby-blue button-down that matched his twinkling eyes. He leaned in, giving her a kiss on the cheek. "I'm Luke Devine, and before you ask, the last name truly describes me perfectly. You know Ryan. This here"—he pointed to the third guy, who had a buzz cut and a lopsided smile—"is Diego."

"This is my friend Josie," said Angie.

"As in the *pussycats?*" growled Luke. Josie tilted her head down, looked up at Luke through her long lashes and giggled. Josie never did seem to mind the cheesy lines. And while Angie wasn't yet sure about Luke, she knew Ryan vouched for him, so she was willing to cut him some slack. Diego scooted over and made room for the two ladies to sit down.

"Don't answer that." Ryan rolled his eyes. "I apologize for him."

"It's okay," said Josie, looking at Ryan and then turning back to Luke. "But I need to know something. Are you going to want to get married?"

Luke practically choked on his own saliva. "Not today," he coughed out.

"No, not today," she replied sweetly. "But someday. You want to get married someday?"

"Yeah. I guess so." Angie could tell from his tone that Luke wasn't sure what Josie was getting at.

"I don't. And I'm afraid once you have me, you'll never get over me. So this," she said, pointing back and forth between them, "this isn't going to happen." Despite the preemptive rejection, Josie delivered the blow with sweetness and a smile. Angie sure admired her for that.

"Ooooh, burn, man," said Diego. "She just put you in the friend zone."

"No," said Luke, clearly taking the teasing in stride. "She just put me in the *fun* zone."

"If you think you can resist my considerable charms . . ." Josie said.

"I don't mind giving it a try. I think I could fall madly in bed with you," Luke said. "I'm all for one night of fun. No strings or attachments. Think it over." He shrugged as if it were no big deal. Angie snorted at Ryan. "Speaking of giving things a try, you ladies got anyone we can set up with Diego here?"

"Hmm," Josie replied, looking Diego over thoughtfully.

"Great guy," said Luke. "Good job. Smart with money." Diego grinned and nodded, playing along.

"Handsome," added Luke. Diego glided his hand across his face, showing off his features. "Big . . ." Luke pointed to Diego's crotch. Diego turned a dark shade of pink.

"What about Regina from the hospital?" Josie turned to Angie.

Angie nodded in consideration. "Yeah, actually, she's awesome."

Josie turned back to the guys. "She's a pediatric resident I work with. Super smart, tons of fun, quirky sense of humor."

"She's obviously smart and successful, and it's a huge bonus she's good with kids," Luke enthused. "Pretty?"

"Gorgeous," Josie said emphatically.

"Big breasts?"

Ryan cringed. "Dude. C'mon. There are ladies present."

Josie didn't seem thrown by the question at all. "Medium sized, but perky and all real," she explained with a thoughtful nod. Angie shared a glance with Ryan. She couldn't believe that Josie and Luke were bantering so easily like this and it looked like Ryan couldn't either.

"Sweet," said Luke. "Let's set it up."

"Uh, hello. I'm sitting right here," chimed in Diego. "Don't I get a say?"

"No," said Luke flatly. "Set it up," he advised Josie. "In fact, why don't you just text me the details. I'll give you my number." *Oh, real smooth.* She watched as Luke and Josie exchanged phone numbers and flirty smiles.

"Do you guys always razz each other this much?" Angie asked Ryan.

"Yeah," Ryan admitted. "You can go from alpha wolf to caribou real fast with these guys. Sometimes you just need to keep the heat off yourself."

"Let me get you ladies a drink. You like beer?" Luke asked.

"We do," said Angie.

"Surprise us with something on tap," said Josie.

When Luke returned, he handed each of the ladies a glass of light amber, foam-topped beer.

"It's Smooth Hoperator, a craft brew," Luke said. Angie rolled her eyes and Josie grinned, then they both lifted the glasses to their lips and sipped.

"Well?" Luke asked. Angie gave him a thumbs-up. "'Good people drink good beer.' Hunter S. Thompson," he shared, in reference to the *Fear and Loathing in Las Vegas* author.

"Mmm. Heaven," Josie said dreamily.

"I was inquiring about the beer, but thanks for the compliment." Luke flashed a wink.

For the next hour and a half, the group told stories, drank beers from the bar's impressive on-tap selection, and engaged in heated debates, such as who would be worse as a sole companion on a desert island—Kanye West or Kim Kardashian. Ryan shared the story of how Luke had taken care of him when he'd had the stomach flu. Luke shrugged as if it were no big deal, but then made a point to praise Ryan for returning the favor when Luke succumbed to it himself. It was evident they were a tight bunch who teased, shared and supported each other with vigor.

"Hey. Feel his sweater," Luke said to Angie, gesturing toward Ryan's arm. Angie reached over, her chest brushing against him, and gently fingered Ryan's dark green cashmere-blend sweater. She didn't like how much she liked being this close to him.

"Know what that is?" asked Luke.

Angie looked deep into Ryan's eyes, and the way he looked back at her, like she was, for lack of a better word, *worthy*, made her break eye contact and look back at Luke. "No. What is it?"

"Boyfriend material," Luke said.

Angie laughed and looked back over to Ryan, who shook his head and rolled his eyes. "He *is* boyfriend material." He really was. He was going to make some girl so happy. Angie couldn't believe she was actually considering that a loving relationship between two people was possible. But Ryan caused her to shed a layer of the cynicism that surrounded her. Sure, she didn't think love was possible for *her*, but at least she was now convinced it was possible for *him*.

"Thanks." Ryan gave her an appreciative smile that lit up his face.

Angie turned back to Luke. "Are you always like this?" she asked, finding it hard to believe he was always this much of a player and seeking a distraction from her confusing feelings about Ryan. Luke wiggled his eyebrows at her.

"They're called eyebrows because my eyes are browsing all over you," he said mock-seductively.

"So that would be a yes."

"Yes!" said Ryan. The two of them laughed as Luke grabbed Angie's and Josie's empty glasses and rose for the bar.

"Let me freshen these up for you ladies," he said.

Ryan raised his almost empty beer glass and called out after Luke. "I'll take another while you're up there. Thanks." Luke nodded in acknowledgment. Ryan turned back to Angie, and she smiled at him, while Josie and Diego discussed the merits of at-home hair clippers.

"Your friend Luke there seems to be an incurable flirt," she said, laughing. "Full of charisma."

"Yeah. He's one of my best friends, but I don't think you should date him. He sounds a bit like your ex-boyfriend. Loves lots of ladies almost as much as he loves himself."

"Is he a liar and a cheat?" she asked, her voice solemn.

"No," said Ryan immediately.

"Then he's nothing like my ex-boyfriend," she said flatly, searching his eyes for understanding.

"Oh. Sorry." Ryan paused, as if trying to think of an appropriate response. "You don't strike me as the type of girl that would take that."

"That's why he's an ex," she said with a sad smile.

"Well, I can assure you, Luke may be obnoxious, cocky and borderline inappropriate, but he's as solid as they come."

"That's good to hear, because he and Josie seem to be hitting it off."

"Good for them," said Ryan, sounding relieved. "You, on the other hand, deserve someone really special." He gently touched her hand as he smiled at her. *I wish that were true*, she thought.

She really deserves someone great. It made Ryan sad to think Angie not only didn't believe in love but didn't think she deserved love. When she'd told him her ex-boyfriend had cheated on her, sad didn't describe it. He couldn't imagine Angie, this tough-as-nails, spirited New Yorker, putting up with that crap. It was a story he wanted to know, but now wasn't the time. What he really wanted was to show that asshole what it felt like to take a fist to the jaw.

"Hey, you okay?" asked Diego. "You look . . . kinda pissed."

"I'm cool, man." But Ryan didn't feel cool. He took a deep breath and exhaled sharply. If tension continued to roll off him, Diego didn't seem to notice.

"So, Angie's pretty awesome," said Diego, gesturing over to Angie, who was walking back from the ladies' room with Josie.

"Yeah."

"So, do you think she might go for someone like me?" Diego asked hopefully. Ryan didn't like that idea at all. He felt confused by his reaction. Diego was a great guy. Truly one of his best buddies. He had a healthy respect for women and, unlike Luke, wanted a relationship. He wasn't a player or a cheater. He was smart and loyal, and Angie certainly deserved all that.

But as much as he loved Diego like a brother, Angie deserved more. She was outspoken, spirited, funny, talented, charming, and hidden beneath that hard shell, he just knew lurked a gooey center. She needed someone who could keep up with her and challenge her. She needed someone who could crack that tough exterior to unleash the warmth underneath. No, Diego was not the right guy for Angie.

"I thought you were getting fixed up with her friend?" Ryan said, hoping to redirect Diego's interest.

"Yeah, with their doctor friend."

"I think that's great." Ryan slapped Diego on the back and stood up to make room for Angie, who had returned to the table. Yes. It was great for Diego, who so deserved to find his someone special, to have a prospect. As long as it wasn't Angie.

ELEVEN

It was just shy of one thirty in the morning, and it looked as though they were about ready to call it a night. Diego went over to the bar to settle the tab for the last round of beers. Josie and Angie whispered to each other, until Luke extended his hand to help Josie out of her seat. He wrapped his arm around her and whispered something in her ear. She shook her head in disbelief, but the smile across her face gave her away. She wasn't annoyed by him. In fact, she seemed downright lust-filled. She gave Angie a wink and a wave, as if to let her know she wouldn't be coming home that night.

Diego walked past the two of them as they exited through the door. Luke turned and gave a thumbs-up. Diego glanced down at the ground, looking defeated.

"Closing time," Diego said with a shrug and a smile.

"You don't have to go home but you can't stay here," said Angie and Ryan in unison. They looked at each other and laughed. Ryan marveled at how her laugh still did something to him.

"Come on," Ryan said to Angie. "I'll walk you home." She stood up and linked arms with him and Diego, smiling up at both of them. When they reached the bar door, Ryan asked, "Which way?"

"Down here," she said, gesturing with her head to the left.

"I'm this way," said Diego, indicating to the right. "Unless you want me to come with you?" he asked Ryan.

"Nah, man. I got this." The two did a combo man-handshake/bro hug before Diego walked away.

"So, Diego seems like a good guy."

"He's the best," said Ryan. Was Angie interested in Diego romantically?

"I think he and Regina would really hit it off. She's really fantastic." Okay, so she wasn't interested in Diego for herself. *But if she did like him, why should that bother me? It's not like I want her for myself. Right?*

Ryan knew that Angie's interest in him was strictly professional. She was helping him find his dream girl. And from the little he knew about the world of video production and celebrity news, he could tell she was damn good at her job. She'd never given him any indication she wanted anything more than to help him, even if she did agree to come hang out with him and his friends tonight. So why couldn't he stop thinking about her?

"This is my place," Angie said, pointing to a three-story Brooklyn brownstone.

"Looks nice," said Ryan.

"Well . . . thanks for walking me home. And dragging me out tonight. I actually had a lot of fun," she admitted. The more time she spent with Ryan, the more she learned about him. The more she learned about him, the more she liked him. Seeing the comfortable banter among his friends revealed a few more layers to this man who was becoming such a fixture in her life. *He really is boyfriend material.*

"I'm glad. I had fun, too. I guess I'll see you later."

"Sounds good. Good night." Neither of them budged from their places on the sidewalk. Instead, they stood still, staring into each other's eyes as if in some strange standoff. Angie swallowed hard and blinked first, glancing down to his mouth.

God, how she wanted to kiss him. And for him to kiss her back. She hadn't been kissed in months. Hadn't felt the press of soft lips. The slide of a tongue stroking hers. The delicious anticipation of those few perfect seconds before lips connect. Ryan was such a good guy and undeniably attractive. Why did he have to be so darn attractive? She was finding it hard to resist his charms, which ironically he wasn't even using to woo her. He was just by nature an amazing guy, and she wanted him.

She glanced down at her feet. *What is wrong with me? He isn't mine to have. He really isn't even mine to borrow.* He belonged to the Subway Girl—at least he would belong to her if they could find her. But she really did want him . . . badly.

She licked her lips and looked up to find him staring at her mouth. Although the light outside her building cast a shadow that cut across his face, she could see his lips slightly parted as if he desperately wanted to know how her lips tasted, too. Her heart thundered in her chest. Did he want this as much as she did? Could someone like him—so honest, kind and committed—be attracted to her?

Angie leaned her body forward, eyes still trained on Ryan's mouth. His tongue peeked out to wet his lips, and she worried that the image would cause her to combust. She leaned in further, lifting her head slightly. *Am I doing this? Am I really doing this?*

Like magnets, Angie felt herself and Ryan being drawn together. The first touch of their lips was just a whisper. After their lips brushed, Ryan pulled back to look into Angie's eyes. Of course he was doing the good guy "check-in." Making sure she was okay with this. She resisted rolling her eyes and instead reached forward and laid her lips on his again, this time with more pressure and more intent.

It went from ember to inferno in mere seconds. Ryan responded by threading his hands in her hair, using his fingers to pull her face closer.

"I've been wanting to kiss that sassy mouth of yours all night," he rasped.

"Less talking. More kissing," she moaned as she pressed her body closer to his, aligning as much as possible given the significant height difference. Looking to readjust the angle of her body, so she could get more comfortably closer to him, Angie pulled back, only to see a look of concern flash across Ryan's face, as if she were having second thoughts. She wasn't having second thoughts. She was having naughty thoughts.

She grabbed his hand, unlocked the front door and guided him up the three flights to her apartment. If Ryan was talking, she didn't hear it. Angie's heartbeat thundered in her ears. Once they reached her door, Angie held onto the knob, turned around, reached up onto her toes and kissed him. While his lips skated over hers, she managed to open the door and pull him over the threshold.

He stretched his arms around her—which wasn't difficult given how tiny she was—grasped her behind and lifted her up. Angie wrapped her legs around him as he spun her around. *Damn.* It felt good to be cradled against his hard length. She rocked her hips back and forth, causing Ryan to grow harder with each thrust.

With Angie still wrapped around him, Ryan kicked the door closed, turned toward the hallway and backed Angie up against the wall. Her legs squeezed tighter around him as he hoisted her up further, getting better leverage. Her arm jutted out, rattling a framed black-and-white photo of downtown New York that hung on the wall. Ryan's denim-covered erection pressed against Angie's most sensitive spot. She rocked her hips against him again, creating an unbearably sweet friction.

She moaned as he pushed back against her, one hand holding her up by the ass against the wall, the other gently squeezing her breast.

"You are so sexy," he panted, trailing his tongue along the hollow of her neck while she continued to rock against him. She'd never felt anything close to this level of yearning.

She moaned again, letting her hand roam under his shirt over the hard muscles of his back. Ryan slipped his free hand under Angie's ass and moved back, as if he were going to walk her toward a bedroom.

Angie had other ideas. Both of her hands dipped further south and she pushed him closer to her, grinding unabashedly. She hadn't kissed anyone in months, and it had been even longer since she'd felt the hard length of a man pressed against her.

With another rub, Angie bit down hard on her lip, tilted her head back and let out another slow moan while her body shuddered and shivered.

Ryan stilled. "Did you just . . ."

"Oh my god. I can't believe I just did that," Angie groaned in embarrassment. Clearly it had been much too long since she'd been with a man if she was able to have an intense orgasm through some fully clothed heavy petting. "I've never done it like that . . ." She bit her lip and trained her eyes on the floor.

"Hey, don't get all shy on me." He lifted her chin for her to look into his eyes. "That was insanely hot," he said, resting his head on her forehead.

"You feel so good," she breathed, both in confession and a sigh of relief that Ryan wasn't as turned off as she'd feared by her shockingly quick release.

"We're not done yet. I want you," he said.

"Thank god." *I want you, too.* While she wanted to keep him forever, she was willing to take what little borrowed time she could.

"Where's your room?" he asked, trailing kisses down her neck and across her shoulder where he had pushed the fabric of her blouse to the side. Angie continued to writhe against him and whimper at the feel of his warm breath on her sensitized flesh. "Angie." He laughed. "Which way to your room?" Angie pointed down the hallway, and he effortlessly carried her along it.

Ryan used his foot to push open Angie's door and lowered her to the ground. She instantly missed the heat and body contact. He reached behind his neck, grabbing his sweater and white t-shirt and pulling them over his head. Angie gasped at the sight of his smooth chest and toned abs. He shivered when her hand caressed his skin.

"Your turn."

Angie stepped back and unbuttoned her blouse, one small button at a time, to reveal a white lacy bra. Ryan let out a shaky exhale as she stood in front of him with her blouse open. He moved toward her, pushing the blouse off her shoulders. It slid past her arms to the ground.

"Wow," he whispered.

She had never felt more beautiful. The way he stared at her, the small vein in his neck throbbing with his increased pulse, set her on fire. He shifted closer to her, trailing his fingers across her collarbone and neck. It was tender and loving. Angie didn't know what to make of it. She didn't want to think about it. She just wanted to feel more of what she'd felt in the hallway.

She eased backward, bringing Ryan with her, until the back of her knees hit the edge of the bed. She sat down, pulling herself up on her knees and scooting back to make way for him. He crawled up the bed, toward her body, until they couldn't go any further.

Ryan gave her legs a gentle tug, pulling them out from under her, and wrapped them around his waist. Angie squealed, leaned back and pulled Ryan down by his shoulders until he was resting on top of her. He pushed up onto his elbows to look down at her. It wasn't just lust she was seeing in his eyes. That was certainly there. But there seemed to be so much emotion, too. *It must be because of the friendship we've developed.*

The room was silent except for their heavy breathing and the sound of Ryan's belt buckle clanking against the hardwood floor after Angie whipped it through his pant loops and tossed it on the ground.

Ryan grabbed his wallet from his back pocket as Angie used her feet to push his pants down. While he pulled out a condom, she shimmied out of her skirt and panties.

As the kiss deepened, Ryan used his strong fingers to caress her cheeks and jaw or to stroke her hair. Angie ran her short nails down Ryan's back, eliciting a low grunt. This right here. This was what she had been missing for so long.

Ryan reared up on his knees, and straddled Angie. She stared up at his impressive physique and licked her lips. He sheathed himself in a condom and lowered himself back down to her.

"I want to be inside you so badly," he moaned.

"Yes," she said, grabbing hold of him and guiding him into her warm channel. It didn't take long for them to adjust to one another—Ryan to the warm wet heat of her, and Angie to both his girth and length.

"Holy . . ." Ryan's voice trailed off. He leaned down onto his elbows and kissed her, while he rolled his hips against her, pushing in and out. Angie, wanting to feel the full weight of his body against hers, pulled him closer.

As he dropped down on top of her, she let out a whispered "Yes." Ryan placed his hands underneath her bottom and tilted her hips up, pushing himself further into her. Sweat formed on his brow as he thrust over and over. Angie closed her eyes from the intensity, both physical and emotional.

"Watch," he commanded.

"I can't," she panted. "It's too much."

"No way. This is going on my mental highlight reel."

Angie moaned. "I'm gonna come."

"Not yet," Ryan begged. "You feel so amazing."

"Oh god. I can't . . ."

"Just a few more minutes. I don't want to go over yet," he said, his voice rough with lust. He continued to piston in and out of her, taking her higher with each drag and pull.

"Ryan," she called out as wet heat flooded her and took Ryan into his own climax. He thrust into her a few more times, then collapsed onto her, being sure to rest on his elbows lest his body crush her small frame. He rested his forehead against hers before rolling onto his back.

"Damn," he said, catching his breath. "We're gonna have to do that again."

"Oh yeah, we do," she agreed. "Mmm," she whimpered, laying her head on his chest. "I'm just going to need a minute to recoup my energy."

"Me too." He yawned.

He doesn't do it like a nice guy, that's for sure. She was in such a state of relaxation she didn't even have the energy to panic or question what this encounter meant. Instead, she drifted toward sleep. She wasn't sure how long she had been out when Ryan's warm breath tickled her ear. She burrowed the side of her face further into the pillow, giving him better access to kiss her neck.

"More?" he whispered. Angie, blissfully in between the state of sleep and wakefulness, gave a groggy "Mm-hmm," though in her mind she was shouting *hell yeah!* "More. Everything," she mumbled. She eased onto her back and raised her arms above her head. She heard the sheets rustle and felt the bed dip with Ryan's movements before being teased with the feeling of a thick finger and wet tongue right on the spot where she ached most.

"I'm going to make you feel so good," he whispered, his breath expelling cool air over her core, which only fueled her desire further.

"Yes. I want to feel so good. I *need* to feel so good," she groaned. Ryan lifted up, draped her legs over his shoulders, and caught her eye.

"I only had one condom, but I need to hear you whimper again," he said with a wolfish grin. He lowered his head and continued to lick and suck on her swollen flesh.

"There's a box in the bathroom, under the sink," Angie panted as his tongue rolled up and down.

"Good to know," he said, before continuing with his ministrations. He knew exactly what he was doing—in terms of both how much he was driving her wild and how to do it properly. Ryan added a second finger and stroked her from the inside, finding that perfect spot to bring her to the brink. Angie let out a few short pants, gripping his fingers tightly with her muscles.

"You're so close," he growled.

"Yes," she whimpered. "I'm so clo—" Before she could complete her thought, blinding white light and an explosion of warmth spread through her. Her body thrashed and shivered against him. Ryan's fingers maintained their penetrating rhythm, allowing Angie's ecstasy to go on and on until she was completely spent.

Once he stopped stroking her, she flung one arm over her eyes and the other across her chest, trying to catch her breath. She opened her eyes as Ryan hustled back into the room—naked—carrying a three-strip of condoms with him.

Angie woke that morning deliciously sore from the orgasms she'd had the pleasure of experiencing over the past few hours. She could feel Ryan's warm, hard body pressed against her. *What is wrong with me?* She'd had multiple orgasms in the span of a few hours, and she already wanted more. Ryan was *that* good.

And that wasn't something she'd expected. Not that she had previously given much thought to how Ryan would be in bed. He was clearly more experienced in that department than she would have given him credit for. But thinking about Ryan with other women wasn't something she wanted to focus on right now.

Likely sensing she was awake, Ryan mumbled, "Morning."

Angie rolled over and wrapped her arm around him, pushing up to rest on his chest. "Looks like we fell asleep again."

"Looks like it." Ryan ran his hand down her hair to her back, drawing little circles across her skin as he did. Angie broke out into goosebumps as he went. She knew she should get up, but she just wanted to enjoy this closeness, the feel of him, for a few moments longer.

She'd thought she might be embarrassed in the light of day, but she wasn't. Was it wrong to sleep with him when she was supposed to be helping him meet a different girl? Yes or no, she didn't care. Things with Ryan felt so right, so perfect, she just couldn't see it as a mistake. Somehow, she felt like this—here with him—was where she was supposed to be. *Maybe*, she thought. *Maybe . . .*

"Angie," he started. "I have to—"

"Of course," she said. "You have to go." *Of course, he has to go. Why would he stay?* Angie knew Ryan had to leave. Thinking of "maybe" was foolish. It wasn't like anything was going to happen between them. She was supposed to be helping him find the love of his life, not hopping on *his* subway car. He was just so kind . . . and funny . . . and sexy . . . and perfect.

"Angie, I—"

"It's just sex," she said, rolling onto her side and lifting up to look at him. *It was just sex*, she thought sadly. She wished it could be more. Somehow, she knew, though, that it would never be more. Not with Ryan. Not with anyone. It wasn't love, just attraction.

"Good sex," he corrected her.

She smiled. "Really good sex."

"Great sex," he challenged.

"Phenomenal sex."

"Really phenomenal sex."

"Yeah," she said wistfully. Angie had had several partners, and two one-night stands in college, and this thing with Ryan hadn't been anything like those experiences. It wasn't hard for her to admit to herself—or apparently to Ryan—that it had been truly phenomenal. "But I know you need to get going." She slipped out of bed and grabbed a floral cotton robe from atop her dresser.

Pee. I was going to say I have to pee. Ryan sighed in defeat as Angie hastily covered herself up like she couldn't get him out of her bed fast enough. She walked out the bedroom door, leaving him alone to get dressed.

They had been lying in bed when she shifted onto him, her silky hair tickling his chest. Each time he'd run his hand down her back, she'd let out a little moan and tightened her hold on him.

Had she even known what she was doing? Ryan had known *exactly* what he was doing. Her skin was so soft, and feeling her curled up against him had shown a vulnerable side to her that he wanted to explore. He already knew how much he enjoyed spitfire Angie. This different side to her was so intriguing.

Do I even still want to find the Subway Girl? Being with Angie felt so good and so right. He'd honestly thought she was feeling the connection between the two of them, but then she dismissed what had been building between them and what they had shared as "just sex."

For her it was just something to do, or rather he was *someone* to do. Angie wasn't looking for love, so of course this was just about sex. Not that he was going to complain about the sex. It was, by far, the hottest night of his life.

Last night when they'd stood outside her building, the chemistry between them was palpable. Like a living organism with a mind of its own. *Was that only last night?* It seemed like a lifetime ago. Ryan shook his head in disbelief that Angie could so easily brush him off after the night they had shared.

He reluctantly stood and grabbed the boxers Angie had thrown across the room earlier that evening; they had landed on a chair. The chair where she had been in his lap last night, riding him in alternating slow steady circles and deep, well-timed thrusts. Being with Angie had felt both like the first time and like they had been there a thousand times before.

"Close," she had choked out as his hands had gripped her waist and beads of sweat had fallen from his brow onto the valley between her breasts. "Really. Fucking. Close." He recalled how she tightened her inner muscles around him like a vise and then how he bucked up into her, pushing her over the edge and chasing his own release. She had leaned her perspiring brow against his shoulder, and he had stroked her back as she continued to shudder. He had never felt so in sync with someone.

Just the thought of it was getting him hard again. He wasn't convinced one night would be enough, but he didn't have a choice. She'd made it clear through her words and actions that it was just a one-time—or rather multiple-times-in-one-night—thing. No, he needed to get his head in the game—his other head. He needed to find the Subway Girl. That's what this whole thing was supposed to be about anyway. That's what fate had been pushing him toward. That's what all of the effort had been for.

He pulled on his boxer briefs and jeans and tossed on his white t-shirt. His head poked through the hole, and he ran his fingers through his hair, which he could tell was sticking up in various directions. He'd grab a quick shower at home before going into the office. With Luke and Diego enjoying the spring Saturday, it would be quiet. He could put on some Kings Quarters music, hunker down and catch up on work.

"You're here?" Angie squeaked out as she walked into the kitchen to find Josie sitting on a bar stool, sipping on a mug of coffee.

"I'm here," Josie responded with a bright smile and a raised brow. Angie knew that look. It was the "do we need to talk?" look. She'd rarely been on the receiving end of the look. It was more likely she'd be flashing the look to Josie.

"Hey, Josie," said Ryan, walking into the living room and pulling his sweater down his torso with one hand while he carried his shoes in the other.

"Good morning," Josie called out in an overly cheery tone. Ryan turned his back to them to sit down and put on his shoes. Josie took the moment to give Angie a wink. "Can I get you a cup of coffee, Ryan?" Josie asked sweetly.

"No, thank you," he replied with his usual politeness. "I need to get into the office."

"On a Saturday?" asked Josie.

"Yeah, I've been taking a lot of time at *Celebrity Monger* and need to catch up on a few things."

"Ah." It looked as though Josie was about to comment further, her mouth open and her finger poised in the air, but Angie glared at her. She put her finger down and just grinned.

"I'll walk you out," said Angie, who was trying to be polite but usher Ryan out at the same time.

"Bye, Josie," Ryan said with a small wave.

"Bye." Josie raised her hand and wiggled her fingers back and forth.

Ryan and Angie walked down the three flights in silence, and it wasn't lost on Angie that it was precisely the way they'd walked up those stairs just last night. At the time, of course, she had been overcome with a raging lust. Now she was fueled by emotions she didn't quite understand.

She wasn't embarrassed, per se. It wasn't like she had made an advance on him and he'd turned her down. She wasn't angry either. *We both know the score.* Her job was to find the Subway Girl for him. Her continued employment, her mom's house and her career prospects depended on it. So what was she feeling? Frustration? Dejection? Hopelessness?

Ryan stopped as they neared the building entrance. He turned to face her, eye level with her given their positions on the stairway.

"So," he started.

"I'll call you Monday after I get in, and we can see how many more videos we got."

"Okay."

"This doesn't need to be awkward," she said. "It was just a release . . . from all the stress." She shrugged. *Yeah, keep telling yourself that.*

"Sure." Ryan turned and walked the last few steps to the door. He opened it without a word and walked through. "See ya," he said, turning back to her one more time. Angie waved and smiled until the door closed behind him.

Once she heard the thud and click of the lock, her smile faded. She took a deep breath and walked back to her apartment, readying herself for Josie's inquisition. She determined that offense was the best defense.

"What are you doing home?" Angie asked, walking into the apartment and turning to the refrigerator so Josie couldn't see her uneasiness. "I figured you would still be sweating up the sheets with Luke."

"Oh, no you don't," Josie admonished. "What the ever-living grace is going on with you and Ryan?" Angie turned to see Josie still sitting at their small kitchen island, her chin in her upturned palms, as if her complete and rapt attention were rooted to this moment.

"Nothing," Angie said with a quick shrug. "He just fell asleep after too many beers." She hated lying to Josie, but she couldn't bear to have this conversation, not when she didn't understand it herself. How could she explain it to someone else?

"Bullshit," Josie replied with a snort.

"Exactly when did you get home?" Angie asked hesitantly.

"Early enough to know you guys did it more than once and it was damn good. You can thank your squeaky bed and these thin walls for that." She smirked. Angie groaned, her shoulders sagging in defeat.

It *was* damn good. The most amazing night of her life. She had been so tempted to tell Ryan that the Subway Girl was never going to contact him and he should be with her instead. That was until he bolted from the bed saying he had to go. She was just something to relieve the pressure of waiting for this girl to get in touch.

"It was no big deal." Angie shrugged.

"It sounded like a big deal. All night long," said Josie, raising her eyebrows.

"When did you say you got home?" Angie asked, her voice rising to a nervous pitch as her heartbeat accelerated.

"Like I said, early enough to know there's a lot of something going on between you two."

Angie brushed her off. "It was just physical."

"Get over yourself, Ange. Not all guys are like Harrison. Ryan seems like the real deal."

"He is. He's great. But my job is to find him the love of his life."

"It doesn't have to be that way."

"This whole thing is getting out of control." She let out a loud exhale from her nose. "It reminds me of this video we posted last year of some guy getting run over, completely flattened, by an oversized tire that came out of nowhere. I feel like that's my life right now." She sagged onto the couch, and Josie sat down next to her. Angie leaned her head on Josie's shoulder.

"C'mon," Josie pressed. "Talk to me."

"You know," Angie said. "You're just going along and minding your own business when BAM! You're just knocked flat by a runaway tire."

"Is this tire your job or your love for Ryan?" Josie said.

"What?" Angie gasped. "You're being ridiculous. This is about the job—plain and simple, although this mess with Barry and my mom and the mortgage and everything is anything but plain and simple."

"Well, if you ask me, I think this has more to do with Ryan than you want to admit."

"Of course, it has to do with Ryan," Angie snapped, although she knew the explanation about to follow was not what Josie had in mind. "I need to find his Subway Girl. That's the solution to this mess, and that's why I've been fixated on him lately. Nothing more."

"If you say so," Josie responded with skepticism.

"I do."

"Okay then, find his girl."

Angie intended to, but she knew she needed to do something more. She needed a new approach to make this happen.

"This chicken piccata is to die for, Ma," Angie said in a garbled voice, as she shoveled another bite into her mouth. Angie, looking for any excuse to avoid thinking about her night with Ryan, had trekked out to Sunnyside to visit her mom. Talking about the mortgage would be just the motivation she needed to cross Ryan off her to-do list and replace it with actually finding the Subway Girl.

"Well, I know it's your favorite," her mom replied, adding more pasta to Angie's plate.

"Ma," Angie warned. "That's plenty."

"Oh, what are you talking about?" Her mom furrowed her brow and shook her head. "You're beautiful just as you are, but put a little more meat on those bones and we won't be able to keep the men away."

"Yeah, because there seems to be a long line of eligible guys lining up to date me," she huffed.

"You wouldn't need to be looking for a man if you just—"

"No! We are not going to talk about Harrison." Why couldn't her mom get it through her thick skull that she and Harrison were like that popular Taylor Swift song that came out a few years back and we were never ever getting back together.

"What about Joseph Finnane? You know, Sharon's son? He's always had a thing for you."

"Joey Finnane? Seriously? The guy is like forty."

"He's thirty-eight and he has a good job."

"Isn't he married?"

"Divorced. Wife cheated on him with their next-door neighbor."

"Damn," Angie muttered.

"Angie. I just want you to find someone to take care of you."

"You shouldn't want me to find someone to take care of me. You should want me to be able to take care of myself."

"Oh, you know what I mean," her mom scoffed. *Yeah, sadly, I do know what you mean.* "So, there's no one special to speak of?" There was someone special. The most special man she had ever met. But she didn't want to talk about that mess with anyone, especially not her mom.

"Let's talk about something else. Read any good books lately?"

"Oh, for god's sake, Angie. You know I don't read books. Is there really no safe topic for us to discuss?" she grumbled.

"We could talk about the mortgage extension," Angie suggested with a raised brow, knowing it was more taboo at the moment than her non-existent love life. While she was pleasantly surprised her mom had been able to get a reprieve from foreclosure, knowing the clock was ticking caused her head to pound and her stomach to roil.

"You know, I read *Moby Dick* when I was in high school . . ."

Angie burst out laughing.

TWELVE

Crew_Haley5: did you SEE yesterday's featured videos?!?!?!?

Make_upB: @Crew_Haley5 Gag! Ryan could do wayyyyyy better . . . me!

Crew_Haley5: @Make_upB Youll have to fight me for him. Gladiator style.

CarneAsadaFan: @Crew_Haley5 @Make_upB Add some mud into the ring and I'll watch you 2 fight.

Make_upB: @CarneAsadaFan @Crew_Haley5 Hello? Perv much!

Load 5,385 more comments

"You can see here from this brief exchange that people are passionate about and engaged with the Subway Girl story. We have thousands of other conversations like this. We're not only a trending topic on social media, garnering conversations on our own channels, and a catalyst for topics among the general public, but other media outlets are devoting their air-time to our story."

Barry cued up a television news story on a TV mounted to the conference room wall. It showed two hosts of the *Today* show prepared for an interview. A banner reading "Guys Tell All" was displayed behind three men, one of whom was a popular late-night television comedy host. Barry pushed play, and his mouth curled into a smile as the network executives watched his contribution to the zeitgeist.

HODA KOTB

So, we've been hearing a lot about Subway Girl, which is one young man's attempt to find a girl he saw on a crowded New York subway. What are your thoughts on this?

PANELIST #1

He's giving guys a bad rap. Either he's a crazy stalker or he's a total romantic. Either way, the rest of us are screwed.

PANELIST #2

Well, he can't really be a stalker because he doesn't know who she is . . . yet.

HODA KOTB

(giggling)

That's true. I guess he needs to *know* her to stalk her.

PANELIST #1
And the inevitable restraining order is only going to help him, right? If he's got to keep fifty feet away from her at all times, he has an excuse to always know where she is.

JENNA BUSH HAGER
I hadn't thought about it that way. Not sure that's what the police had in mind.

PANELIST #3
It used to be that we called these individuals 'secret admirers.' There's clearly been a cultural change in how we view these interactions.

PANELIST #2
Yeah. That's true. A good-looking dude comes along and gives you flowers and he's a romantic. An ugly dude does that and he's a stalker.

HODA KOTB
Well, I know we are only joking here, but stalking can pose real dangers. We don't want to diminish the seriousness of it as a crime.

PANELIST #1
I read the other day that you can't make somebody love you. You can only stalk them and hope for the best. So, I wish this guy luck.

HODA KOTB
I don't know. I think it's kind of sweet, and this just may end up being the love story we've all been looking for.

JENNA BUSH HAGER
Up next, we'll be talking with Chef Laura and Clint Eastwood about their new charity cookbook, *Bake My Day.*

Barry clicked off the television and referred back to the next slide of his presentation. "And here you can see how our site traffic has grown four-fold since we started the Subway Girl series. During this same period of time, we've been the first to break the Dean Caterwall DUI and the arrest of the suspect in the Shawn Leifer nude-photo hacking case. People continue to turn to *Celebrity Monger* for all their celebrity news," he said proudly. "I don't need to tell you what all this means to advertisers who covet the 18- to 35-year-old demographic."

"This is all very impressive. Where are you on start-up financing?" asked suit number one, one of the generic TV executives Barry was meeting with again.

"I've secured private funding to cover the first three months of operating costs and salaries. We can raise an additional two months of costs through a Kickstarter campaign. That gives our sales team time to fund the remainder of the year with ad revenues," he explained, referring to charts and graphs on the screen behind him.

"So you're looking for a one-year contract?" asked an unassuming man who was dressed far more casually than the other executives. Barry knew not to let his appearance be deceiving. The man before him was JP Rawlins, head of the network and the man who could make or break his career dreams.

"Yes. Twelve months," Barry said confidently. "We don't do re-runs. We're prepared to produce a half-hour show, seven days a week, all year long. The news doesn't stop, and neither do we. It's all detailed here," he said, referencing the binders littered around the table which housed his detailed proposal.

The impressed executives looked at each other and then turned to Rawlins.

"Let us review all the numbers. But from what I can see, if you can find this girl and further double your weekly traffic in the next few weeks, we just might have a deal," he said. A broad smile crossed Barry's face, hiding the worry he felt inside—that he needed Angie to make things happen. He shook hands with the executives and walked out of the network building to his awaiting town car. Upon his arrival back at *Celebrity Monger*, he went to Angie's office and walked in without knocking.

"We've got a few weeks to find her and dazzle them if we have a chance of making this deal happen," he said in a strict tone.

Angie took a deep breath. "I'm on it."

THIRTEEN

Ryan, Luke and Diego were seated at an outdoor café, ready to enjoy a leisurely lunch, having either caught up or gotten ahead of all projects in the office. Ryan figured that was what happened when he was actually doing his job, as opposed to hanging out at *Celebrity Monger*. After his unplanned tryst with Angie, and the awkward morning after, he had avoided going in to watch more videos, instead letting her weed out the ones obviously not from the Subway Girl, which appeared to be all of them. In fact, he and the other guys had spent more time in the office this week than they had in the past two weeks combined.

The waitress delivered a round of iced teas as the three guys perused the menu. Diego closed his with a flourish.

"BLT," he announced with a nod.

"What a surprise there," snipped Luke.

"What's your problem?" Diego asked. "You've been acting weird all week."

"*I've* been acting weird?" Luke responded with incredulity. "If anyone has been weird this week, it's been Ryan here." He jerked his thumb in Ryan's direction.

"Don't drag me into this," said Ryan.

"No, he's right. You have been acting strange all week," said Diego. "In fact, you've been around all week. Something happen with you and Angie?" *Something happen? Yeah. Something happened.* Ryan wasn't sure what Josie might have told Luke about his sleepover at Angie's place. In fact, he wasn't even sure that Josie and Luke had spoken again. It would surprise him if there had been any contact beyond their one night together. Love 'em and leave 'em—with their full advance knowledge and consent, of course—was Luke's style.

"Did Josie say something?" he asked Luke, who was sipping his tea.

"Josie," he choked out, lowering his glass and using the napkin in his lap to cover his cough. "What . . . why . . . I . . ."

Diego's brows furrowed. "I've never, *ever*, heard you tongue-tied over a woman," he said with a laugh.

"Neither have I," said Ryan. "I mean, I've heard a lot about tongues and being tied up, but never *tongue-tied*." Diego reached over for a silent fist bump, and Ryan obliged.

"I'm not tongue-tied," Luke said defensively. "There's just nothing to tell. Josie and I shared a night together. End of story. Like always."

"End of story?" Diego chuckled. "We usually get more of a story before it ends."

"Yeah, since when don't you kiss and tell?" Ryan asked just as the waitress stopped to take their order. She raised a brow, examining Luke. He grinned up at her and winked.

"I'll have a burger, well done. No fries. Small side salad," Luke told her.

"BLT for me," said Diego.

"May I please have the turkey club, and I'll take the fries. Thank you," said Ryan. The waitress took the three menus back and left the table to place their order.

"May I please have . . ." Luke mocked.

"Uh-uh," said Ryan, shaking his head. "No trying to derail the conversation by making fun of my manners. What's the deal with Josie?"

"Like I said, no deal." Luke shrugged. "We had a fun night and that's all." Ryan wondered if that *was* all. "Why? Did Angie say something to you?"

Ryan didn't want to talk about Angie. Not with the guys. Not since he didn't know how to explain things to himself, let alone to these two knuckleheads.

"Angie didn't mention anything to me." Ryan was trying to sound nonchalant. "And Josie didn't say anything to you?" Luke seemed to be going through the same effort to sound casual, but Ryan could tell there was a story there. He couldn't press without risking a reveal of information he didn't want to share.

"Nope."

"All right then," said Diego, closing the door on the conversation. "So where are we going tonight to celebrate all our recent good work? Bar None? Malone's? Hangar 12?"

"I think I'm going to pass," said Luke, taking a sip of his tea and looking around the restaurant, avoiding eye contact with Ryan or Diego.

"What?" exclaimed Ryan. "Luke Beauregard Devine is passing on a night on the town?" He spoke slowly, mouth gaping open.

"Don't Beauregard me," warned Luke with a laugh.

"You feeling okay?" Diego asked, putting his hand on Luke's forehead.

"Get off me, man!" Luke swatted his hand away. Diego leaned back into his chair and laughed. Ryan joined in and gave him a high five.

"Seriously, man. It seems like there's more to this story about you and Josie. What happened? Couldn't get it up?" Ryan joked.

"I get it up just fine," Luke shot back. Ryan knew that Josie wasn't getting clingy with him. She hadn't spent that night at Luke's place, because she was already home the next morning when Angie had ushered him out. Not that he wanted to let the guys know that. Then he'd have to answer a bunch of questions he didn't want to. So, if she wasn't hung up on him and making waves, then what was it? He pondered a moment, then it came to him.

"You like her!" Ryan said triumphantly.

"What? No!" Luke rushed out.

"You totally like her."

"No," Diego said. "He doesn't like her. He loves her." He stretched out the word "love" and followed it up with kissing sounds.

"Asswipe," Luke muttered.

"Never thought I'd see the day when Luke Beauregard Devine was whipped," Ryan said with a chuckle.

"I'm not whipped! And don't Beauregard me."

"What happened to 'I got ladies in the 212,'" crowed Diego, making fun of Luke's boasting of female companionship in every area code in the five boroughs. "I got ladies in the 917. Ladies in the 347. The 718. The 929.' Huh?" The waitress returned at that exact moment and looked at Diego aghast. Ryan howled with laughter, and this time Luke joined him.

"Whatever happened with that doctor Angie and Josie were going to fix you up with?" Luke asked, clearly looking to take the heat off himself and light a fire under Diego.

"You guys are assholes," Diego muttered.

"Ain't that the truth," agreed Ryan.

FOURTEEN

Out of the corner of her eye, Angie watched Ryan's leg bounce up and down while he twisted back and forth in the swivel office chair. She began a grocery list in her notebook, doing anything to avoid having to make eye contact or conversation with him.

She'd always thought that being tied up in knots over a guy would relate to indulging his kinky side for a night or two. She'd never imagined this all-consuming, nagging sensation that sat low in her belly and caused her to be distracted from everyone and everything. Everything except the feel of Ryan's tongue, the timbre of his voice as he groaned in pleasure, the warmth of his body covering her like a warm blanket, and the feeling of positivity that had bloomed inside of her. *Stop this. This isn't productive.*

So, they'd slept together . . . and then he'd bailed. She knew he'd been avoiding her the last few days, claiming a tight deadline that prevented him from coming down to watch videos. Yeah, this was awkward. No two ways about it. And even though she was feeling hurt, mourning what could have been, she knew she needed to raise her chin, get past this weirdness and do her job. Yes! Her job! That's what this all had started with. Finding the Subway Girl for Ryan.

"So . . ." she began, unsure of what she was going to say.

"So . . ." Ryan echoed, finally looking up to make eye contact with her.

"Listen, this doesn't need to be awkward."

"Even though it totally is?" he said with a raised eyebrow.

"Yes." She laughed in relief. "It's totally awkward," she acknowledged. "But it doesn't need to be. We had a fun night together." She shrugged. "But we both know it was just a fun night." Even though she wanted to tell him it was more than a night of fun for her, she knew he didn't feel the same way. She wanted to tell him it was more than a physical connection. It was an emotional one. Was it unexpected? Yes. Highly unusual for her? Indeed. Genuine and all real? Absolutely. However, she knew what he needed to hear.

"Right. Just a fun night."

"And we're both mature adults. We can compartmentalize this and now focus on the task at hand, which is finding the Subway Girl, right?"

"I've seen you do the Chicken Dance at Thuy's wedding, so I'm not sure I would classify you as a 'mature adult,' but I suppose you're right."

"Oh, that's rich. If I recall, you were quacking and do-si-do-ing right alongside me," she fired back.

"Yeah," he conceded. "But in my defense—and yours, I might add—that bridesmaid was persuasive."

"Oh." Angie shuddered. "It was an act of self-preservation."

"Self-preservation?"

"Yeah. If Green Organza—that was my affectionate nickname for her—didn't stop pestering me, I was going to go off on her, and I didn't want to be arrested for assault." She chuckled.

Ryan considered her admission and nodded. "Yeah, I can see it."

She playfully tapped his arm. "So . . . about us . . . no regrets?" She didn't regret sleeping with Ryan. And if she were being honest with herself, she didn't regret opening her heart up to him, even if her feelings were unrequited. She'd dealt with a broken heart before, so it wasn't an entirely foreign feeling. What was new was the feeling of hopefulness. He'd actually given her a gift—a restoration of faith in people and the belief that maybe, just maybe, she might find love one day.

"None. You?"

"Absolutely no regrets." Angie glanced down at her feet and grinned. It had never felt like this. Like she wanted nothing more than to see him smile and know he was happy. That feeling propelled her conviction that she must succeed in this search. Ryan deserved to be happy, and if he didn't think she could be the one to do it, she'd find the girl who could.

"No regrets about what?" Harlan walked into the conference room with his ever-present camera and tripod.

"About searching for the Subway Girl, of course," said Angie, with an inaudible sigh of relief that Harlan hadn't walked in any earlier.

"Exactly," said Ryan. "This is where I'm supposed to be."

Out in the lobby, Gina, the receptionist, had her head buried in a set of Excel spreadsheets she was proofreading for Barry when a large shadow crossed over her. She looked up, and standing in front of her was a tall, foreboding police officer. She had to stretch her neck up in order to take him all in.

He was dressed in a blue uniform complete with shiny gold badge and holstered gun. A matching navy cap with a gold emblem sat atop his head. He removed the cap, tucking it under his arm to reveal a shiny, clean dome. A worried look crossed Gina's face.

"Uh . . . can I help you?" she asked.

"I'm here to see Angie Prince about the Subway Girl," he said, his deep, intense voice panicking the young receptionist.

"Let me get her for you. Please wait here," Gina muttered. She rushed down the hall, taking a few deep breaths. She knocked on the conference room door hard enough to push it open. "Angie!" She beckoned Angie into the hall with her pointer finger and looked suspiciously at Ryan. Once she was sure Ryan was out of earshot, she continued. "There's a very large and very scary-looking police officer here who wants to talk with you about the Subway Girl."

Angie smiled and walked down the hall.

Trailing her, Gina continued, "Maybe Ryan's wanted for a crime? Maybe the girl ended up dead?"

Angie held up her hand to silence her. Angie stopped in front of the ominous figure, a serious look on her face. Then her mouth broke into a smile.

"Spence!" She leaned in and gave the officer a big hug. "Thanks for coming on such short notice."

"Anything for you, Angie," he replied. Leaving behind the dumbfounded receptionist, Angie guided the police officer to the conference room where Ryan was sitting on the office chair, still nervously twisting back and forth. Harlan was unsurprisingly seated on a couch, his video camera trained on the conference room table.

Angie looked at Ryan and found his discomfort endearing. In fact, if she was being honest with herself, she found most everything about Ryan endearing. *No. Knock it off.*

She'd spent most of the week reliving her night with Ryan, and she'd considered begging him to give up this futile search and just be with her. But then she thought about how he'd bolted from her bed, about the visit with her mom over the weekend, about the very temporary reprieve from the bank and about the pressure from Barry to come through.

Now, with Ryan sitting in the conference room, looking so delicious in a vintage t-shirt and faded blue jeans, she was conflicted all over again. She blinked back a few tears and smiled brightly.

"Ryan, this is Officer Spencer, one of New York's finest, and one of the best sketch artists around," she said. Ryan stood to shake the officer's hand and, despite his own admirable height, like the receptionist he had to crane his neck up to see the police officer in his entirety.

"Nice to meet you, Ryan," said Spence, handing Ryan a book entitled the *FBI Facial Identification Catalog*. "And thanks for the kind introduction, Angie," he added, smiling at her.

"So how do you two know each other?" Ryan asked.

"Oh, Spence and I have known each other for years."

"Yeah, years," he added. Angie smiled at Spence and glanced at Ryan only to see a tightness to his features. If she wasn't mistaken, he looked a bit jealous. *Well, that's curious*. On one hand, she liked the idea of the green monster rearing its ugly head where Ryan was concerned.

But that soon turned to frustration. How dare he be jealous when he was the one who'd leaped out of her bed like it was on fire? Angie took a deep, calming breath. She needed to get past it.

"So, let's go ahead and get started," Spence said. "Why don't you flip through the first few pages"—he indicated the guide he'd brought—"and see if there's a face shape that matches hers."

"I'm surprised you don't do this stuff on computers," Ryan said.

"Spence here is old school," said Angie with pride. "He is a true artist. He attended the Rhode Island School of Design before becoming a cop."

"Impressive," remarked Ryan as he flipped through the booklet and stopped on a page, pointing. "Her face was kind of like this one." Officer Spencer made notes on a number chart listing face shape, eyes, nose, lips and chin. Angie tried to keep her own chin up, knowing realistically, in her head, that Ryan finding and being with the Subway Girl would be for the best.

Knowing it in her heart, though. That was another matter altogether.

"That's A-3925. Good. What about her eyes?" the officer inquired.

"Oh, her eyes were a beautiful, sparkling green. They just sort of . . . burrowed into you," said Ryan wistfully.

"I think he means what shape were they? How close together or far apart?" Ryan could tell that Angie was barely holding in a snort, but she hadn't managed to keep the sarcasm from her voice. Officer Spencer put up a hand to silence her.

"They sound beautiful. My Serafina–we've been married for fourteen years–has green eyes, too. They haunted me for weeks until I had the courage to ask her out. She's still the most beautiful woman I've ever known." *Ah, so Officer Spencer is happily married,* thought Ryan cheerfully.

Why this made him so happy, he didn't know. That was bullshit. He did know. He liked Angie. Cared for her. Wanted to see her happy. Thought *he* could make her happy. Those feelings weren't reciprocated. She'd kicked him out of her bed like it was on fire. No, this was where fate had dictated he be–finding the Subway Girl.

"Take a look at these photos and let me know if you see something similar in shape, size, spacing," Officer Spencer continued. Ryan flipped through the resource book and described facial features to the sketch artist for several hours. During that time, any awkwardness between Angie and Ryan seemed to disappear, as the two talked and laughed while Officer Spencer's charcoal pencil scratched across the paper. *Would things be this easy and comfortable with the Subway Girl? This fun?*

Officer Spencer turned his sketch pad to Ryan and waited for Ryan's response.

Ryan studied the sketch. "Her nose was a little . . . cuter."

"Cuter?" said Angie, laughing.

"Perhaps a little shorter? Less severe?" suggested Officer Spencer. Ryan nodded as the cop/artist erased a few pencil marks and made a few new ones.

"Cuter?" repeated Angie.

"What?" Ryan said, a playfulness in his tone. "I don't know the lingo."

"Really? There's not some movie with a sketch-artist scene?" she teased. Officer Spencer turned the paper again toward Ryan.

"That's it. That's her," he said. Angie grinned at Ryan. He could sense her excitement at getting closer to the Subway Girl and felt a little sad that she didn't seem at all bothered about helping him meet someone else.

It wasn't like he expected some grand gesture. Or even an admission of feelings. But he wouldn't have minded seeing a hint of regret cross her face. Just a tiny sliver of something to show that he meant more to her than one epic night in bed . . . and on a chair . . . and up against a wall. Harlan, meanwhile, smiled broadly.

"So, what next?" asked Ryan, clearing his throat and trying to clear his head.

"We'll show it at the concert tonight and get it up on the website as soon as possible, and hopefully someone will recognize her," replied Angie.

"Great," sighed Ryan. *This is great, right?* This was what it was supposed to be about. So why did he dread the exposure this would bring? Why did he feel compelled to spend more time with Angie? "So, do you want to grab some dinner before the concert? Or do you have some other work to do?" The words came out before he could stop himself. He held his breath as he waited for her response.

"No. Dinner sounds good. Give me a minute to shut down my computer."

The rabid concert crowd cheered at the band, who waved in thanks as they left the stage. Ryan stood backstage with Angie, Barry, Harlan and a few interns wearing *Celebrity Monger* t-shirts, watching as roadies removed set fixtures and instruments, while others took new pieces onto the stage.

The emcee, a thin man wearing pinstriped pants, a burgundy t-shirt and old-fashioned spats, emerged from stage left.

"Let's give it up one more time for Fitz and the Tantrums! Now, I know you are all excited for our main event, but while we set up, I have a special guest. Put your hands together for Barry Osler, owner of *Celebrity Monger*," he called into the microphone. Barry and a set of interns walked onto the stage to limited applause.

"Good evening, New York! How many of you are excited to see Jase Connors?" Barry asked, trying to whip up some enthusiasm. The crowd, which had dwindled slightly as concertgoers went to the bathroom and snack stands, applauded and cheered mildly.

"And how many of you would like a free *Celebrity Monger* t-shirt?" Barry called into the microphone. The thinned-out crowd began to cheer more wildly. The interns lifted up cannons with balled up t-shirts inside and shot them into the crowd as fans caught them to cheers.

"Now, how many of you are familiar with the Subway Girl?" asked Barry. There was an audible increase in applause and cheers. "Well, tonight Ryan is here to ask for your help in finding her." Barry motioned for Ryan to come out on the stage. Ryan shuffled out as the crowd began to cheer and several women screamed, "I love you, Ryan!" The flashbulb from a high-end camera went off, causing Ryan to blink rapidly a few times. When he opened his eyes, he noticed a sea of camera phones. To the untrained eye, Ryan probably seemed to be enjoying the attention, what with his good-natured and sincere smile. But he most definitely wasn't comfortable, instead rubbing the back of his neck and shifting subtly from one foot to the other.

While he was hopeful the sketch would jog someone's memory or convince the Subway Girl herself to come forward, he hated having all of these people looking at him. Talking about him. Photographing him. Judging him. The screen behind the stage filled with Officer Spencer's composite sketch of the Subway Girl.

Barry continued, "Today, one of New York's finest helped us put together this sketch of the Subway Girl. If you know who she is–or if you are the girl we're looking for–please contact *Celebrity Monger*." Barry turned to Ryan. "Ryan, do you have anything you want to say?"

Ryan hesitantly took the mic and glanced over at Angie for encouragement. She gave him a smile and lifted her head up, indicating to him to go ahead. Yeah, Angie certainly wasn't itching to spend more time with him. "Just thanks to everyone who's helping me find her," he said, looking over at Angie again with a grin. *Angie.*

"We love you, Ryan!" called out some of the women in the crowd. Ryan blushed, which seemed somehow to elicit a few more cheers and whistles from the audience. He stepped back and handed the microphone to Barry.

"Don't forget to visit *CelebrityMonger*.com daily for updates on Ryan's search for the Subway Girl and for all the other celebrity news you want and need." The emcee walked forward and took the mic back from Barry as Ryan walked backstage. Harlan continued to film the scene unfolding, so it could be posted to the website in the morning.

"Looks like you've got yourself some fans," Angie joked. Too bad she wasn't one of them.

Lovegirl89: Tell Ryan to give up his search for the Subway Girl and be with me. I will treat him right.

DrillTeamBabe: I LOVE YOU RYAN!!!! I want to have your babies!!!!!

DHP329: Could "Saint Ryan" be more annoying. Don't believe a bit of this drivel. No one—believe me—no one is THAT good.

> LiveWell2: @DHP329 just because you're a total douchebag doesn't mean that other guys are. Why don't you crall back under that rock and shut up.
>
> DHP329: @LiveWell2 when you fucking learn how to spell "craWl" then you can tell me what do to. Moron!

TreeGirl: I just think Ryan is the cutest thing evah!

DeenaDoe: Let me preface this by saying I love Ryan soooooo much. I think he's funny and cool and so down to earth. He's an amazing human being. So when I see threads saying that someone saw him doing something wrong, I just get really mad. People are just trying to tear him down.

> PhotoLover: @DeenaDoe yeah, the downfall is inevitable. People need to remember he's just a man. It didn't take long for people to start making up nasty rumors about him. Don't believe everything you read. But don't not believe it because he's just a man.

RichRich: I heard that Ryan has a porn addiction.

> Xan888: @RichRich where your proof? Don't say shit isn't true.

> RichRich: @Xan888 Your grammer sucks. Are you even from this country?!?

> Forlorn12: @RichRich–It's "grammar" idiot.

HamiltonFan8: Is anyone else thinking this is just a big ploy for ad dollars. If this chick doesn't turn up soon, I'm out.

Insanity9: Why is everyone hating on him all the sudden? Jeezzz

Load 13,765 more comments

To: Ryan.Carlson
From: Jessica Hearn-Dooberman
Subject: What the what?

Hey Ry. Imagine my surprise when I opened up a celebrity tell-all magazine while getting my nails done at Cute-icles today and saw a picture of you from some concert. Everyone back home is now following along. My (perfectly manicured) fingers (LOL!) are crossed you find her. When are you coming home for a visit? We all miss you!!!!

Jess was a childhood friend and married to one of Ryan's best buddies back home. The fact she and everyone in his Iowa hometown were "following along" just further ratcheted up his need to find the Subway Girl. He had to stop thinking about "what ifs" with Angie. His people were watching. His people were expecting. His people were invested. He wouldn't disappoint them again.

To: Jessica Hearn-Dooberman
From: Ryan.Carlson
Subject: Re: What the what?

Hey Jess. Good to hear from you. Miss everyone too and hope the gang is doing well. Will be home for Finlay's graduation, so we'll definitely all meet up.

FIFTEEN

Six dancers dressed in leggings, leotards and jazz shoes warmed up along two ballet barres in front of a mirrored wall in the small dance studio on the Lower East Side. A low hum of chatter came from three of the dancers, who were discussing a recent audition for an off-Broadway musical rumored to be the next *Dear Evan Hansen*.

Two of the dancers shared a pair of earbuds while watching a video on *Celebrity Monger*–Angie on their screen:

> *"Thank you again to Officer Spencer with the 73rd Precinct for offering us his services with this composite sketch of the Subway Girl. As always, if you have information about her, you can use this link to contact us."*

The video ended with the sketch that Ryan had provided two days earlier. The two dancers whispered to each other and pointed at a lone dancer in the studio–Misty Waites.

Misty sat in a butterfly pose, using her elbows to push down her knees, and lowered her head to the floor. She looked up into the mirror and noticed the two dancers, still wearing a shared pair of earbuds, looking at her and whispering.

Having other dancers, actresses, or hell, just other women, talk about her behind her back wasn't a new occurrence for Misty. When she'd moved to New York City from Buffalo to become a famous Broadway actress, she'd known it was going to be competitive. It had taken a year of temp jobs, from cater waiter to boutique salesclerk, before she'd landed her agent. And even then, she'd had to sleep with the sweater-vest-wearing pit bull before he would take her on.

At least he'd gotten her a few roles in some off-off-off-Broadway shows. She would have had that swing role in the *Godspell* revival too, if her former friend hadn't slept with the choreographer before she could.

She'd learned quickly that talent could only take you so far and that you couldn't be as attractive as she was without bringing out the green-eyed monster in other women, especially in the competitive world of New York theater.

Normally she didn't let it get to her. But Misty couldn't help noticing that they continued to stare at her, and then they giggled. Fed up with their rudeness at her expense, she approached them.

"Excuse me. Is there a problem here?" she demanded, placing her hand on her hip. The two dancers removed the earbuds and giggled again.

"No. No problem," said the first dancer, who looked contrite. The other dancer shook her head.

"Then why do you keep looking at me and whispering?" Misty asked with a huff.

"It's just . . . you look at lot like . . ." The now-shy dancer thrust her phone at Misty.

"What the . . ." Misty said, grabbing the phone and playing the video from the start.

SIXTEEN

Takeout Chinese containers littered the desk and table. A very tired and frustrated Ryan clicked through videos from the Subway Girl search. This was it. He was officially pulling the plug. He couldn't take this anymore. And there was so much he had been taking. First were these insipid videos from women who clearly weren't the Subway Girl. He didn't know if they were hoping to generate some spark within him, seeking fame, or just mocking him.

And don't get me started on the message board comments. Luke and Diego had made him promise to stop reading them. While many were supportive and kind, some were downright cruel. The judgment and assumptions about his life were hurtful. A few even went so far as to suggest he give up the search and just "off himself."

It was one thing for the guys to tease him, but something altogether different for strangers to completely question all his life choices. While his parents had tried to be supportive, he could sense the hesitation and concern in their voices when they asked about it.

He continued to get emails from friends back home, eager to know all of the details, from how things started to how things were progressing. He felt so much pressure to deliver what everyone wanted.

Then there was Angie. He'd given their night together a lot of thought—and not just when he was reviewing the highlight reel while jacking off in the shower. *What to make of all this with Angie?* She had become one of his best friends, and he enjoyed their time together. Would ending the search end their friendship? He wasn't ready to walk away from her.

Never mind the fact he had seen her naked, heard her breathy moans, felt her body clench around his. He knew that ship had sailed. Didn't keep him from mulling over the possibilities in his mind of how it would be if things had been different.

He was a ball of confusion, but he didn't think he could give up now. Angie had put so much time and energy into this. He looked over his shoulder at her, asleep on the couch. Even stretched out, she didn't take up all the cushion space. She really was a tiny little thing. He smiled until movement caught his eye. Harlan, who had been sitting in a chair scrolling through his cell phone, looked at him with a cocked brow. Ryan gave him a "what's up" nod and turned back to the computer monitor. He clicked on the next video to see a gorgeous brunette appear on screen.

"Hi, Ryan. My name is Misty, and I think I'm the girl you've been looking for . . . the Subway Girl. I sometimes ride on the 1 when I go on auditions, like a few months ago when I was going for the role of Eliza Doolittle in *Pygmalion.* I was practicing my lines—probably a bit too loudly—in an English accent. Anyway, I would love to talk with you, so call me."

Yes! Ryan stood, raising his arms in triumph. His heart thumped with adrenaline-fueled enthusiasm. The excitement at finding her—at realizing this entire search hadn't been in vain—energized him. Pride surged in him at having accomplished what he had been beginning to think was impossible.

"This is her! Her name is Misty! She's not British," he sighed. "She's an actress!"

Harlan looked up, a broad smile crossing his face. He let out a slow clap, which reminded Ryan of the cheesy teen movies from the '80s and '90s that he secretly loved.

Angie woke up to the commotion to find Harlan applauding and Ryan throwing exaggerated fist pumps. She jumped off the couch and leaped into Ryan's arms. Although there was a stationary camera capturing the moment, Harlan turned on the video of his cell phone to secure different angles of this genuine show of emotion.

"Wow! We did it! We found the Subway Girl!" Angie said.

"Yeah," said Ryan excitedly. He hugged her a bit tighter then pulled back, hands on her shoulders, to look in her eyes. "Yeah," he repeated, a tinge of sadness in his voice as it occurred to him that he would no longer be spending time reviewing video submissions with Angie. *Will we remain friends? How is this going to change things between us?*

"Yeah," echoed Angie, but her tone didn't seem to match Ryan's uncertainty. "I told you we would find her."

"You did," he said. "So, what now?"

"We call her. I mean, I call her and arrange for you two to meet," she replied.

"Okay. I guess I won't need to come here and watch videos anymore, huh?"

"Guess not." The silence that passed between the two of them was deafening. Harlan cleared his throat, breaking the stalemate.

"Well, I'll call her first thing in the morning and set something up for as soon as possible," Angie said.

"Sure. That works." Ryan swallowed hard. A hollow feeling filtered through his chest. It wasn't hard to admit to himself that he was going to miss Angie. Miss their talks and daily exchanges. Miss her snarky snips. Miss her witty remarks. Her boisterous laugh. Her eye-rolls. But as his mom always said, "When God closes a door, he opens a window." This relationship with Angie may have been coming to an end, but things with Misty were just starting, and that was what the search had all been about. *Misty*. He liked the sound of that.

"Why don't you head home and get some sleep and I'll call you?" Angie suggested.

"Okay." He gave Angie a hug and smiled in gratitude and disbelief as he walked down the *Celebrity Monger* hallway. He was moving forward, as he should be, and fate was bringing Misty into his life.

"Hey, Angie," Ryan called out. Angie turned, surprised to see he'd returned to the doorway.

"Yeah?" Her voice sounded breathy. She never sounded breathy. What did she want him to say? *Forget Misty. She's not as beautiful as I remember. Let's you and I give this a go.* Angie knew it wasn't realistic to think Ryan was going to forgo his dream girl—the dream girl she had been charged with finding—to be with her.

No. This was about Ryan, and Ryan wanted Misty. At least he would be happy. Barry would be happy, too. This would ensure the network deal got approved, which would make her mom happy as well. *Yes, this will make everyone happy. Everyone else*, she thought sadly.

"Thanks for everything. This has been . . . really fun."

Angie smiled, but she had the feeling it didn't quite reach her eyes. She turned to see Harlan's phone shoved in her face and pushed it away with a shake of her head.

"Of course. Happy we found her," she said. *No, this is how things are supposed to be.* Ryan would get to meet Misty, and the rabid online fans would get their happily ever after. Ratings would soar, the site would go network, and she would have enough money to pay off her mom's mortgage and quit her job. If she didn't have to peddle this crap anymore, she would have time to focus on the stories that were important to her and would be important to the city and beyond. After Ryan walked out, Angie turned to Harlan.

"So, looks like we're done," she said with a mixture of relief and sorrow. Ryan was moving on, and she resolved to move on, too. Sure, she would miss him. But it would be easier to get over him when they weren't side by side at the computer monitor. When she couldn't hear the sound of his laugh. When she couldn't smell his cologne or witness how he treated everyone with kindness and respect. She sighed. She was completely out of her depth here.

"Not even close," replied Harlan with a chuckle. "Barry's going to want to see this thing all the way through." He pulled out his phone and dialed. "We found her," he said, and Angie could almost hear Barry's sleazy grin on the other end.

SEVENTEEN

Misty sat in the diner booth, thumbing through audition postings on one of the Broadway websites. She glanced up each time the bell above the door chimed to signal a new patron walking into the restaurant. She was eager for her meeting. Eager to learn more about moving ahead with Ryan.

She'd never had a man go to so much trouble to meet her before. Sure, guys stopped her all the time. On the street. On auditions. In restaurants. She'd even had a man hit on her while she waited in the ER with a sprained ankle. This, however, was something on a whole new level.

At first, she'd thought Ryan must be some kind of nut job. Who believes in love at first sight? Lust at first sight? She was familiar with that one. Ryan didn't come across like a player though. He was more like a lovesick puppy. She was afraid that once he knew who she was, she would never be able to shake him.

She almost didn't respond to his inquiry. It wasn't until she saw the thousands of comments from people eager to see them connect that she understood the opportunity in front of her. Even if he ended up being a stalker, the exposure could only help her career.

Although maybe Ryan was doing this to further *his* career. Maybe they could help each other out. She hadn't known what to think, but she'd agreed to meet with Angie.

The bell tinkled over the door, and Misty caught the eye of a handsome man in a business suit, tie loosened, walking by. Misty gave him a once-over. He had deep-set eyes, broad shoulders and shiny black shoes.

He raised a brow and flashed a sly smirk. Misty glanced down at her phone and then back up to see the man still checking her out. A ghost of a smile crossed her face as he walked right past her table. She could feel his eyes on her even though he was now past her sightline. She considered turning around, but the diner door bell rang again.

One look and she instantly recognized Angie. The only way to describe her was *cute*–tiny with a sweet-looking face, especially in contrast to the shrewd-looking man who accompanied her.

"Misty. Happy to meet you. I'm Barry Osler, owner of *Celebrity Monger*. This is Angie Prince, who you spoke with on the phone." He reached his hand out to shake hers.

"Nice to meet you," cooed Misty, standing and shaking hands with both of them. Barry sat down and gestured for the two women to follow.

"Thanks for meeting us here today. We showed your video to Ryan, and he confirmed you are the girl he's been looking for," Barry said.

"I'm the Subway Girl."

"Yes," confirmed Barry.

"So, what do I win?" she asked, her head tilted to the side.

"What do you mean, win?" asked Angie. Misty could sense the attitude right away. *Hmm. Shouldn't have been fooled by her innocent appearance.*

"What do I get?" Misty said, giving Angie a sideways glance.

"You get . . . Ryan," Angie said incredulously.

"Oh, come on. He seems like a sweet guy and all, but you and I know there's more to this than finding true love. So what do I get?" she repeated, ignoring Angie and focusing on Barry. Barry smiled knowingly at her.

"Exposure," he said. "Certainly something your fledgling acting career could use. Believe me, we checked you out." Misty nodded her head and smiled. "We have millions of subscribers that visit *Celebrity Monger* every day, many of them eagerly waiting for updates on Ryan's search for love. And I anticipate we'll only have more when we reveal he's found you and your romance can begin," he explained dryly. Misty sat thinking about the opportunity, while Angie looked disgusted.

"I'll need a clothing allowance and a weekly stipend," Misty said. "And a car at my disposal."

"You've got to be kid—" Angie began, aghast.

Barry interrupted her. "I can agree to all except the car service. I can't have my subway lovebirds all of a sudden shunning public transportation."

Misty considered his position. It made sense. "It's a deal."

"I'll have our attorney prepare an agreement for you to sign," said Barry, his eyes narrowing. Misty rose and reached out her hand to shake Barry's.

Angie sat in the booth, looking dumbfounded. As Misty was set to walk away, Barry turned to her.

"This is going to be great. Angie will be in touch."

"Great. And if I have any problems, I'll be sure to let Angie here know," Misty said with faux sweetness. Angie gave her a fake smile as Misty turned and walked away.

"She's perfect," said Barry.

"Perfectly awful. Barry, you can't seriously—"

"She's going to take us all the way to network TV, Angie. I can feel it." He pulled out his cellphone and dialed.

"It's Barry. I need you to draw up a contract for our newest online star, Misty Waites. Make sure we have rights to footage and include a $500 weekly stipend and $1,500 monthly clothing allowance. I need it by end of day." He hung up the phone and turned back to Angie with a smarmy smile. "Gold!"

EIGHTEEN

A few days later, Barry charged into Angie's office with a series of faxed papers, licking his lips and grinning.

"We just got Misty's signed agreement. It's done. I need you to call Ryan to set up their first date for tomorrow. And I'll need you to record a promo spot to start running ASAP." He walked out of her office, and Angie followed him down the hall.

"Listen, Barry. Ryan's a really nice guy, and I don't think he signed on for—" It was one thing for Ryan to fall for someone other than her, and an entirely different thing for him to be manipulated.

"Don't fuck with this, Angie. The network deal is on the line. This is my future. Either roll with it or, mark my words, get rolled over. Got it?"

"Got it." She nodded reluctantly, since her mom's house was on the line, too. Barry motioned to the office where Harlan was waiting with a camera set up to record her call.

"Now go play matchmaker!" he commanded, expecting Angie to not only facilitate Ryan and Misty's courtship, but monitor, edit and share it for the world to see. He walked out of the room leaving Angie with a quivering lip and tightened chest.

"What was that all about?" asked Harlan.

"Nothing," Angie mumbled.

"Oooo-kay," said Harlan, clearly not wanting to get into a discussion about it.

"Can you just give me a minute?" she asked. Harlan walked out of the office. Angie's eyes welled with tears.

How can I be a party to this charade? Would her broken heart survive bearing witness to this day after day? Ryan deserved more. He deserved better. He was a good guy. He was also a smart guy. *He'll see through her phony charms, right? Will anyone be good enough for him?* She figured probably not, but Misty was awful. Wretched. Beyond the pale. Harlan knocked on the door, distracting Angie from the growing ire rising in her.

"Ready?" he asked.

Angie wiped away her tears. "Yeah. Come on in," she said, picking up the phone and taking a deep breath. She dialed Ryan's number and waited for him to pick up.

"Angie. So great to hear from you."

"Hey," she eked out.

"Are you okay? You sound strange."

"Yeah, I'm fine."

"So, what's up?"

"We got hold of Misty, and she's very excited to finally meet you. We've arranged for you two to have dinner tomorrow night."

"Will you be there?" he asked, with what Angie thought was a hopeful tone.

"No. Harlan will. And I'll cut the piece the next day." She didn't tell him she would be sitting outside the restaurant in a truck, watching the closed-circuit feed live as it unfolded.

"Oh. Okay. Well, I guess this is good, right?"

"Yeah. This is what it was all about," she said. "Good luck tomorrow," she added before hanging up and hanging her head.

The next day, Ryan sat at a table for two in a small Italian restaurant on the Upper West Side. He wore a pair of black trousers, slip-on loafers and a powder-blue button-down shirt. He'd debated wearing a tie but decided that wasn't his style, and he wanted Misty to get to know the real him. He fiddled with the collar of his shirt, took sips of his water and nervously watched the door. Harlan was standing nearby capturing it all on film.

This was it. The past few months had all been leading up to this. *Don't blow it.* He glanced back up from his drink as Misty walked into the restaurant, removing her coat and the adorable pink beanie that had captured Ryan's attention all those months ago.

She wore a pink halter-style dress with a deep V and wide straps that tied around her neck. The low dip in the front showed off all the smooth, creamy skin between her small breasts. She had a dancer's body. Slim. Slight. Ethereal. She carried herself like a dancer too, practically floating through the restaurant entrance.

"Hi, Misty. I'm Ryan," he said, clearing his throat so that his voice wasn't accompanied by a squeak. Unsure if he should hug her or shake her hand, he made some awkward starts and stops. Misty, likely sensing his uncertainty, leaned in to give him a warm hug and kiss on the cheek. She smiled toward the camera and took a seat across from him.

Now, staring into her eyes, it was hard for him to believe he was really here . . . with her. Watching videos for hours, enduring the ridicule of the message boards, assuring his parents he knew what he was doing (though, really, he didn't have a clue) and exposing his vulnerability to the world had finally paid off. He'd found her. It was fate. *Right?*

"I'm so flattered you went to all that trouble to find me," she said coyly.

"It was worth the effort," he said. It had to be worth the effort, especially since *Celebrity Monger* was continuing to record and share this with the world.

"I'm glad you feel that way." She smiled at him.

"I was getting worried that maybe you knew you were the Subway Girl but were too scared to contact me."

"Oh, no. This"—she gestured toward the camera—"doesn't scare me at all. I love having the cameras on me."

"I meant that you might have thought I was crazy."

Hesitating slightly, Misty said, "That's what I mean. I felt safe meeting you because of the cameras."

"Oh, good. I can assure you I'm definitely not a serial killer," said Ryan.

"Good-looking guy like you? I bet you're actually a real lady-killer."

Ryan blushed. He actually blushed. Angie watched his and Misty's date while she sat outside in a nondescript white van, reminiscent of undercover vehicles that law enforcement used on stings, complete with headphones and TV monitors. She couldn't believe this phony wannabe actress was trying to get away with such a cheesy line.

And every time Misty flashed a smile at the camera, Angie let out an audible gag. At this rate, Barry could make a soundtrack to fake a bulimia video—and she wouldn't put it past him to do something so unscrupulous. Kai, the audio tech who was sitting in the van with her, chuckled each time Angie groaned.

"Are people seriously going to buy this shit?" she asked.

"Is that a rhetorical question?" Kai replied with a quirked brow.

"I know." Angie let out a loud exhale and lowered her head into her hands.

"You do know, Ange. Either way, it's a winner. They either lap it up or bash it online. Who cares? It means page views."

With Barry's network meeting coming up, and the mortgage foreclosure deadline looming, increasing page views was critical. So Angie watched Ryan and Misty's date unfold, making note of the timestamp during certain parts of their conversation so it would be easier for her to edit a recap reel tomorrow.

NINETEEN

It had been a few weeks since highlights of Ryan and Misty's first date appeared on the *Celebrity Monger* website. Since then, the couple had shared several meals, visited a flea market in Chelsea and done yoga in Central Park. Angie had reluctantly watched each date unfold and edited the footage to share with the rabid fan base on *Celebrity Monger*.

FoxyRoxy22: That Misty chick is dumb as a post.

SinnerSeven: @FoxyRoxy22 No way. She's HAWWWWWTTTTT!

FoxyRoxy22: @SinnerSeven Haters gonna hate

514UCLABruin: I give them two months, tops.

CleanQueen78: @514UCLABruin Ha! Should we set up a pool.

> MaryJoJacobs: @CleanQueen78 I'm in. I give it three more dates.
>
> 514UCLABruin: @MaryJoJacobs @CleanQueen78 I say two LOL

MateRater4: What a horrible actress. Ryan could do so much better . . . like me.

PerdyGirl!: If she is trying to be an actress, she shouldn't quit her day job. She sucks.

MoreIsMore9: Painful. Watching the two of them is just painful.

59832!: Squeeee!!!! I'm so happy he found her. They are soooooo cute together. I can already imagine how gorge their babies are gonna be.

DrillTeamBabe: @maribel5 @everychance @gogo18 @ameliarb @karilb @ PicklesNTickles8 THEY FOUND HER!!!

Imposter666: He looks so happy. I'm so happy for him.

LoisLaneLover: Dump Misty. Pick me.

Blessed4Life: Oooooh. I am so in love with this story.

AkashaAA: I love her sweater. Where can I buy one?

Load 54,762 comments

Now Ryan and Misty were seated at a small French bistro, with Harlan chomping on a baguette two tables over. Thankfully, his camera was connected to the microphones attached to his subjects and wouldn't pick up the sound of his teeth grinding down on the crunchy crust.

"I mean, they had me wait for an hour and then only let me sing the first few notes before calling 'next.' And my agent is no help," Misty whined to Ryan, who sipped on a glass of red wine.

"I'm sorry that you had a bad day, but it seems to be the nature of the beast," he responded with genuine concern. "There's this famous Alfred Hitchcock quote where he says actors shouldn't be called cattle but it's okay to treat them like cattle." He laughed.

"Who's Albert Hitchock?" Misty asked, confusion etched on her brow.

"*Alfred Hitchcock*. He's one of the most famous movie directors that ever lived," Ryan informed her, the disbelief evident in his voice. *How can anyone not know who Alfred Hitchcock is?*

"Do you know him? Could you introduce me?" Misty asked hopefully.

"He's dead. He made some of the most famous movies of the '50s and '60s," he said, still unsure how Misty had never heard of him. He looked at her blank face. "You know. *Vertigo. North by Northwest. Rear Window. The Birds. Psycho,*" he rattled off.

"Oh, I saw *Psycho*. With the guy from *Wedding Crashers*, right?"

"Yeah. Vince Vaughn. But that was the remake in '98. The original from 1960 starred Anthony Perkins."

"Whatever," groaned Misty.

"Speaking of Hitchcock, this conversation is for the birds," Ryan mumbled under his breath while he rubbed his temple with his fingers.

"What?"

"Nothing."

Sitting in the van across from the restaurant, Angie and Kai let out howls of laughter. Misty may not have heard Ryan muttering under his breath, but the microphone had picked up everything.

"Wow!" remarked Kai. "She's something else." He shook his head in disbelief.

"She's awful." Angie cringed. "I just don't understand what Ryan sees in her." She didn't get it. Ryan was a smart guy. How could he be so blinded to reality by this misguided notion of fate?

"Really?" Kai said with his characteristic quirked brow. "You don't get what he sees in her? She's hot. Like, super hot."

Angie expelled a loud exhale. She would give Misty that.

"Okay, so she's hot," Angie conceded. "But shouldn't there be more?"

"I'd take more of her." Kai wiggled his eyebrows, which only reminded Angie of Ryan's friend Luke. She let out a little chuckle, which Kai likely thought was directed at him. She didn't want to hurt his feelings, so she didn't let on.

"Of course, you'd take more. You're a man-whore," she chided playfully.

"Card carrying man-whore since 2003 and damn proud of it."

Angie laughed out loud. "Yes. A proud man-whore. I understand. I do. But really, don't you need more than a pretty face and a nice body? Don't you want someone to talk to, who challenges you, who inspires you to be better and be more?"

Kai nodded a few times, taking in Angie's words, but then shrugged. "Nope." He shook his head. "Pretty face. Nice body. That's all I need."

"Well, Ryan's not like other guys. I think he needs more. I know he *deserves* more."

"You sure seem to be taking a particular interest in this story," Kai noted, again quirking an eyebrow in her direction.

"Of course, I am," she replied defensively. Little did Kai or anyone realize how personal this had become for Angie. How strong her feelings for Ryan ran. How much she wanted for him to be happy. "As with every story I produce, I want it to engage the audience, evoke some emotion, cause some change in people's behavior or perceptions."

"Really?" That quirked brow made another appearance, which was really starting to piss Angie off. "You do know you work for *Celebrity Monger*, right?"

"I know." Her shoulders slumped in defeat. She knew the only emotions her stories on the tabloid site were likely to evoke were derision, ridicule and disgust. This wasn't where she'd imagined her career would be. That coupled with her frustration over the progression in Ryan and Misty's relationship put her on the verge of tears.

"So, it's not Pulitzer material we're working on." Kai shrugged. He had no idea that for Angie this was about so much more than her career.

"No. But it's still my job, and as long as I have it, I will work to create the best stories I can," she said with resolve. Before Kai could respond, the van door opened and Harlan climbed inside. He tapped the back of the driver's seat, and the van lurched forward.

"Follow the cab," Harlan commanded the van driver as he pointed to a taxi that Ryan and Misty had just entered. They followed the taxi in silence, Harlan hopping out just as Ryan paid the fare. Angie watched Ryan place his hand on the small of Misty's back and usher her up toward what she assumed was Misty's apartment. All the while, Harlan filmed the trek with a handheld camera that was linked to one of the monitors in front of Angie.

With an accelerated heartbeat and trembling lips, she turned away from the monitor. So, fine. She was jealous . . . and hurt. She could admit that to herself. She wanted to feel Ryan's hand pressed against *her* back as he walked *her* up the stairs. Actually, she wanted to feel that hand pressed into a lot more intimate places. Wanted to know his thoughts were consumed by her. That his pulse beat harder when she walked into a room. That his heart–and other parts– felt bigger when he thought of her.

She turned back to the screen as Misty ran her fingers through Ryan's hair while they kissed. Without realizing it, Angie's hand went to her own lips, which tingled as she recalled how it felt to have Ryan kiss *her*. She continued to watch as Misty's hand roamed up and down Ryan's back, and recalled the feeling of his warm skin beneath her, over her.

She let out a shaky breath and hoped that Kai wouldn't notice, schooling her features so as not to give anything away. Because as much as she was willing to admit to herself that she was in love with Ryan, she certainly wouldn't admit it to anyone else. So, she watched as Ryan and Misty's kiss turned more passionate, and allowed herself to wither a little bit on the inside.

"Damn! This is hot!" Kai said. The van driver leaned back so he could catch a glimpse on the monitors. Ryan took the keys from Misty's hand and opened her front door. He held it open for her to walk through and followed her in. Harlan tried to muscle his way inside, but Ryan held his hand up to stop him. He closed the door in Harlan's face. The sight of Misty's wooden door with the tarnished "4E" lingered on the TV monitor, suggesting Harlan had turned off his camera and was mustering up the energy to walk down the four flights of stairs. Angie stared at the "4E," knowing what was likely happening on the other side of the door, and she willed the tears not to fall until she was in the privacy of her own home.

TWENTY

Angie felt an arm wrap around her waist as she got out of the cab that had brought her home from the dental surgery clinic where she'd had three of her wisdom teeth removed. The impacted teeth had not only impacted her pocketbook, but the timing hadn't been great. She was still super busy with the Subway Girl series (much to her disdain), but her oral surgeon said she couldn't put it off any longer. She was grateful that Josie was working four tens this week–meaning four shifts of ten hours each–and was able to take her to the appointment.

She closed her eyes and leaned into the body that was helping her up to her third-floor apartment. Josie didn't smell like she usually did. Rather than her light, floral fragrance, it was a bit more woodsy. She wasn't sure whether it was the pain meds or the fantastic scent, but her legs buckled. She grabbed the railing to steady herself. Her feet felt like lead weights, and she was having trouble lifting them off the ground. Before she could protest–not that she was about to complain; she could barely walk—those arms moved from her waist, lifted her up and cradled her like a baby.

Josie must really be hitting the gym. Angie giggled to herself. *Josie used to hit the Jim.* Jim was the closest thing to a boyfriend Josie had ever had, a few years ago. She listened to Josie's footsteps pad along the wood floors until they reached Angie's bedroom. Josie must have used her foot to kick the door open wider, because Angie heard it rattle against the wall.

"Oops, sorry," Josie said.

"S'okay," Angie mumbled back. Angie felt Josie gently lower her onto the bed and take her shoes off. Angie wiggled her toes, which felt lighter and looser than they had when she'd tried walking. *I like wiggling my toes. And I like the way that sounds. Wiggle my toes. Wiggle my toes.* She let out a small giggle.

Angie sensed the room darken and figured Josie had closed the curtains so she could presumably sleep off the rest of the powerful and quite lovely painkillers the oral surgeon had given her. But Angie didn't want to be alone. "Come lie down with me."

"I'm not sure—"

"Please," Angie whined. She knew it was annoying. She was quite certain of it. But she also knew Josie wasn't immune to her begging. And it wasn't like they hadn't curled up in bed together before, watching TV and eating ice cream. "Girls' Night In" was a mainstay. "Please," she repeated, rolling to her side to make room for Josie to lie down. Angie felt the bed dip as Josie sat down next to her and stroked her hair. "I'm a kitty cat," Angie purred before dissolving into giggles.

Angie opened her eyes to look at Josie and had to blink a few times to ensure she wasn't hallucinating, because she wasn't lying next to Josie. No. She was snuggled against Ryan. "You're not Josie."

"No." He laughed. "Josie's friend Della needed her to cover a shift. Something about Della's son being home sick. Josie asked me to take over her nursing duties here."

"Della likes miniature horses," Angie said dreamily. Ryan chuckled and continued to stroke her hair. Angie burrowed further into Ryan's chest and sniffed. *Damn! He smells good. Really good.* "I should have slept with you again when I had the chance."

"What?" he spluttered. His cheeks were tinged pink and his mouth gaped open. He clearly hadn't expected *that* anesthetic-fueled confession. If she hadn't been plied with an apparent truth serum, she certainly wouldn't have uttered it aloud.

"These abs are seriously lickable," Angie said, unconcerned that he seemed embarrassed, as she pulled his shirt up and ran her hand across his toned stomach. Ryan gasped and pulled her hand away, tugging his shirt down. *Welcome to Rejection Town–population, one.*

"Okay, Princess Demerol. Easy there."

"Hrmpf." Angie groaned. She was certain she was pouting. No one had ever found that look attractive on her, so she couldn't imagine it was working now. "It's too late. You're with Misty now," she complained.

"Believe me, sweetheart. If I were single and you weren't high as a kite right now, I'd want to roll you over, strip you naked and pound you into the mattress," Ryan muttered so softly she could barely hear him. She was certain she wasn't meant to hear him.

"You say the sweetest things," she sighed. "I love miniature horses, too." And that was the last thing she remembered before she awoke that evening.

Angie lifted her head from the pillow and could feel the swelling around her jawline. She gently touched the affected area, and, sure enough, she was rather puffy. She sat up and determined she was alone in her bed. But she hadn't been alone when she got home.

That's when it hit her. Ryan. *Oh god, Ryan. I begged him to cuddle with me and then I told him I wish I had slept with him. Ugh! If I could die of embarrassment, they'd be writing my eulogy right now.*

She just hoped her mom picked irises for the floral display. She was always partial to irises. As the painkillers began to wear off, Angie was shocked out of planning her funeral by the clank of a spoon against a pot in the kitchen.

She padded out of the bedroom, stopping by the bathroom to inspect her appearance. Yeah, if Ryan hadn't friend-zoned her before, he certainly would now. One look in the mirror confirmed her suspicions that she looked like a chubby-cheeked chipmunk. *Only a sadist would find this attractive.* She groaned at the sight reflected back at her and tried her best to flatten her hair, which was sticking up on one side. Why hadn't he just gone home?

Angie poked her head into the kitchen. Standing with her back to Angie, stirring a pot on the stove, was Josie. *Oh. It's Josie.* She should have been happy Josie was there. Happy she didn't have to endure an awkward encounter with Ryan. So why did she feel awash with disappointment?

Maybe Ryan was never there. Maybe she'd just imagined it all. The doctor had given her some pretty powerful drugs. She sagged in relief. Yes, it must have been a crazy–hyper-realistic but crazy–dream. No cuddling. No confession. No Ryan telling her he wanted to pound her into the mattress. *Wait, what?* She rubbed her temples, trying to remember her dream. Ryan had said that if he weren't with Misty and she weren't on painkillers, he'd have wanted to "pound her into the mattress." *Damn, that sounds hot.* No one had ever said anything like that to her before. Not even in her drug-fueled hallucinations–until today. But she couldn't trust that what she'd heard was the truth.

"Hey, sweetie," Josie said when she turned and saw Angie staring at her back.

"Hey." Angie offered a weak smile.

"You blew up!" Josie said. Angie swatted at Josie's arm and tried pouting, although she wasn't certain Josie could tell through the puffy layers of skin surrounding her mouth. "How do you feel?"

"Surprisingly, not too bad. I think I look a lot worse."

"You do look pretty bad." Josie grimaced, darting out of the way before Angie could swat at her again.

"Brat," Angie muttered.

"Yes, but I'm your brat and you love me."

Angie tilted her head from side to side. "Yeah, I do," she conceded. "Whatcha got cooking?"

"I think the expression is '*Hey, good lookin*', whatcha got cookin'."

"Always fishing for a compliment, aren't you?" Angie rolled her eyes.

"I just speak the truth." Josie gestured for Angie to sit down on a bar stool and lifted the lid off a pot on the stove. "Can't help it if I'm beautiful."

"Okay, good looking. What *is* cooking? It smells good and, no offense, but you're not especially skilled in the domestic arts." Angie watched as Josie ladled chicken noodle soup into a bowl.

"No offense taken. I was planning to just order in something from the deli around the corner, but my friend Della made this for you." She handed Angie a spoon and napkin, then turned to ladle a bowl for herself.

"She is the sweetest." Angie dipped the spoon into the bowl, moving the soup around to let some of the steam out.

"She felt bad that I had to bail on you earlier."

"Mmm." The soup was delicious. *Wait, what?* "What do you mean, bail on me this afternoon?"

"While I was in the waiting room, Della's son's school called to say he was sick. I ran over to the hospital to cover her shift. She made him soup and made an extra batch for you." Josie sat down at the table and took a sip of soup, letting out a contented sigh.

"So . . ."

"So . . ." Josie repeated, giving Angie a quizzical look.

"I got home via Uber?" Angie suggested, hoping and praying that her crazy and realistic dream wasn't real.

"Seriously," Josie scoffed. "You think I would hire an Uber to pick you up from surgery and put you to bed?"

Of course, she wouldn't have. That was ridiculous. It was just a better alternative right now than the truth staring Angie straight in the face.

Everything that had happened with Ryan actually *happened* with Ryan.

"I'm joking," Angie said. "You sent Ryan to take care of me." She tried to keep her voice even. She didn't want to give anything away, and by "anything," she meant her humiliation. She didn't dare look in Josie's eyes, certain her friend would see the truth. Instead, she looked down at her bowl of soup and took another heaping spoonful.

"I figured that was a better alternative than your mom," Josie joked.

"Good call. That was nice of him."

"Mm-hmm," Josie agreed, continuing to enjoy her soup.

"So . . . did Ryan say anything?"

"Anything like you wanted to climb his jungle gym?"

Angie gasped. In fact, she raised her hand to her mouth so quickly, she smacked it pretty hard, causing her eyes to water.

"Oh, sweetie. You've got to be careful." Josie leaned over and stroked her hair. Once Angie got her composure back, Josie added, "So, you still have feelings for Ryan, huh?"

"No," Angie quickly—too quickly—fired back.

"Mm-hmm."

Angie exhaled, her shoulders slumping in defeat. "Okay, you have to promise, and I mean promise, you won't say anything to anyone, or bring this back up at a later date." Angie pointed a finger at Josie.

"Promise," she said, holding out her pinky for a swear.

"I may have—in a drug-induced stupor—come on to Ryan."

"Good on you." Josie nodded. "It's about time you two got together."

"We didn't. We can't. He's with Misty now." Angie slumped forward.

"Anyone with two eyes and half a brain—which means Misty isn't included in our definition of anyone—can see that you and Ryan are so right for each other."

"I'm not so sure about that. You've got to remember, I've seen all their dates. And when I say all, I don't mean each one. I mean the *entirety* of each one." Angie recalled watching Ryan and Misty making out in front of her doorway a few nights ago.

"I can't imagine how hard that must be for you." Josie squeezed Angie's hand.

Angie's lip trembled. "It is what it is." She shrugged.

"Luke and I have talked about this, and we think you and Ryan would be perfect for each other."

If only Ryan felt that way.

"You and Luke? Really?" Angie perked up.

"We're just friends," Josie assured her.

"Well, I'm not sure if I'm flattered by the attention or feeling sympathetic that you and Luke have nothing better to do than worry about me and Ryan." Angie knew she was deflecting. It was a common avoidance technique of hers. Unfortunately for her, Josie knew all of her tricks.

"First of all, Luke and I *are* just friends. Nothing's going on between us. Second, the two of you just need to get together already. The sexual tension is obvious to everyone around you."

"There's no sexual tension."

"Believe me, from what Luke tells me, Ryan's tense."

"What does that mean?"

"It means that it's been a while since he's gotten the kind of *release* that guys need."

"What?" Angie giggled.

"Shit! Luke's gonna kill me. Listen, this is just between you and me, but Luke's all but certain Ryan and Misty haven't slept together."

"And he knows this how?" She cringed, unsure she was prepared for the answer.

"You don't want to know. I didn't want to know," Josie said with a grimace before turning it into a bright-eyed look. "But he's pretty sure."

"Really?" Angie's voice held both hope and humor.

"Truth," Josie said emphatically. At that possibility, Angie smiled before wincing in pain, from both her teeth and her heartache.

TWENTY-ONE

Gina blew out sharply and pushed her chair back from the receptionist desk at *Celebrity Monger*. She shook her head at the series of small flat-screen TVs that lined the lobby wall. She walked to Barry's office, fearful he would take the brunt of his frustration out on her. She tentatively rapped her knuckles on the door, pushing it open as she did.

"Dammit, Gina. I'm on the phone," Barry barked.

"You'll want to see this," she said, her voice trembling. She turned on the television and changed the channel to NBC, where Misty sat across from Savannah Guthrie on the set of the *Today* show. Barry pulled the headset off his crown and lowered it to the table.

"And how is it that you discovered you were the Subway Girl?" asked Savannah.

"I was in dance class. I'm a dancer and an actress," said Misty, turning her head coquettishly to the side and smiling for the camera. "Some of the other dancers recognized me from the website. I don't pay attention to that tabloid stuff. I'm too focused on my acting career."

Barry furiously punched his thumb into the remote, silencing the TV. He glared at Gina, who scurried out of the office before Barry could say a word. He yanked the headset out of the phone jack, picked up the handset and yelled, "I'll call you back." He slammed the handset down and ran his fingers through his slicked-back hair. His jaw tightened and the vein in his forehead visibly throbbed before picking up the handset again.

"Hey, Barry," said the attorney on the other end.

"Why the hell am I seeing Misty Waites on the *Today* show talking about the Subway Girl? Doesn't she have an exclusivity agreement with us?" he shouted.

"Uh . . ." said the lawyer, with the audible sound of papers being shuffled on his desk. "I don't recall you asking me to draw one up for her—"

"You're fired. Clear your shit out!" Barry slammed the phone down. He pushed the intercom button and barked, "Get Misty in here," to Gina.

If that little bitch thinks she is going to derail my plans, she is in for a very rude awakening. No one and nothing is going to stop me from taking Celebrity Monger *to network television, especially some two-bit whore actress.* He just needed to remind her that he called the shots and that without him, she would be nothing.

Gina led Misty, who had at Barry's insistence come straight to *Celebrity Monger* from her TV appearance, into Barry's office, seating her in a black leather chair across from his desk. Misty stretched out her long legs and examined the polish, which was starting to chip, on her nails.

"Barry will be right in." Gina walked back to the reception desk. Normally she would have offered a guest a cup of coffee or a glass of water, but Misty wasn't going to be on the receiving end of a friendly visit.

Barry stormed in, shaking his head, processing Misty's complete betrayal. After all he'd done for her and her career. While he glowered at her, silently fuming, Misty lowered her eyes, unable to meet his intense glare, and once again picked at the nail polish on her thumb.

"What the hell were you thinking, going on the *Today* show?" Barry demanded.

"I was thinking what great exposure it was for you and *Celebrity Monger*," she said with a smile, which Barry could tell was fake. It didn't surprise him that Misty wasn't a great actress.

"Bullshit!" he barked at her. "You were thinking what great exposure it was for your *acting* career, or lack thereof."

"Well, my new agen–" she began, sitting upright in her chair.

"Your new agent?" he hissed incredulously. What the hell made her think she or her "new agent" were in control of any of this? This was his show! His opportunity! His future!

"Yes. My new agent thought it would be a good idea. He thinks we can parlay this into a stint on *Dancing with the Stars*." She shrugged and gave a slight grin, as if suggesting that maybe this *was* indeed a great opportunity for Barry.

"Listen to me, Misty," he said in a menacing tone, pointing a long bony finger at her. "This is bigger than your *acting* career. I need you to stop doing interviews and focus on Ryan."

"And how are you going to make that worth my while?" she said, tilting her head and glowering at him. Barry could tell by her response that she'd taken offense to his suggestion that her attempts at acting were more hobby, less career. While he admired her pluck, he knew that no one, *no one*, picked a fight with him and survived. A big backbone only made for a louder snap.

"Are you extorting me? *Me?*"

"We don't need to use ugly labels." Misty's voice wavered. Barry guessed she was starting to regret her forthrightness.

"Your ungratefulness is what's ugly," he scoffed.

"Listen Barry," said Misty, standing up to leave. "I appreciate all you've done for me. But I think I'm ready to move on." Her lip subtly quivered in fear.

Staring at her with intense eyes and gesturing for her to sit back down, Barry said, "You're ready to move on when I say you are."

Misty didn't take a seat. Instead, she took a deep breath, squared her shoulders and shook her head slightly.

"Don't threaten me, or I'll expose you as the puppet master that you are," she challenged.

Barry stared at her, and Misty's shoulders hunched forward. Barry took that as a signal that she didn't have the stones to stand toe to toe with his imposing form.

"You think you can turn this thing around on me? Believe me, I am a puppet master, and you won't believe the strings I can pull," he said calmly. It might have been a bit too calmly for Misty. She lowered herself into the seat.

"I . . . I . . ." she spluttered.

"You're going to continue dating Ryan until I say so. And you're going to keep your mouth shut. I've broken little whores like you for fun. Trust me, you don't want me as an enemy." Misty gulped as he stood over her, staring intently. "Now get the hell out of my sight, and keep your goddam mouth shut until I tell you what to say and who to say it to. Got it?"

"Yeah, I got it." She scurried out the door.

Damn right, you got it, thought Barry. Now if he only knew what his next move needed to be.

"Hey, slobs. Can you try and remember to date your food in the refrigerator?" Diego held out a takeout container with a stained bottom. He scrunched his nose and tossed it into the trash can.

"I tried dating my food in the fridge, but it only thinks of me as a friend." Luke's well-timed quip was enough to pull

Diego out of his foul mood over the foul odors in the fridge. He tossed Luke an air high five, grabbed an apple, and sat back at his desk.

Ryan glanced up in time to see Misty stride into the graphic design office wearing a black leotard, black tights, a loose-fitting ballet skirt and a pair of pink leg warmers. He couldn't help but think she looked like a stock character from *Flashdance*, one of his favorite classic '80s movies. He wondered if Angie had seen that one, and then gave himself a mental slap for letting Angie invade his mind when Misty was standing right in front of him.

"Hey, this is a surprise," Ryan said, wrapping his arm around Misty and giving her a kiss on the cheek. "Guys, let me introduce you to Misty." Misty demurely held out her hand for a shake.

Diego stood and shook her hand. "Nice to meet you, Misty."

"You must be David," she cooed. "Ryan has told me so much about you. He says you're his partner in design crime."

"I would be the criminal here," said Luke. "Diego, not David, handles the books."

"Oh, I'm sorry." She cringed.

"That's okay," soothed Ryan. "Diego is a financial whiz and keeps the operation funded and running. Luke here"—he gestured to Luke—"is the other half of our design team. He's an amazing talent. Just ask him," he joked.

"True," said Luke. "Well, it's nice to meet you." He politely shook Misty's hand, turned back to his desk and began working at his computer terminal. Diego stood there for a beat, looking unsure. Then he nodded at Ryan and Misty and went back to work himself.

Huh. I wonder what's up with the guys? Ryan had never seen them so focused on work, especially when they had a guest in the office. Typically, they would do anything for a distraction, especially one as beautiful as Misty.

"I hope you don't mind me just stopping by, but I wanted you to know that I was thinking about you," she said breathily.

Luke groaned. Ryan whipped his head around to him.

"Everything okay?" *Yeah, there is definitely something up with the guys.*

"Oh, just trying to get this coding sequence right," Luke said.

"Do you need help?" Ryan moved away from Misty and stood over Luke's shoulder, running his finger along the monitor, trying to find the error. Misty sidled up next to Ryan, linking her arm through his and using her other hand to rub his shoulder.

"I thought maybe we could grab an early dinner," she suggested.

Ryan grasped her hand and gave it a firm squeeze. "I wish I could, but we're a bit swamped this week with a big project."

"Okay," she said with a pout. "I should probably let you get back to work then."

"That would probably be best," agreed Luke. Diego coughed as if he were choking.

"Sorry, went down the wrong pipe," Diego said, pointing to the apple sitting on his desk. He cleared his throat a few times and smiled. "I'm good now."

Ryan gave him a questioning look before pulling Misty toward the door. "Thanks for stopping by."

"Happy to see you." She licked her bottom lip and tugged it between her teeth.

"I'll call you when I'm done here, maybe around seven or eight."

"Okay." She placed her hand around Ryan's neck and left a lingering kiss on his cheek. Ryan watched her leave the office and felt guilty. Not that he couldn't spend time with her, but because he wasn't sure he wanted to. He was confused about his response to Misty, which reminded him of the guys' reaction to her. Ryan stalked over to Luke's desk, noticing how he was particularly focused on his monitor.

"So, what gives?" He swiveled Luke's chair around and leaned down to get closer to his face. "What. Gives?" he repeated.

"I'm not sure what you mean."

"Really?" Ryan mocked. "Misty?"

"What about her?" Luke shrugged.

"I have never seen you act so cool around a woman before."

"Dude," Luke said. "I'm always cool with the ladies." Luke spread his arms out to the side. Ryan sensed the return of Luke's typical swagger.

"Yes! That right there is what I'm talking about," he said in triumph. "You weren't cool like that; you were downright cold. None of your normal banter. No 'how-you-doin'-Joey-from-*Friends*' flirting."

Luke glanced over at Diego. Ryan looked back too.

"You got something to say?" he asked Diego. Diego swallowed hard and slid his chair across the workspace to where Luke and Ryan were seated.

"It's intervention time," Luke said grimly.

"Intervention? You can't be serious." Ryan shook his head and chuckled. "Okay, so you don't like Misty. That much is obvious. But why? You just met her." He couldn't help coming to her defense.

"Dude, you know I love you like a brother," said Luke. "And I'm not one to question who people hook up with. Lord knows I'm not the most discriminating," he added, trying to lighten the mood with some self-deprecating humor.

Taking the bait, Ryan replied, "That's true. As you often quote Twain, 'Familiarity breeds contempt.'"

"'And children,'" finished Luke with a firm nod. "But listen, you're not like most guys," Luke explained. "You don't just hook up. You get *hooked*. And Diego and I," Luke continued, motioning to Diego, who gave a grim grin and a nod, "we don't want to see Misty getting her hooks into you."

Diego cringed. "What I think Luke here is trying to say is that when you love, man, you love with your whole heart, and we aren't getting the sense that she's worth it."

"That was beautiful, man." Luke wiped an imaginary tear from his eye.

"Why, thank you," Diego replied, holding his hand to his heart.

"Are you two done having a moment?" Ryan said with a laugh.

"Yeah, I just get a little choked up when we start talking about true love," Diego joked, fanning himself with his hand.

"Seriously, though. We just want you to keep your eyes open, Ryan," said Luke.

"Yeah," Diego said. "Eyes open."

"I know this probably isn't what you want to hear, but . . ." Luke rubbed the back of his neck, his jaw tight.

No one in the history of time has ever liked where "I know this probably isn't what you want to hear but" has led. Ryan expelled a deep breath.

"Probably not." But if anyone was going to tell him something he likely didn't want to hear, but perhaps *needed* to hear, it was his best mate Luke, who had nursed him through everything from heartaches to stomachaches. "But if it's something I need to hear, I'm open to it."

"Just because Misty turned out to be the girl on the subway, doesn't mean she's necessarily the one for you," Luke said. "For fools rush in where angels fear to tread." Diego and Ryan stared at Luke with furrowed brows. "Alexander Pope." After a beat he added, "Eighteenth-century English poet."

"Who the fuck are you?" scoffed Diego.

Ryan ignored Diego's comment. "Are you calling me an angel?" Ryan asked.

Luke shrugged. "Angel. Boy Scout. All-around good guy. However you want to label it. The point is, you don't owe her anything. You owe it to yourself to be happy."

Ryan thought about this. What would make him happy?

"What does Angie think of all this?" asked Diego.

"Angie? Why would it matter what Angie thinks?" Ryan asked, although he already had Angie on his mind.

"She's the one who set this whole thing up. Doesn't she have an opinion?" Luke replied.

"She hasn't said anything," said Ryan. "Aside from helping her the other day, I haven't spoken much to her since Misty and I met." Although he'd wanted to.

"Maybe you should see what she thinks. You know, get a second opinion," Luke suggested.

"Third opinion," Diego corrected. Luke rolled his eyes, which reminded Ryan of Angie and her ever-present eye-roll.

"Third opinion," Luke reluctantly agreed.

Ryan stroked his chin in thought. "Okay, maybe I will."

"Now, if we're done exploring our feelings, maybe we could get some work done," Luke said.

While the other guys went back to work, Ryan considered what they'd had to say. He did want to talk to Angie, but not for the reasons Luke and Diego thought. If he was being honest with himself, he struggled to keep her out of his mind throughout the day. He was supposed to be thinking about Misty. He was supposed to be focused on building a relationship with her. Fate, after all, had brought them together, right?

How could he do that if he not only kept thinking about Angie, but talking to Angie, and—worse yet—accidentally confessing his attraction to her while she was high on painkillers. At least she was so out of it, she couldn't have heard him.

Maybe this wasn't fair to any of them. Maybe he was wrong about fate being at work in this instance. Maybe it *was* time to acknowledge that Misty wasn't right for him after all and figure out a way out of this that would keep his dignity intact.

TWENTY-TWO

Angie paced back and forth at the foot of Barry's desk as she waited for him to finish his call with the analytics firm. He'd hired the company to monitor site traffic, calculate ad revenues, capture organic and inorganic searches for the Subway Girl online, as well as identify other metrics to help him sell *Celebrity Monger* to a major TV network.

The web series had been going on for a while now, and people were enthralled by Ryan and Misty's relationship. It didn't matter if they loved the couple or hated them, rooted for love or a crash and burn, believed the story to be fairy-tale magic or a master manipulation. No one could stop talking about it, and Barry couldn't be happier.

But was it enough for the network? Barry was convinced that if Misty hadn't gone on the *Today* show there would have been even more eyeballs on the site. He didn't believe her little stunt had helped drive interest in her and Ryan's story.

Now, sitting on the phone waiting to hear the latest report, he was beginning to panic. And if he was going to panic, that just put Angie in full-blown crisis mode. With the deadline of

Barry's next network meeting approaching, they *needed* good news here.

"Two points still?" Barry asked in disbelief. "Run the numbers again," he growled into the phone, running his fingers through his hair.

"Shit," Angie muttered under her breath.

"That damn Misty!" He scowled. "Well, Angie, any ideas? We need two points and have eight days to get them"

Angie tapped her finger against her temple. She knew the bank issue needed to be resolved by then, too.

"I'll find another way, Barry," she said confidently.

"Good! Go!"

Angie rubbed her temples, then grabbed her cell phone and scrolled through the contacts until she reached Doug Harp. Her thumb hovered over the call button. She put the phone down and picked it up—repeating the pattern several times. She wasn't sure she could do this. Sweat beaded on her brow. She knew she shouldn't but couldn't think of another option.

She needed the network deal to go through. And if this worked, success wouldn't be dependent on Ryan and Misty continuing down their path. She could talk to Ryan and open his eyes to what was happening.

She took a deep breath and pressed call. She stood and paced the room while the phone rang.

"Hey, Angie," said the voice on the other end.

"Hi, Doug. I have a job for you, if you've got the time."

"Yeah, always have time for you guys. What's up?"

"This is a rather sensitive matter—"

"Aren't they all?" Doug chuckled.

"Well, yes, that's true. But this one especially so."

"Okay, I could meet you in an hour, if that works."

"Don't come to the office," she blurted. "Um, how about we meet somewhere else?"

"I'm just wrapping up a stakeout on the Upper East Side. Meet you at the Starbucks on Lexington?"

"That works. I'll see you in an hour." Angie hung up the phone and let out a loud exhale before burying her head in her hands.

An hour later, Angie sat at a table at the Starbucks across town from *Celebrity Monger*. She didn't want to hold this meeting at the office or even near the office. Anonymity was key for this. It wasn't going to be her finest moment, and the thought of anyone knowing about it filled her with dread. But this was about her mom and Ryan. Too bad she would have to live with herself forever.

As she agonized about this moment she wouldn't be able to turn back from, a man approached her table. He had a plain face, wire-framed glasses and sandy-brown hair. He was completely forgettable, which made him excellent at his job.

"You wanted to see me," he said to Angie, sliding into a chair across from her.

"Yeah, Doug. See what you can dig up on this guy." She pushed forward a folder. Doug opened it and pulled out the photos and brief dossier she had prepared.

"Who is he?"

"JP Rawlins. He's the head of programming for one of the major networks."

"Looking for anything in particular?" His pointer finger traced down the list of information Angie had gleaned from a basic internet search.

"Anything useful. Illegal nanny. Drug problem. Mistress. Whatever you can find," she said, taking a deep breath and knotting her fingers in her hands. "And I need it by Friday."

"A rush job is gonna cost you extra."

"It's okay. Whatever it takes."

Doug grabbed the folder and walked away without saying goodbye. As Angie walked out of the coffee shop to head back to the office, her eyes began to water, the decision to enlist Doug's help weighing heavily on her mind.

She'd worked with the private detective before, mostly to fact-check story details or confirm an anonymous tip. But this . . . this was something altogether different. This was blackmail. There was no way to pussyfoot around it. She was about to draw from Barry's playbook, and that thought alone scared the wits out of her. She bolted a few paces and braced her hands against a trash can, fearful she was going to vomit.

There is no other way, she thought as she righted herself. If Doug found something, then Rawlins would deserve what was coming to him, she tried rationalizing as she trekked back to *Celebrity Monger*. But in her heart, she knew she had crossed a line that would change her forever.

While she was waiting by the bank of elevators in the lobby of the office building, Harlan appeared. He took one look at her face and asked, "What's wrong?"

"I just sold my soul to the devil," Angie managed before falling into his chest for a hug.

TWENTY-THREE

Barry had always been confident in Angie's ability to get the job done. Sure, she could be an annoying pain in the ass when pitching him stories he had no intention of telling, but she also had a nose for news and was a solid writer. So he kept her around. Plus Harlan had let it slip that she was under some financial pressures, so he knew she was just as invested in making this network deal a success as he was. That didn't stop him from worrying about how the meeting with the network would go. There was only one shot to make sure it was a success, which meant he was going to take matters into his own hands.

Those were the thoughts going through his mind as he paced the small room, glancing through the one-way glass. Across from him, but unable to see him behind the mirror, were a group of women in their twenties and thirties. Each thumbed through a non-disclosure agreement while seated around a dark wood table. The room was otherwise empty, except for a long credenza against one wall, covered in soft drinks and snacks provided by the research facility.

"I'll go ahead and collect your non-disclosure agreements when each of you are done signing," said the focus group leader,

Janette, a plump woman in her late fifties with jet-black hair and a pair of red cat-eyeglasses. She adjusted the glasses on her nose and continued, "Again, these are binding contracts where you agree not to reveal anything we discuss here today without opening yourselves up to major litigation."

Barry ran his finger back and forth across his lower lip as he watched. When Janette had gathered the signed forms, Gina walked to the door and grabbed them from her. Barry glanced through, ensuring all the papers were signed, initialed and dated as needed. He gave Gina a nod, and she alerted Janette that she was cleared to proceed.

"Now that we've got all the paperwork out of the way, we can get started. We'll be spending the next hour and a half talking a bit about the Subway Girl, which you all mentioned you were fans of. After we conclude our discussion, Gina will provide the $125 payment we discussed as compensation for your time and thoughts."

Barry watched as all the women nodded in agreement, seeming eager to earn some cash for providing their opinions—opinions he would use to shape the future of the series, in order to move the needle enough for Rawlins.

"I'd like to start out by gauging your perceptions of Ryan. What do you think of him?" A young woman wearing a Harry Potter-inspired t-shirt paired with skinny jeans and brown lace-up boots raised her hand.

"Yes," Janette said, pointing at her. "Please start out by telling us your name."

"Hi, everyone," she said with a wave. "I'm Casey. And honestly, I just love Ryan. He's like the perfect combination of a guy's guy and a girl's guy." Other focus group participants around the table nodded.

"I agree," said a blonde whose tight ponytail showed off a severe forehead. "He's so sweet. I would totally go for him."

"Tell us your name," requested Janette.

"Oh, I'm Laurel."

"Thanks, Laurel," said Janette.

A sassy brunette spoke up next, her thick New York accent coming out. "I'm Evie. Sometimes I think he's too sweet. I think Misty is kind of taking advantage of him and he doesn't realize it." Again, heads around the table nodded.

"Speaking of Misty, what do you think of her?" Janette asked.

"Hate her!" interjected Evie, almost before Janette finished her question.

"I sometimes feel . . . oh, I'm Margot . . . sometimes I feel she doesn't even like Ryan," suggested a thin redhead, gesturing enthusiastically with her hands.

"Yeah," said Casey. "I know she's supposed to be some sort of actress, but I don't think she's a very good one."

"Truth," added Evie with a sassy tilt of her head. Behind the mirror, a mischievous smile crossed Barry's face as he listened to these women confirm his initial suspicion that Ryan was a hero and Misty was the perfect villain.

After an hour of eliciting opinions about everything from Ryan's background to Misty's intentions, Janette moved into the critical component of the day's focus group—determining what to do next.

"So, what would make you more sympathetic to Ryan: if Misty cheated on him or if you found out that she had been hired to date him?"

Iris, a dark-skinned African American woman, looked devastated. "I thought Ryan's search for love was real, but now that we're here talking about his breakup, I realize it isn't."

"And how does that make you feel?" asked Janette brightly, careful not to betray any of her own feelings, but instead just facilitate the discussion among the participants. She pushed her glasses up on her nose again, waiting for the group to discuss.

"Honestly, it bums me out," said Laurel, with Iris and Evie shaking their heads in agreement.

"Yeah," said Evie. "If I had known this was all fake, I wouldn't have wasted my time on it." Janette nodded.

"Okay, given your position, would you rather find out that Misty's part of the romance was orchestrated or have Misty break up with Ryan and preserve the illusion that this was all real?" the focus group leader posed to the group.

Iris blew out a sharp breath. "I'm sure other people would be bummed or angry to find out this is all fake. So, I guess it would be better for Misty to dump him."

Casey gasped. "I don't want to see him get hurt," she said solemnly.

"He's going to get hurt either way," retorted Evie. "Either she cheats on him or he finds out she was paid to date him."

"I think he should break up with *her*," suggested Laurel. "Really tell her off."

"Ooooh, that's good," said Iris.

"That's an interesting option," said Janette. "Let's explore. If that could be orchestrated, how bad a breakup would you like to see?"

TWENTY-FOUR

Misty wrung her hands as she stood outside Ryan's apartment while Harlan strapped a wireless microphone to her shirt, linking it to a battery pack that sat low at the back of her waist. He turned her around, adjusting it against her dark-wash skinny jeans.

Angie stood in the hallway, exhaling deeply and shifting from the ball of one foot to the other.

"Why don't you go home, Ange?" Harlan said, giving her a sympathetic nod. "Or at least go wait in the van."

"Three's already a crowd," she said solemnly. If Harlan was going to be here to witness and record Misty's confession—and if Angie was going to have to edit and release it for the world to see—the least she could do was be here for Ryan in the aftermath. More than wanting to soothe his ache, she wanted to support his dreams . . . and motivate his kindness . . . and lick his abs. *No. Mind, stop going places you have no business going.*

"I can call you when it's over," he offered.

"No. I'll wait in the hall," she said with a sad smile.

"Suit yourself." He shrugged.

"I . . ." Misty rubbed her temples.

"Just like Barry said," Harlan advised her.

"But I'm going to look like such a bitch," she whined.

"If it looks like a bitch and acts like a bitch . . ." said Angie, taking no care to hide her disdain for Misty.

Harlan turned to Angie. "That's enough," he said in an admonishing tone before facing Misty. "Make it easy on yourself. Just do what Barry said, and then get out."

"Think of it as an acting job. A *continuation* of your acting job," Angie hissed. Misty glared at her, and Angie looked away.

"Okay," said Misty, taking a deep breath. She knocked on Ryan's door and took a step back. Ryan opened the door and kissed Misty chastely on the cheek.

"Thanks for coming over. I wanted to talk–" he said, opening the door further and allowing her to pass. Harlan walked in right behind her while Angie remained hidden in the hallway. "Oh, hey, Harlan," said Ryan, his voice flush with confusion. "Is it really necessary for you to be here tonight? I mean, you're a cool guy and all, but three's kinda becoming a crowd."

Angie, overhearing Ryan's quip, so similar to her own, smiled to herself. Despite Ryan's clear interest in having some alone time with Misty, Harlan pushed his way in.

"Sorry, man."

"All right. Well then, come on in." Ryan gestured for Harlan to make his way further into the small apartment.

"So, listen Ryan . . ." began Misty before Ryan could close the door.

Harlan, in the process of setting up his camera on a tripod, called to her. "Just hold on a second, Mist. Let me get set up." Angie, still standing out in the hallway, put her hand over her mouth to muffle an impending sob. Her stomach plummeted in anticipation of what was about to go down. Of the heartache to come.

"You look upset. Is everything okay?" Ryan, sensing that something was wrong, walked toward Misty. He was planning to end things with her, but he wouldn't do that on camera. And even though he didn't think she was the right woman for him, he didn't want to see her hurting. He rubbed his hands up and down her arms consolingly.

"I'm really going to need you two to hold on a minute," said Harlan as he continued to set up his equipment. Ryan turned to Harlan and scowled, then looked back at Misty with concern. "Okay. You're good to go." Harlan gave Misty a confirming nod and thumbs-up. "Hey, Ryan, do you think you can repeat that?"

Frustration enveloped Ryan as he ignored Harlan and kept a concerned eye on Misty. "What's wrong?" he asked her, grasping her hands in his and guiding her over to the couch.

"I'm sorry, Ryan. I . . . I . . ." She looked at Harlan, who gestured for her to continue. Misty took a deep breath, waited a beat and turned to Ryan. "I'm sorry, Ryan. I just don't deserve you. It breaks my heart to tell you this but I . . . I hooked up with my ex-boyfriend last night."

"I don't believe it," said Ryan, almost in a whisper, still holding onto her hands.

"Harlan has the tape if you want to see it," she huffed.

"Wha . . . why would you . . . why would you do that?" he asked, pained. He dropped her hands and paced the room.

"I just don't love you, Ryan. You're wonderful, and you deserve someone much better than me. I'm sorry I hurt you. I should go." Misty turned to walk away.

"Wait," called Ryan. "I just . . ." Harlan looked at Misty and jerked his head a few times, motioning for her to leave.

She offered one final goodbye and walked out. Harlan kept the camera trained on Ryan as Angie walked in.

"Hey," said Angie in a gentle tone, placing a consoling hand on Ryan's shoulder.

"I just . . ." started Ryan before being enveloped in a hug.

"I know. I'm sorry. So sorry," she soothed.

"Obviously you knew." Ryan shuddered. *And now everyone knows. Cheated on again. Publicly humiliated . . . again.*

"I knew she was coming here tonight to tell you. I thought I would tag along so I could be here for you," she said reassuringly.

"Thanks," he eked out, his small smile not matching the appreciation he felt at the moment. He turned to Harlan. "Could we turn the camera off now?"

"Oh, sure." Harlan turned his back to them, shielding the camera with his body as he appeared to fiddle with the buttons. "I'll be right back. Let me just get the case from my truck." He walked out the door.

"You're in shock right now," said Angie.

"Yeah. I was planning to . . . I just didn't think she would . . ." Ryan stared out the window, his voice tinged with disbelief. He felt Angie wrap her arms around him from behind.

"It's okay. She just wasn't the right girl for you."

Logically, Ryan knew this. He had been so convinced Misty wasn't a match, he'd been planning to break up with her. It still didn't take away the sting of being cheated on.

Angie's arms slipped away from him, and he immediately missed the comfort and contact. She shifted around so they were face to face and placed her hands on his shoulders. He looked down to see softened eyes full of emotion.

"You deserve someone who's going to appreciate your sense of humor and all your movie references . . . and how kind-hearted you are."

If all that was true, and those qualities were valued, why didn't Angie want to be with him?

"I brought some movies about cheating women," Angie said. "Thought we could have a marathon. I've got *The Postman Always Rings Twice*, *Indecent Proposal* and *Dial M for Murder*," she said, pulling the CD cases out of her purse.

"Hitchcock?" sighed Ryan.

"Yeah," Angie said brightly. "I know you like him."

"Of course you do. The whole world does," he said, recalling his unfortunate and admittedly painful conversation with Misty about the famed director. He dropped his face into his hands. "I'm such an idiot."

"You're not an idiot." Angie grasped his hands so he would look up at her.

"I just really hoped . . . I mean . . ." He turned away from her. He so badly wanted to meet the right woman for him. For a while there, he felt like he had . . . in Angie.

"It's okay," she reassured him. "You deserve so much more." Did he?

"Why do they keep cheating on me?" he whispered.

"I don't know. I'm just glad it's all over," Angie said. Harlan returned and packed up his equipment while Angie and Ryan silently watched. Angie led Ryan over to the couch. He sat down, his head slumped forward, elbows braced on his knees. Angie put her hand on his back.

"Did I ever tell you the story of my ex-boyfriend, Harrison?"

Ryan looked up to see her face scrunched up in disgust. He shifted his body so he could watch her. "No. You mentioned once that he cheated but didn't elaborate."

Angie nodded. "We were living together. Had been for about four months. It was a Thursday evening, and I was lying on the couch with my feet in his lap. He was reading something on his iPhone, and I was on his iPad, shopping for supplies for the baby shower I was throwing for his sister." She swallowed hard.

"You okay?"

Angie nodded again. "I was scrolling through a party website when a text for him popped up on his tablet. He responded on his phone, not realizing I was seeing the texts in real time. They started out innocent enough, with 'hey' and 'what are you doing,' before moving on to 'miss you' and 'when can I see you.' It escalated pretty quickly to a request for nudes."

"Shit," Ryan said. *Damn. What a fucker.* "And all the while, you were sitting right there?" He didn't know whether the infidelity or sheer disrespect angered him most.

"Yup. Him rubbing my feet in his lap the whole time, as if he were just reading the Yankees highlights."

"What a dick. I'm guessing you ripped into him pretty good." He was eager to hear her response.

"No. My uncle is an exterminator. You don't kill the rat until you know how big an infestation you have. I took the next day off work and used his iPad to review all of his old texts. Turns out, he was a pretty big rat."

Ryan grasped her hand and squeezed, pouring as much comfort, sympathy and outrage into that one touch. "More than one?"

Angie nodded grimly. Ryan huffed out a breath of air. He rubbed his knees with his palms and continued to breathe hard.

"So, while he was gone, I removed all of my stuff from the apartment. The only trace I left behind was printouts showing his lengthy and varied infidelity plastered all over the walls."

"That seems awfully restrained for you." Ryan side-eyed her.

"Oh, I also cut the crotch out of his favorite Tom Ford suit. Figured since he couldn't keep it in his pants, I would make sure he wouldn't be able to keep it in his pants."

Ryan leaned back and laughed a genuine laugh, finding some relief from his own personal anguish. "That sounds more like it."

Angie grinned smugly.

SaturdayNite2: someone needs to teach her a lesson.

JokersWild10: No!!!!! How could she do this to Ryan?!?!

LMW2870: Told you so!

DrillTeamBabe: @maribel5 @everychance @gogo18 @ameliarb @karilb @ PicklesNTickles8 I heard Ryan hangs out at the Finch on 33rd. We should totally stake the place out.

> PicklesNTickles8: @DrillTeamBabe @maribel5 @everychance @gogo18 @ameliarb @karilb YAAAASSSSS!

> Everychance: @PicklesNTickles8 @DrillTeamBabe @maribel5 @gogo18 @ameliarb @karilb GNO!

VegasVirgin: I knew it!

HazmatHattie: @FloraJ22963 You would make such a good Subway Girl. You should apply.

> FloraJ22963: @HazmatHattie Awww. Thanks, hon.

> HazmatHattie: @FloraJ22963 Of course! And when u and Ryan get married, I get to be the maid of honor.

> FloraJ22963: @HazmatHattie Absolutely!!!!

FlyByNite33: Thank god this national nightmare is over. Now can we all get back to things that really matter.

WWCD41: Never trust anything that bleeds for a week and doesn't die.

> FemFatale5: @WWCD41 Misogynist asshole!

> RollingRoll: @WWCD41 Right on, brother.

> FemFatale5: @WWCD41 @RollingRoll: Are you even remotely serious with this shit? You'd think it was the 1800s.

> ChicagoLover: @WWCD41 You're a disgusting pig!

> WWCD41: @ChicagoLover Why don't you go back to the kitchen where you belong.

> ChicagoLover: @WWCD41 How do you even know I'm a woman, idiot. Maybe I'm just a guy who respects women.

MondayMan: Look up liar and cheat in the dictionary and you'll see Misty's picture.

> Dunitz9: @MondayMan Yeah, but it's a super-hot photo.

LeePatel: @Dunitz9 Oh so it's okay to be cheated on if the girl is hot?!?!

MondayMan: @LeePatel @Dunitz9 I say it's okay for ME to cheat if the girl is hot. LOL!

ClaireCoy01: Call me, Ryan. I would never diss you like that.

TheRealRR: @ClaireCoy01 Oh really. If ur who I think u r, u slept with my boyfriend.

ClaireCoy01: @ TheRealRR Who is this?

TheRealRR: @ClaireCoy01 This is Renee. Josh's girlfriend!

MondayMan: @ClaireCoy01 @TheRealRR GIRL FIGHT!!!

TexArkana5: Soooo tired of women always playing the victim. See? This is how women show their true colors.

DDesign86: @TexArkana5 Misty cheats on her boyfriend and you condemn all women? Do you even understand why women feel so marginalized in society?

TexArkana5: @DDesign86 Hear that sound? It's my tiny violin playing a sympathy song for you.

JJBarnes: @DDesign86 FemiNazi!

DDesign86: @TexArkana5 @JJBarnes I don't know why you even bother. You can't argue with stupid.

AleyaArndt: *Crushed* I'm so sorry Ryan. Please know that not all woman are like Misty. Stay hopeful.

Load 56,003 comments

TWENTY-FIVE

A pair of Charles David heels clicked on the marble floor in the lobby of *Celebrity Monger* as Frankie Lee strode confidently through the door. Her shoes were complemented by an olive-colored Eileen Fisher cocoon dress, and her hair was pulled into a sleek, high ponytail.

"Can I help you?" asked Gina, looking up with admiration at the beautiful and well-put-together woman standing before her.

"Yes, I would like to speak with someone about the Subway Girl series."

"Regarding?"

"I'm Ryan's ex-girlfriend and think I could be of value to you," Frankie said.

"Sure. You'll need to speak with Angie. Will you please come with me?" Gina said, gesturing for Frankie to follow. As Frankie sat down in one of the plush leather swivel chairs around a large glass table, the receptionist flipped a switch that started a hidden camera rolling in the conference room.

"Thanks," said Frankie. She looked at her phone, staring at an old picture of her and Ryan.

Back at the front desk, the receptionist called Angie.

"Angie, there's someone in the conference room for you," she said before hanging up and calling Harlan. "Hey, Harlan. It's Gina."

"What's up, Gin?"

"Ryan's ex-girlfriend just came in wanting to talk with Angie about the Subway Girl."

"No shit."

"I put her in the conference room and started the cameras rolling."

"That was good thinking."

"Maybe you could mention that to Barry," she suggested.

"Sure. I'll let him know. Just give me a call when she leaves, and I'll check the footage out." Gina hung up the phone and left the conference room as Angie walked in.

"I'm Angie. How can I help you?"

"Hi Angie. My name is Frankie–"

"Lee?"

"Yeah. Frankie Lee. I see Ryan's mentioned me," she said in a conceited tone.

"Oh, yes. He's told me all about you," Angie said, shaking her head and scowling.

"Then I'm sure he's told you that I was his first love and that he will always love me," retorted Frankie.

"What can I do for you, Frankie?" Angie asked exasperatedly.

"I've been following Ryan's online exploits with the Subway Girl and am just so bothered to see him getting hurt that way." She furrowed her brow at Angie and clutched a perfectly manicured hand to her heart.

"Oh really," said Angie. "Grown a conscience, have you?" She couldn't believe Frankie had the audacity to show up in here and claim to feel sympathy for Ryan over Misty's infidelity.

"Listen, I don't know what you think you know. But believe me, I know Ryan, and I know he's hurting."

Angie did know Ryan was hurting. She knew Ryan better than she knew almost anyone, and not just because they had slept together. She knew of his loyalty to his friends. His affection toward his sister, Finlay. His penchant for terrible puns and movie quotes, which she secretly loved. She also knew Ryan knew *her* in a way few others did and recognized that opening up to him was unexpected for her.

"I also know getting back together with me would make him feel a lot better."

What's in this for Frankie? Although she was meeting her for the first time, Angie could spot a phony when she saw one, and the insincere, conniving woman in front of her fit the bill. Couple that with what Ryan had told Angie about Frankie, her fame-obsessed friends and her infidelity with a pro baller, and Angie figured she was looking for internet notoriety. She already felt responsible for bringing Misty into Ryan's orbit. She wasn't going to make the same mistake twice.

"Sorry to disappoint you, but we've officially pulled the plug on the Subway Girl series. Your services won't be needed, and believe me, Ryan doesn't need you either," said Angie.

"Don't be so hasty. I think you should hear me out. This could really help your ratings."

Ratings. Angie certainly needed those to increase if she had any hope of getting out from under the mortgage mess. No. She'd find another way. Doug would come through with some dirt on JP. He'd have to. Partnering with Frankie wasn't an option.

"You can't say anything I would want to hear," barked Angie.

"Ryan is a great guy, and he—"

"He *is* a great guy. He's sweet and romantic and wants to believe in the very best of people," Angie said. She believed every word of it, too.

Frankie laughed a low, throaty chuckle. "Oh, that's rich." She shook her head and rolled her eyes toward the ceiling.

"You've fallen for Ryan, haven't you?" she said, nodding her head knowingly.

"I don't know what you are talking about," Angie responded defensively. Never mind that she couldn't fall asleep without seeing his face, hearing his voice, missing his smile. For one, he hadn't been interested in her when he'd had the chance. And two, he was just getting over a heartache. No good could come from starting a relationship with him right now.

"Don't you?" said Frankie, tilting her head down and looking at Angie with incredulity. "You think *I'm* going to use him, but you're the user."

"*I'm* using him?" repeated Angie in disbelief. *Who the hell does this woman think she is?* "You don't know anything about our relationship."

"Listen, lady. I don't know what your angle is–whether you really like him or just want to hog more of the spotlight for yourself–but believe me, you're not his type." Frankie pointed a menacing finger at Angie.

"Judging by the last two schemers and cheaters he's picked, I'm proud to say I'm not Ryan's type," Angie fired back. "So you listen to me, *lady*. You may think you're all tough and shit because you've lived here for a few years. But I'm a New Yorker. So don't mess with me. The exit is that way. And if I need to call security, I will." Angie pointed to the door.

Gina, pressed against the wall just outside the conference room, could tell that Angie and Frankie had concluded their "conversation." She scurried back to her desk in time to see Frankie walk off in a huff.

Angie followed Frankie into the office lobby to make sure she left, then turned to the receptionist. "If she comes back, call security. Got it?" Gina nodded. After Angie left, Gina walked back into the conference room and turned the camera off. She returned to her desk and called Harlan.

"Ryan's ex just left, and I think the footage is something you and Barry will definitely want to see."

An hour later, Barry, Gina and Harlan sat in Barry's office watching the footage of Angie and Frankie's feud.

"For a second there, I thought we were going to have a girl fight on our hands," said Harlan with a chuckle.

"We should be so lucky," replied Barry, smiling devilishly. He turned to the receptionist. "Good work, Gina." Gina blossomed at the praise.

"Find this Frankie Lee and get her in here tomorrow. And make a reservation for the spa at the Four Seasons for tomorrow, too."

"For me?" she asked hopefully.

Barry smirked. "No. That's for Angie."

That night, Angie and Ryan sat on the couch of his apartment, the coffee table before them littered with Chinese takeout containers. Neither of them bothered with a plate. Instead they shared cartons back and forth.

"It just brings back all that shit with Frankie, you know?" Ryan said, reaching for another egg roll. He took a bite, savoring the crispy shell and mixed vegetables inside. While he hadn't initially wanted to move to New York, he had to admit he loved the international food options. *You won't find egg rolls like this in Iowa.*

"I do. I've been there," replied Angie with sympathy. Ryan remembered how Angie had confessed that her previous boyfriend had been unfaithful. His blood boiled at the thought of Angie–spirited Angie–enduring the broken heart he had suffered and was suffering again today.

"I know you have." He patted her bare knee, and for a brief flash, he thought back to their night together. The way her naked body pressed against his. The little whimpers of pleasure he elicited from her. The smell of her release mixed with sweat and her sweet, natural scent. *Why am I thinking about Angie when*

I'm supposed to be analyzing my breakup with Misty? He couldn't get Angie out of his mind, and it was more than their one night together. He'd never felt so close to anyone before. Never felt that perfect of a connection—physically and emotionally.

It was never like that with Misty. Sure, she was attractive, and the little they'd shared physically had been nice. But there was little chemistry beyond that. While he and Frankie had a truckload of good memories and shared experiences, their young love hadn't been destined to last as they grew apart. But Angie? Angie was . . . everything.

Since Misty's confession, the guys had wanted to take him out. Get him drunk. Have him hook up with someone for a night of hot revenge sex. But he only wanted to be consoled by Angie. Even if Misty hadn't been in the picture, Ryan knew that Angie wasn't interested in him in that way. She'd made that perfectly clear the morning after they got together. And while Ryan felt like Angie genuinely liked him, he also sensed she thought he was too good of a guy. *She deserves a good guy*, he thought. *Even if she doesn't believe she's worthy.*

"So, Frankie. Have you heard from her lately?" Angie asked.

"No. Why?" Ryan hadn't spoken to Frankie since right after their breakup almost a year ago. *Why would Angie ask that?*

"Just curious," she said nonchalantly. "Wanna start the movie?"

"Sure. What did you bring?"

"*Chinatown*. Hence the Chinese food," said Angie proudly.

Ryan laughed. "I think you're gonna like it. A classic neo-noir film."

"So, not about Peking duck?" she joked.

"No." He chuckled. "Seriously though, I'm impressed that you are committed to seeing all the American Film Institute's top 100 films in one year."

"What can I say? You've inspired me."

If only I could inspire her to take a chance on us.

Whew. Angie was relieved that Frankie hadn't reached out to Ryan. Dealing with his horrible ex was something Ryan didn't need. He needed to move on past all the schemers and cheaters. *He needs to hang out with me. He needs to need me.*

But Angie knew Ryan didn't want her. She was probably too rough, too New York for him. She only had to think back to their awkward morning-after to know that she had been nothing more than a momentary distraction. Those thoughts alone were themselves becoming a distraction.

She turned her attention back to the movie, only taking her eyes away from the TV to briefly inspect Ryan—his rapt attention focused on Jack Nicholson investigating a suspicious murder. Angie herself became increasingly absorbed in the story, absentmindedly polishing off an entire carton of cream cheese wontons in the process.

As she put the last fried treat in her mouth, Faye Dunaway's character confessed that Katherine was both her sister and her daughter. Angie gasped, dropped the takeout container and grabbed Ryan's knee.

"Didn't see that coming?" he said with a chuckle. He looked down at her hand grasping onto him.

"No," she managed, still shocked by the sudden plot twist. As she came to her senses, she noticed she was still holding Ryan's knee. She looked down at her hand and then back to his face, and noticed him swallowing hard.

Shit! I'm making him uncomfortable. She unclasped her hand and ran it through her hair.

"Wow. Now there's an unexpected plot twist," she remarked. She certainly hadn't seen that turn in the movie. Now, finding herself physically drawn to Ryan? That didn't surprise her.

"Yeah," Ryan agreed. "Sometimes you don't see something coming, but when it does . . . well, watch out."

Angie wondered if Ryan was talking about more than the movie. She wasn't sure if they were on the same page.

"So . . ." She didn't know what she should say. She knew what she wanted to say. *Ryan, I've fallen in love with you. I think about you all the time. I would do anything to make you happy. I realize that love is possible.*

"Great movie, right?" he said.

So, not on the same page. Not even in the same book.

"Yes. Fantastic movie."

"There's a sequel, called *The Two Jakes*, but it isn't nearly as good as this one."

"I probably should focus on my list."

"Well, if you like this type of film, we should watch *The Maltese Falcon* next."

"Yes, that's the Humphrey Bogart one, based on Dashiell Hammett's novel."

"Look at you, busting out the movie trivia." He smiled broadly and reached his fist out for a bump. *A fist bump? Really?* If that didn't cement her position in the friend zone, she didn't know what could.

"I do my best." She shrugged.

"The student becomes the master. I like it."

If only he liked me.

TWENTY-SIX

Barry placed his hand on the small of Frankie's back as he ushered her from the *Celebrity Monger* lobby into the small conference room. He gestured for her to take a seat next to Harlan.

"Thank you for taking the time to come back in." He sat opposite Frankie. She was wearing a BCBG Max Azria jumpsuit and a pair of red-soled stiletto heels, which bounced as she slowly kicked her leg up and down.

"Well, after the way I was treated the last time I was here . . ."

Barry thought back to her and Angie's exchange and fought back a smile. He loved a good fight, and that had had the makings of a fierce cage match.

"Yes, I apologize for that. Angie can be rather spirited when it comes to the stories she works on," he explained with faux sincerity. What he really thought was *Angie nearly fucked this opportunity up*. Clearly she was thinking about Ryan's feelings and not about the business. That was something he would need to address at a later date. But for now, he thanked his lucky stars that Gina had had the foresight to record Angie and

Frankie's interaction and call Harlan's attention to it. With Angie enjoying the spa services he'd ordered as a "thank you" for her recent hard work, she wasn't around to cause any more problems.

"I don't think 'spirited' is how I would describe it. She was downright rude," Frankie huffed. She glanced down at her hands and rubbed her thumb across the rose-pink nail polish on her middle finger.

Harlan snorted. "Excuse me." He covered his mouth with his fist and coughed in an exaggerated manner to mask his reaction.

"Yes, be that as it may, Angie doesn't make the decisions around here. I do. And I think you're just the breath of fresh air we need . . . Ryan needs," said Barry. *Yes, you're just what* Celebrity Monger *needs to keep this series alive,* he thought, *and drive that much-needed audience engagement.*

"Thank you. I'm glad *you* feel that way," said Frankie, brushing the hair off her shoulder with a smile. Barry could tell Frankie knew the way the game was played and would have no problem going along with it.

"Don't worry about Angie. She'll toe the line," he said flatly. Angie *would* toe the line. He wasn't fucking around anymore. Despite the popularity of the Subway Girl and growth in online engagement, clicks and views still needed to increase to meet the network's threshold. Angie wasn't going to stand in his way, that was for certain.

"So how do you want to proceed?" she asked.

Barry had given this a lot of thought. He needed to ensure Ryan was caught up in the emotion of seeing Frankie again and was reminded of their first love.

"Harlan will meet you at Ryan's tomorrow at seven-thirty. From there, it will fall to you to make a reunion happen," he said.

"I'll make it happen," she confirmed.

On one hand, Barry had no doubt Frankie could use her considerable charms to sway Ryan back into her arms and bed.

However, he knew through his quick background research on her that she had cheated on him with an NBA player. He couldn't risk Ryan rebuffing her advances.

"I'd like you to sit down with one of our consultants, who can coach you through some different scenarios and how you can respond to each," he said.

She shrugged. "If you think that will help."

"I do. I'll need you to sign this non-disclosure agreement, video release *and* an exclusivity agreement . . ." Barry shoved the forms and a pen in front of her.

Three hours later, Frankie strolled into the Bloomingdales break room, an hour before she was set to start her shift. She knew it would be empty right now, as the afternoon crowd had died down.

She sat down on one of the padded chairs at the table and pulled a Post-it note out of her pocket. She got out her phone and dialed the first of several phone numbers scrawled across the paper.

"Hi, Lynda," she said sweetly. "This is Frankie Lee over at Bloomingdales. Do you have a moment? I have an interesting proposition for you."

"Sure, Frankie. What can I do for you?" said Lynda. She sounded slightly muffled, as if she were balancing the phone on her shoulder while doing something else.

"Are you familiar with the Subway Girl?" Frankie asked.

"You mean that guy who is looking for his dream girl online?" Frankie could hear her clacking away on her computer keyboard.

"That's the one."

"I'm familiar with it but don't follow it. Why?" The sound of shuffling paper accompanied Lynda's distracted voice.

"Well, his name is Ryan, and he's my ex-boyfriend or, should I say, soon-to-be-on-again boyfriend. The Subway Girl turned out to be a horrid wannabe actress, and he and I are getting back together. The producers of the series have assured me that they will be following our reunion and relationship progress for the foreseeable future," she explained.

"And . . . what does this have to do with Stella McCartney?" asked Lynda with an audible exhale, as if she were growing tired of this conversation. Frankie knew she'd have to spell it out for Lynda.

"The website has millions of followers and commands thousands for rotating banner ads. Everyone from the *Today* show to *Page 6* has been following it. I'm giving *you* the opportunity to have *me* wearing Stella McCartney for the world to see."

"Hmm. I'm intrigued," she responded. Frankie smiled to herself in triumph. "Let me bring this up to our head of marketing and I'll call you back."

"Just don't take too long, Lynda. I would hate for you to miss out on this great promotional opportunity," said Frankie smoothly.

"I'll call you back later today."

Frankie hung up the phone and smiled to herself. She dialed another number.

"Hi, Yuri. This is Frankie Lee over at Bloomingdales. Do you have a moment? I have an interesting proposition for you . . . "

TWENTY-SEVEN

Angie was hoping to power down her computer and head home for a girls' night in with Josie. Over the past few weeks, she'd heard Josie talking in hushed tones and giggling girlishly on the phone at night when she went to bed. Tonight Angie was determined to find out what was going on. She wasn't above using her investigative journalism skills to get to the bottom of things.

She had just finished writing captions to accompany three photos of a prominent pop artist's car wrapped around a light pole when an email alert popped on her computer screen.

To: Angie
From: Jeanie
Subject: Approval request

Hey Angie. Let me know if the attached graphic is approved to run ASAP per Barry.

Angie opened the attachment to see a promotional graphic reading:

Ryan finds comfort in the arms of his ex-girlfriend, Frankie. See the exclusive update Wednesday

Angie stormed into Barry's office. Not finding him there, she stomped off to the conference room, where Barry sat with Harlan reviewing papers.

"We need to talk!" Angie shouted as she burst in. Barry nodded to Harlan to excuse himself. As Harlan left the room, Angie thought she saw him touch the room's AV controls as he did, but she was too angry to give it much thought "What's going on? I thought we ended the Subway Girl series?" she demanded.

"After you dismissed Frankie, she and I came to an understanding of how she can help us resurrect this ratings winner," Barry said coolly.

"She's awful," Angie said. "Worse than Misty. How can you get into bed with her?"

"If she gets into bed with Ryan, it's worth it." A smile crossed his face.

"I just don't feel comfortable with this," she said with hostility. She was already plagued with guilt over enabling that charade with Misty to go on for as long as she did.

"This is bigger than you, Angie. Need I remind you my network meeting is Monday and we need a spike."

She didn't need reminding what was at stake.

"It's bigger than your ambition, Barry. You're screwing with this man's life. Ryan's been through enough. He didn't sign up to be used by you. All he wanted was to find happiness. I can't be a part of this anymore." What was she saying here? Was she really giving Barry an ultimatum?

"So, what are you saying?" Barry side-eyed her.

What am I saying? Was she really willing to give up everything she'd worked for? Was this even work she could feel proud of? Hadn't pride already prevented her from telling Ryan how she felt about him? How badly she wanted him to be happy?

"I quit!" She stomped toward her office, storming past Harlan, who stood back against the hallway wall.

Angie grabbed her purse, slammed her office door and tore down the *Celebrity Monger* hallway. A few people sitting at cubicles in the open-plan workspace looked up and murmured to one another.

She needed to call Ryan. To warn him. She pulled her phone out of her purse and dialed his cell with shaking hands. After ringing a few times, it went to voicemail. She figured he was either in a meeting or had turned his ringer off, which he was prone to do.

"Ryan. It's me. Please call me as soon as you get this message." Her voice wavered.

Once out on the street, the gravity of reality hit her. She'd just quit her job. The job she needed to pay the bills. The job that would ensure the network deal went through. *Shit!* What if her payout was contingent on her still being employed at *Celebrity Monger*? She leaned over, bracing her hands on her knees, and took a few deep gulps of air. *What the hell am I going to do?*

Harlan and Frankie stood in the hall outside Ryan's apartment, while she checked her hair and makeup in a compact mirror. She was dressed in a pair of skinny jeans, tall boots and a soft-to-the-touch sweater—an outfit in homage to her Iowan roots.

"Okay. Give me a quick sound check," Harlan requested.

Frankie cleared her throat. "Gucci. Prada. Hermes," she said, speaking clearly and slowly so that Harlan could check the sound levels. "How's that?"

Harlan shook his head in both disbelief and amusement. "Perfect. Ready when you are."

Frankie pushed up her breasts and knocked on the door. Ryan stood motionless—in shock—when he opened it to her.

"Frankie. Wow. Uh, what . . ."

"Hey there. I know it's been a while, but it's been hard to miss what's been going on with you, and I felt like you could use a friend," she said with a saddened smile on her face. "Can I come in?" she asked sweetly.

"Yeah," said Ryan, trying to get over the surprise of seeing her at his apartment. She looked beautiful and was dressed much more casually than the last few times he had seen her. Much more like that girl he remembered from back home. "Of course." He opened the door wider for her to walk in. Harlan traipsed behind her and put down his camera tripod. "Harlan, what are you . . ." started Ryan, confused to see Harlan in his apartment.

"Don't worry about him," Frankie said, turning Ryan around to face her. With great concern she asked, "How are you?"

"I've been better." He shrugged.

"I know. And I'm so sorry. Seeing what Misty did to you made me realize how much I must have hurt you, and that's just gutted me. I hope you can forgive me and know I'm here for you." Frankie leaned in to hug Ryan, and he let her put her arms around him, sighing into the comfort and familiarity of her embrace. They stood for a few silent minutes, just holding one another. Ryan was taken back in time to when things were simple and good.

"This feels nice," he whispered.

"It does. Reminds me of that summer at Juniper Falls."

"Mmm," Ryan mumbled.

"It feels right." Frankie leaned in, placing a few light pecks on his cheek. When he didn't pull away, she shifted over to gently kiss his lips. Ryan sighed. It felt good to be wanted. Frankie raised a hand to the top of Ryan's head and ran her fingers through his hair. Her kisses became more potent and urgent, spurring Ryan on. Ryan's hand moved up from her waist to grasp her jaw, his tongue tangling with hers.

"Let's go to the bedroom," Frankie moaned, a carnal expression in her eyes. She grabbed his hand, pulling him down the hall. Ryan's body had no problem responding to Frankie's touch, but his mind couldn't stop the nagging feeling that something was off. As good as it felt to be wanted, was she who *he* wanted? He gently pushed her away.

"Why are you stopping? This just feels so right," said Frankie. But it didn't feel right. Not at all.

"Why is Harlan here?" Ryan tried to process it. *Why is Harlan in my apartment with my ex-girlfriend?*

"I just thought your fans would want to see how happy you could be. You *should* be. You can't deny how great we are together," she said.

"My fans?" repeated Ryan, his head tilted to the side in confusion.

"Yeah. All the people who are rooting for you to find happiness," she said passionately. He did want to find happiness, but at what cost? "I love you, Ryan. You know we are fated to be together."

All the people rooting for me? We are fated to be together?

"That's bullshit," he whispered after considering her for a moment.

"So what are you saying?" she asked, shaking her head slightly in disbelief.

"You don't believe in fate." Never once, in all the time he and Frankie had dated, had she ever once believed in fate. If anything, she would roll her eyes whenever the story about his parents' first meeting would come up. The thought of her rolling her eyes made him think about Angie, who had just asked if he had heard from Frankie. *What the fuck is going on?*

"I do now," she said hopefully.

"This doesn't make any sense." He had to be missing something here. "This isn't about love." *Frankie isn't in love with me. So what does Frankie want?* "This is about you getting fame and attention," he snapped.

"People want to see you with someone like me–who appreciates how great you are."

"People don't want to see me with a girl like you. Who cheated on me and broke up with me over the phone. If anything, they want me to find real love," he said with disdain. *They would want to see me with someone like Angie.*

Frankie stood silent for a moment, then turned to Harlan.

"I tried," she said flatly. "Well, I've got to give you credit," she said, turning back to Ryan. "I didn't think you'd figure it out. Maybe the big city has wised you up."

"I'm not a country bumpkin anymore. Is that what you're saying?" he blasted out.

"You've grown savvier," she admitted. "But that's good. Think about how great it could be. Everyone wants a piece of this. I'm talking restaurants, clothing brands, endorsement deals. We could take this thing so far." She grabbed his hand, her eyes filled with greed.

"This isn't about fame and getting free stuff. It was never about that. This was about feeling like there was a connection there." He shook his head at her. The girl he fell in love with a long time ago was completely gone.

"Of course," she sneered. "It was all about love and fate."

"What's wrong with that?"

"This isn't one of your classic romance films. And you can't keep living in the shadow of your parents' *perfect marriage*," she said, making air quotes with her fingers. "I wouldn't be surprised if your dad was fucking that nurse of his." She smirked.

Disgusted by her words, Ryan shook his head. "You are just awful. Go. Just go!" he yelled.

Frankie looked at Harlan and shrugged before walking out the door. Harlan kept the camera trained on Ryan, whose shoulders sagged. *More public humiliation? More dirty laundry being aired for the world to see? For my parents to see?* Was he ever going to catch a break? He just wanted to be alone and for this dating experiment, this failed attempt at fate, to be over and out of the public eye. Why wouldn't Harlan just leave? There was nothing more to see here. Ryan's hands balled into fists. His nostrils flared. "Go!" he yelled at Harlan. "Get out of here!"

Ryan slumped onto his couch and lowered his head into his hands. How had everything gotten to be such a confusing mess? As he picked his head up, he saw a missed call from Angie. Angie, who had just been asking about Frankie. He'd give her a call tomorrow. He wasn't in a place to talk with her right now. He needed to think through what all of this meant.

TWENTY-EIGHT

Diego looked like he was going to vomit. He and the guys had all been working at their respective computers in the office when he got a pop-up ad on his screen.

"Uh, Ryan. I think you better come see this," he said.

"What? Still having trouble with that Excel sheet?" Ryan asked.

"No. Just come here. Both of you," Diego replied. Ryan and Luke walked over to Diego's computer, concern on their faces. Diego motioned to a banner ad on the *Celebrity Monger* website that read: "Subway Girl Ryan's True Colors." He looked at Ryan, who lifted his head in a small nod, indicating Diego should click on the link.

A video screen popped up displaying creatively edited footage of Frankie and Ryan's encounter in Ryan's apartment, which played out like a movie:

FRANKIE LEE
I'm here for you.

Frankie and Ryan kiss passionately. Ryan pushes Frankie away.

RYAN CARLSON
I'm not a country bumpkin anymore.

FRANKIE LEE
I love you, Ryan. You know we are
fated to be together.

RYAN CARLSON
This isn't about love. This is
about wanting fame and attention.

FRANKIE LEE
So what are you saying?

RYAN CARLSON
People don't want to see me with a
girl like you.

CUT TO: Devastated Frankie.

RYAN CARLSON (CONT'D)
Go! Get out of here!

What. The. Fuck. Ryan's eyebrows rose to his hairline, then his face fell and his shoulders slumped forward. He leaned over and clicked the video off.

"That is just messed up, man," said Luke with a mixture of sympathy and anger.

"I can't believe Angie would do that to you. She seemed so cool and fun," said Diego,

"She was just asking if I had heard from Frankie," Ryan said as he stared down at the floor and shook his head. *How could she do this? There's got to be some explanation.*

"That's just cold!" said Luke.

"After all those nice things you said about her. Why would she set you up and sell you out like that?" asked Diego.

"Isn't it obvious? She's just a schemer like the rest of them," Luke said.

"This is bad." Diego cringed. "You've got to get out in front of this and fast. They say when a lie is out running around, the truth is still getting its boots on. What are you going to do?"

Dammit, thought Ryan. His parents were going to see this. And all of his friends back home. Everyone was going to think it was the truth. That had been the very reason he'd hesitated to even sign on for this crazy search.

"I tell you what you should do. You should sue," interjected Luke.

"I have to talk to her." Ryan grabbed his cell phone and rushed out the door.

He raced to *Celebrity Monger*, forgoing the subway and opting for a cab, which would get him there faster.

"I need to see Angie," he demanded of the receptionist.

"She's not here. Let me get Barry for you." Gina picked up the phone and eyed Ryan as she dialed. "I've got Ryan Carlson here asking to see Angie." She paused for a beat and turned to Ryan. "He'll be right out. Can I get you some coffee?"

"No, thank you." Ryan paced the lobby waiting for Barry, breathing in and out through his nose. The more he thought about things, the more worked up he became.

Barry entered the lobby. "Ryan. What can I do for you?"

"What can you do for me?" Ryan's voice was hot with agitation. "You can leave me the hell alone."

"Where's all this anger coming from?" Barry held his palms up and shrugged his shoulders.

"Are you fucking kidding me? You just ran a story that paints me as an arrogant, fame-obsessed asshole." The vein in Ryan's neck throbbed as he seethed in anger.

"I'm sorry you're unhappy with the piece." Barry pursed his lips and nodded slightly as if he was sympathetic to Ryan's frustration. "Angie went rogue. Thought she could make a name for herself. If it helps, Angie is no longer working here so . . ."

"The buck stops with you, and I'm putting you on notice that I want you to stop covering me." Ryan stabbed his pointer finger at Barry. "You did not have my permission to film me with Frankie, and if I see anything else online, you'll be hearing from my lawyer." Ryan stormed out.

Barry turned to Gina and rolled his eyes. It wasn't the first time someone had threatened to sue him, and it definitely wouldn't be the last. As he was set to walk back to his office, he saw Doug Harp enter the lobby.

"Doug," Barry said in surprise. "Did we have an appointment today?"

"No. I'm working on something for Angie and she mentioned it was sensitive. Didn't want to send it through email and figured I would drop it off. She around?"

"No, she's not in today. We're under a time constraint, so you can just pass the info along to me."

"Sure." Doug shrugged. He handed an envelope to Barry and waited while the businessman looked inside.

"Ah, yes." Barry's thin lips curving into a smile. "If you want to wait around a few minutes, I can have Gina here get you a check."

"Yeah, sure. That would be great. Invoice is inside," Doug replied, gesturing to the envelope in Barry's hands.

Barry removed the invoice. Even with the rush billing rate reflected in the price, it was money well spent. He handed the invoice to Gina and nodded toward the hallway, indicating for her to get a check cut right away.

Ryan took another cab over to Angie's brownstone in Greenpoint. The cab fare was going to kill him, but right now he didn't care.

"Yes?" Angie inquired through the intercom.

"It's Ryan," he said, trying to remain calm. Angie buzzed him up. She opened the door and leaned in to hug him, but Ryan pushed her away.

"I just saw . . ."

"Barry told me everything. How could you do that to me?" he said, exhaling deeply.

"It wasn't me," she said, shaking her head and reaching out to touch him.

"I don't believe you." He moved out of her reach. "You're a liar, just like Misty and Frankie. But you're worse because you manipulated me, used me and made a fool out of me in front of the world. And I expected more from you. *Wanted* more from you."

"I . . ."

"What?" he said, giving her the opportunity to respond. When she stood silent, he continued. "Don't tell me you were just doing your job, because that's bullshit."

"You're right." She hung her head. "It started out that way, and I should have stopped it earlier, but I didn't. And I'm sorry. But I don't think you're a fool, and I never wanted to see you get hurt. I tried . . ."

Ryan closed his eyes and shook his head, pained by what he was hearing.

"More lies. Like I told Barry, leave me the hell alone."

59832!: Noooooooooo!!!!!

DrillTeamBabe: I have no words!!!
#RyanYouFucker

maribel5: @DrillTeamBabe @everychance @gogo18 @ameliarb @karilb @PicklesNTickles8 WHAT?!?!?!?!?!?

> PicklesNTickles8: @maribel5 @DrillTeamBabe @everychance @gogo18 @ameliarb @karilb What an asshole! I read one of his clients is Bank of New York we should totally boycott them.

> Everychance: @maribel5 @DrillTeamBabe @gogo18 @ameliarb @karilb @PicklesNTickles8 Devastated. I'm absolutely devastated.

> Gogo18: @maribel5 @DrillTeamBabe @ameliarb @karilb @PicklesNTickles8 @everychance Are they going to do a spin off with Frankie now?

CarboLoad3: Shut the front door. You cannot be serious.

DeliverMe5: I've been played!

> JMR1023: @DeliverMe5 Don't hate the playa, hate the game

> DeliverMe5: @JMR1023 Whatevah

ShoesNStuff9: Oh how the mighty have fallen. It was just a matter of time until his true colors came through.

PartyOnDudes: I'm just waiting for someone to blame this on Obama.

FictionLover10: @PartyOnDudes Or Trump LOL!

HackerSlacker: Saw this coming a mile away. No guy is that good. Anyone acting all surprised by this deserves the misery.

McGeeTwentyThree: I'm no psychologist but this guys sounds psycho.

Load 79,887 comments

TWENTY-NINE

Ryan is right, Angie thought. For a while now, she had felt knee-deep in shame over how she had been a party to this charade. But seeing Ryan, so hurt, in front of her? It felt like the tide was rising and she would drown in regret. She needed something, anything, to distract her from the immense guilt. Helping her mom sort out the mortgage mess would do the trick. She logged into online banking for the first time in months, and what she saw had her fuming. She rushed to her mom's place in Queens.

"What do you mean, you haven't been depositing the checks, Ma?" Angie demanded. *What the hell is going on?* She'd been giving her mom checks for months now. Not necessarily enough to cover the payments in total, but certainly enough to show the bank that she'd been trying. It wasn't like the money wasn't there. So why hadn't her mom made the payments? Why was Angie just finding out that the checks weren't being cashed? She scolded herself for being so busy with the Subway Girl search that she hadn't been keeping her checking account balanced.

"I don't want you wasting your money on me," Angie's mom explained.

"Wasting my money?" Angie said in disbelief. "You took out a second mortgage to loan *me* money. How is me paying you back–giving you the money to make the payments–how is that 'wasting money'?" she nearly shouted.

"I told you that I had it covered." Her mom shrugged.

Angie raised an eyebrow. "You're telling me you've been making the payments on your own?"

"I've been making the payments," her mom confirmed. However, Angie could tell by the way she shuffled her feet and avoided eye contact that her mom was holding something back.

"You've been making the payments?" she repeated.

"Yes, we are not in arrears. We aren't in jeopardy of losing the house, so you can just calm down." Her mom placed a hand on Angie's shoulder. "It's paid off."

"How is it possible that you've been making the payments all on your own? You can barely afford . . . Jesus, Ma, what did you do?" Angie exhaled and pressed her fingers to her temples. She couldn't even fathom how her mom was managing all this on her own.

"Nothing illegal, if that's what you're thinking."

"Well, I should hope not!" Angie retorted with a huff. "Where did you get the money, Ma?" Her mother looked down at the ground, wringing her hands together. "Where?" Angie demanded.

"Harrison."

Angie's shoulders slumped in defeat. "Harrison." She chuckled, not in amusement, but out of sheer frustration.

"What?" her mom said. "He stopped by a few months ago and we got to talking. I asked him for some financial advice, and he offered to help with the balance."

"You just don't get it, do you, Ma?"

"He feels badly you two ended things and–"

"And he wants to get back together," Angie finished. "I will never get back together with Harrison," she spat out. "Ever. He's a liar and a cheat, Ma. Did I ever tell you that? He cheated on me."

"You never told me that."

"He cheated. More than once. He even slept with Sabrina," Angie said.

"Your cousin Sabrina?" her mom gasped.

"Yes. He and I will *never* get back together."

"Okay." Her mom pulled her into a much-needed embrace. "Okay," she repeated. They stood together in silence for several minutes, Angie being comforted in her mother's arms.

"All this time, I didn't know. I never would have encouraged you to get back together with him if I had."

"I know," Angie sighed.

"Well, I'm not giving him the money back," her mom said. "And if he comes slinking around here again, you better believe he'll get an earful."

"Yeah. Thanks, Ma." Angie vowed to find a way to give him the money back. Every last penny. She didn't want to owe him anything.

"You deserve better. You deserve more."

Angie wasn't so sure that was true. Maybe a lying, cheating bastard like Harrison was exactly what she deserved. She was ashamed of how she had manipulated Ryan. She missed him. If she hadn't needed the money, all this could have been avoided. She was appalled by the assignment she'd given to Doug and made a mental note to contact him later today to call the whole thing off. At least she could stop that train from leaving the station.

"The good news is, we don't owe anything else on the house. And all the money you've been giving me—it's yours, doll face. You can do whatever you want with it. Go on a vacation. Buy some new clothes. Anything." Angie began to sob in shame and relief. Now that she had quit her job, she'd at least have a little cushion to find something new, something where she wouldn't have to compromise her values any longer. But could she ever earn Ryan's forgiveness or his trust?

A few hours later, Harlan sat in the conference room, scrolling through his phone while he waited for Angie to finish up in her office. He wasn't sure why, but instinct told him to have the hidden camera rolling.

After a fifteen-minute wait, which felt interminable to Harlan, Angie emerged from her office carrying a cardboard box filled with some personal items, including a framed photo of Angie with a Pulitzer Prize-winning editor she met during high school, and an award for journalistic excellence she received working on her college newspaper.

"Thanks for letting me come by after hours. I couldn't bear the thought of seeing Barry."

"How are you holding up?"

"Not good," she said, her eyes welling with tears.

"That's what happens when you have principles," he said, trying to lighten the mood. His words had the opposite reaction, as Angie broke down into heaving sobs into his chest.

"He won't talk to me, Harlan. He thinks I brought that shrew back into his life for the sake of ratings and manipulated the footage to make him look bad. But I would never hurt him like that. Never."

"I'm sure—"

"He *hates* me, Harlan. He thinks I'm a lying, manipulative piece of shit."

"So he thinks you're Barry," he said, again trying to elicit a smile.

"He probably thinks I'm even worse than Barry because he"—she raised her hands and made air quotes—"*expected more from me*. I've tried calling and emailing him, but he won't talk to me."

"Maybe you just need to let it go," Harlan suggested.

"Let it go?" she snapped. She sighed and looked at him with sadness in her eyes. "Can't he see that he's the love of my life and anyone that comes after him will only be there because they are willing to have me? I love him, Harlan. And he hates me," she said, the tears streaming full force down her face.

"I know," he said, leaning in and hugging her while she continued to sob into his chest.

THIRTY

Today's the day. Barry looked out at the group of TV executives seated around the table. All his dreams were on the line here. Of course, he'd never doubted it would happen. He was a man who got what he wanted, no matter the risk or the cost.

But then Angie, Misty and Frankie came along to muck everything up. For a short while, he began to think he would have to go back to the drawing board. And then Doug dropped by. *Maybe that lovelorn Ryan was right. Fate does work in strange ways.* So now he stood before these suits with an insurance policy in his back pocket.

He talked through the presentation, showing chart after chart illustrating the growth of *Celebrity Monger* and the potential value of the show in terms of ratings and advertising revenue.

When he got to the statistics about the Subway Girl series, he felt a surge of pride. The segments had been a ratings winner, and the online engagement via message boards and social media was beyond compare.

Of course, he would have loved to see it continue. Too bad that do-gooder Ryan wised up and saw things with Frankie for what they really were, rather than what Barry had hoped they would be. He had to admit he was rather impressed that the fool hadn't been fooled this time. Barry was sorry he had underestimated him. It had thrown his plans for another loop.

Casting Ryan as the bad guy–the one who was corrupted by fame? Well, that was just a stroke of genius, if I do say so myself.

"There have certainly been a lot of twists and turns in your Subway Girl series, which has created momentum. And that ending created a big spike in traffic. But given the end of the series, we're just not sure the traffic you're generating can be sustained," explained one of the executives who had not been keen on the idea of a *Celebrity Monger* television series from the start. Barry smirked. This annoying asshole certainly wasn't going to derail his plans. Not when Barry had an ace in the hole.

"I think, JP, you might be interested in these figures," said Barry with a slimy smile, pushing an envelope across the table. JP opened the envelope, his shoulders slumping, as he unveiled photos of himself with his mistress in a hotel room. He kept his emotions in check while responding.

"Ah, yes. These are very interesting figures. I have a good feeling about this deal. Let's make it happen," he said, staring into Barry's cold eyes.

"Fantastic," said Barry. "I'll have my attorney contact your counsel to hammer out the details." Barry leaned his hand forward to shake JP's. JP stood with a forced smile, shook Barry's hand and walked out. The other executives, unaware of the unspoken exchange between the two men, congratulated Barry and each other, ready to bring a new show to the network.

Two hours later, Barry strode into the crowded *Celebrity Monger* conference room, where champagne was chilling on ice. Harlan interrupted the low chatter when Barry approached.

"Settle down! Settle down!" Harlan called out.

"It's a done deal. The lawyers still need to hammer out the details, but a good-faith commitment was signed a half hour ago. *Celebrity Monger* is officially hitting TVs nationwide this fall," announced Barry with pride. The crowd erupted with cheers and applause, and employees patted each other on the back for a job well done.

THIRTY-ONE

Josie walked into the apartment having worked several double shifts and immediately cringed. She was met with a vision of Angie—red-rimmed eyes, nose rubbed raw, swollen lips and a hangdog expression—that leveled her. She'd known Angie was in a bad state but hadn't realized it was *this* bad. Angie glanced up from the quart of ice cream in her hand and tossed Josie a pathetic wave.

"How are you?" Josie asked tentatively, her voice full of sympathy.

"Seriously?" Angie huffed.

"Did you eat all the ice cream in the freezer?"

"No. I ate it sitting on the couch because it's cold in the freezer."

"I'm going to let the sarcasm slide for today because I know it's coming from a place of pain."

"Josie." Angie groaned. "I'm sorry." Angie knew she shouldn't be taking her foul mood out on Josie. If anything, Josie had been her rock through all of this. A shoulder to cry on. A partner to share comfort food. A sounding board for all of her angst.

"I know, Ange."

"Thank you for always looking out for me."

"Of course. It's my job." Josie shrugged, as if it were no big deal.

"And you do it like a boss."

"Hell yeah."

"So, boss, what am I going to do?" Angie groaned again, silent tears falling from her eyes. "My life is like a Taylor Swift song."

"Which one?" Josie said with a grimace, which elicited a rare smile from Angie.

"All of them," Angie lamented before dissolving into a giggle and a cry. She and Josie laughed heartily, and Angie wasn't sure if her tears were falling from the tragedy or sheer silliness of this conversation.

"All right, let's have it."

"It was all for nothing." Angie sighed. "Mom snuck behind my back and took Harrison's money to pay the mortgage. So I put Ryan through that hell with Misty and Frankie for nothing. Even worse, I made it possible for Barry to get his TV deal by sinking to a low I'm not sure I can crawl back from. And now the man I love–the love of my life–hates my guts and justifiably so."

Josie exhaled sharply. "Okay. So we're going to triage this, just like we do in the ER. So let's start with Ryan and Misty. *He's* the one who saw her on the subway. *He's* the one who started the search for her. *He's* the one that continued to date her, despite the fact she is a shallow, vapid user. *He* needs to accept some of the responsibility."

"I suppose," said Angie. It was true that whether she was involved or not, Ryan had been intent on finding Misty. Who knows how long he would have dated her if *Celebrity Monger* hadn't been involved?

"And don't get me started on Frankie. You tried to keep that train from leaving the station."

"Train? Or subway?"

"You clever girl." Josie wagged a finger at Angie. "Okay. You tried to keep that *subway* from leaving the station. You even quit your job over it."

"That's true. But Barry manipulated—"

"Stop right there!" Josie held her hand up to keep Angie from going down that particular rabbit hole. "Barry's gonna Barry. That has no bearing on who you are. And you are the person who stood up to him."

"Yeah, but I also gave Barry the ammunition he used to blackmail the head of the network." Angie shuddered. "Oh god. I think I'm going to be sick again." She put the spoon and ice cream down and clutched her stomach.

"I'm not going to lie to you, Angie. There was a serious lapse in judgment on your part."

"I know," Angie groaned.

"To your credit, you did call it off. You just didn't get to Doug in time. But Barry is like a dog with a bone. He wanted that deal, and come hell or high water, he was going to get it."

"Barry would have found a way, I'm certain of it," Angie agreed.

"And it's hard for me to muster a lot of sympathy for some bigwig cheating on his wife."

"I agree, but I was the one—"

"Like I said, serious lapse in judgment." Josie's tone had more sympathy in it than Angie felt was justified. She appreciated it nonetheless. "But as much as I'm loathe to admit it, *Celebrity Monger* is going to be a huge hit, and the network is going to make a ton of money. People love that stuff."

"But the money . . ."

"Which money? The windfall you got from the network deal or the money from Harrison?"

"Both." Angie sighed.

"There's nothing to say you have to keep the network money. If you feel bad about it, find a way to put it to good use. And as far as the money from Harrison, don't sweat it. After everything he's put you through, that's the absolute least he could do."

"Yeah?" Angie was slightly encouraged by Josie's pep talk. At the very least, Josie had given her a lot to think about. "What about Ryan? He'll never forgive me."

"Fuck him!" Josie shrugged. Those were some pretty harsh words, coming from Josie, who would even brush you off with a smile.

"I figured you were going to say, 'his loss,'" Angie said.

"If there was ever a time to get fired up, this is it," Josie said with a nod. Angie expelled another laugh and cry at the same time. "Seriously, I'd like a word with *Saint Ryan*. I've never met anyone who hasn't regretted something they've said or done. I mean, good for him for never making a mistake or doing something insensitive or hurting someone's feelings. Does he think he deserves a medal? Because you've tried to apologize and make amends. And learned from your mistake. If you ask me, you're the one who deserves the medal."

"But . . ."

"It's okay to embrace your mistakes."

Angie fell into Josie's arms and enveloped her in a hug. Josie pulled back, placing her hands on Angie's shoulders.

"You better not be hugging me because you're embracing a mistake," she mock-warned.

Ever grateful for Josie's advice and support, Angie knew she would get through this. But she also knew forgetting Ryan wasn't an option.

THIRTY-TWO

Ryan slammed back the shot of tequila Luke had placed in front of him. He'd long since given up the salt and lime. A few shots ago, he had welcomed the burn. It made the other pain he was suffering feel less intense. Now, he was just numb to the sting of the liquid.

Logically, he knew this shot—the last three shots, if he was actually able to think about it clearly—had been a mistake. He knew he would be kicking himself tomorrow when he suffered the ill effects of a hangover. But at this moment, he didn't care. *Let Future Ryan worry about that.* Tonight was all about Present Day Ryan. And Present Day Ryan was angry, hurt, and drowning his sorrows with the guys.

"We forgot to toast," slurred Diego, holding his drink in the air.

"Damn. Guess I'll have to redo that one," Ryan said with a laugh.

"No problem," said Luke. "I'm sure that one is going to be coming back up sooner rather than later." Diego apparently thought Luke's quip was the funniest thing ever and sloppily reached his arm out for a high five. Luke tried several times to tag his hand before giving up with a scowl.

Through his tequila-fog, Ryan revisited how it had been a shitty two weeks: Misty cheated on him. Frankie tried to seduce him. Angie betrayed him. Two weeks had brought him to the harsh realization that he had a crappy track record with picking the women in his life. As he looked across the table, to the two buddies who never let him down, he felt grateful to at least have them by his side.

"I miss her, you know?" Ryan didn't want to look up and see ridicule in his friends' eyes. He felt a hand clap on his shoulder and turned to see Luke looking at him with sympathy. "She was amazing and funny and smart, and I just miss her."

"This whole situation is just fucked up, man," said Luke, shaking his head.

"And the sex was epic," Ryan said.

"Yeah. As much as I wasn't on Team Misty, she was pretty hot," said Diego.

"Not Misty. Angie," Ryan confessed.

"Angie?" Luke asked in disbelief, swaying slightly. "I know I've had a few more than usual, but I want to make sure I heard that correctly. You finally slept with Angie?"

"Yup! And it was epic."

"Wow. Cat's out of the bag," said Luke. "Bag here"–he gestured to his side–"Cat waaaaay over there," he added, pointing across the room.

"Dude! When?" Diego asked.

"The night he hooked up with Josie," Ryan answered, jerking his thumb at Luke.

"Mmm. Josie." Luke groaned. "You know we didn't even have sex that night."

"Come again?" Ryan cupped his hand next to his ear and pushed his face toward Luke.

"No, not come again. If he didn't sleep with her, she didn't come at all," cackled Diego. Ryan tried to give him a fist bump but missed and accidentally punched Diego in the arm.

"Nope. We just went back to my place and talked."

"Whoa," whispered Ryan.

Diego bunched up his fingers on both hands and put them to his temples, then pulled them back to mimic an explosion. "Mind blown!" he shouted a bit too loudly.

"I wondered why Josie was there when I got up in the morning," said Ryan. Then, as if they were in a scene from *Beetlejuice* where the spirit was conjured up by uttering its name aloud three times, Ryan looked up to see Josie stride into the bar along with two other women wearing scrubs.

"She's here," Ryan called out.

"Angie?" Diego said.

"No, Josie. I think we beetlejuiced her." Normally Ryan would have given a subtle shift of his eyes or an inconspicuous head tilt. But he was three sheets to the wind. So instead, he stood up, shouted her name and pointed at her.

"Aww, shit," whispered Luke. He and Diego were only one or two sheets to the wind, so after looking in Josie's direction, they both cringed and lowered their eyes to the table to avoid eye contact. Josie whispered something to her girlfriends, who walked to the bar to order drinks. Taking in the three very drunk guys in front of her, Josie took a deep breath and made her way over to their table.

"Gentlemen," she said with a smirk.

Luke scrambled to get up and enveloped Josie in a hug. "Josie," he slurred. Diego gave her a little salute while Ryan debated internally whether to meet her eyes. *Angie is the one who should be lowering her eyes in shame. I'm the victim.* He looked up to see Josie staring at him.

"Hey," she said, and the sympathy in her eyes was like a punch to the gut.

"Hey," was all he could muster in return.

"I know you think you know what went down, but there's more—"

"Save it," he cautioned, lifting his hand to stop her.

"Listen, you're obviously hurting. And it doesn't need to be this way. I know she's tried calling you a bunch of times. I think you should talk to her. Let her explain. Let her tell you what was happening behind the scenes," Josie implored.

"Josie, you know I think you're awesome. And Luke here thinks you're awesome or he wouldn't have talked to you instead of having sex with you. Wait, that didn't come out right. Anyway, there's nothing Angie could say to make this right," Ryan slurred.

"She's hurting too, you know," she said. Ryan didn't know. A part of him felt like Angie was getting what she deserved. The other part hated the idea that she was wounded.

"I don't mean to be rude," he said, not letting the alcohol affect his manners. "I'm just going to suggest that you go back over to your friends and enjoy your evening and pretend that we never saw each other or else I'm going to end up saying something we're both going to regret."

"Okay." She walked back to her friends.

Diego couldn't help noticing Luke sigh as he watched Josie's retreating backside. "Explain to me why you didn't go for that?"

Luke groaned.

"Yeah," said Ryan. "Talking isn't really your MO. What gives?"

"Fuck," Luke muttered. He lifted his shot glass. "This shit is like truth serum."

"Damn straight," agreed Ryan. "So spill."

"I like her, okay?" Luke confessed.

"*Liked her* liked her?" Diego moved his eyebrows up and down suggestively.

"I may be drunk, but I distinctly heard 'like' not 'liked,'" said Ryan.

"I *like* her."

"My head is spinning," Ryan said. "And it's not just the tequila."

"We've hung out a few times since that night—just as friends—and I like her, okay? I really like her. Like, *a lot* like her," Luke admitted.

"This is all too much," said Ryan. "I'll be right back." He stumbled to the bathroom, relieving himself and splashing some cold water onto his face. He looked at himself in the mirror. If sober, he would have wondered why all the women he trusted ended up betraying him. He would have questioned why he'd thought it was a good idea to seek out a date on a New York subway. He would have challenged his notions of love and fate. But he was drunk. So instead, he rubbed his eyes, rinsed out his mouth and started for the table where Luke and Diego were lining up another round of shots.

He passed by the table where Josie sat with her friends. A guy in his late twenties, dressed in a tailored business suit with an expensive-looking tie loosened around his neck, stood over Josie, gesturing wildly with his hands. Ryan heard Josie say, "I told you, she's not here. And even if she was here, she doesn't want to talk to you, Harrison."

Harrison? Angie's Harrison? That piece of shit Harrison who cheated on her? Oh, hell no. Ryan may have been furious with Angie, but that didn't mean this lying bastard could get away with hurting her like that.

"Harrison?" he said, charging to the table.

"Who the hell are you?"

"The guy who's going to teach you a fucking lesson about how to treat a lady." Ryan made a fist and reared back his arm, ready to strike. Channeling his outrage toward Harrison and his frustration in general with the infidelity and manipulation he had suffered at the hands of the various women in his life, Ryan took a wild swing, which Harrison dodged easily given how drunk Ryan was. Ryan faltered, trying to right himself, and Harrison turned the tables.

His fist connected with Ryan's jaw, and as Ryan's head snapped to the side, Harrison grabbed Ryan's shirt and punched him in the stomach. Ryan went down . . . hard. Josie rushed to him, pushing Harrison aside and muttering, "Asshole."

Ryan clutched his stomach, agony radiating through his ribs. Despite the pain and the alcohol, Ryan had the presence of mind to grasp onto Harrison's finely tailored wool-blend slacks before violently hurling. He laughed—like Angie, he had now ruined one of Harrison's pricey suits too. Several other bar patrons gagged. Josie, being a nurse, didn't seem put off by the vomit and let out a laugh at Harrison's expense.

Harrison growled with disgust and used one of his now soiled legs to kick Ryan in the ribs again. The pain caused Ryan to roll over onto his back and groan. While Harrison stormed off, Josie, working hard to avoid the puddles of puke, kneeled down and soothed Ryan's brow.

"I got you." Though her calm voice helped mollify the intense sting of each breath, the physical pain was a good distraction from the heartache he was unwilling to discuss with her.

She stood up and called over to Luke and Diego, who weaved and stumbled over. When they spied Ryan and the upchuck on the floor, one laughed uncontrollably and the other recoiled.

Hand on hip, Josie shook her head in exasperation. "Can you stop acting like children for five minutes? Your friend just got the shit kicked out of him."

It was only after Josie explained that Ryan had tried to punch Harrison that the guys understood the gravity of the situation and helped their buddy to his feet. Josie got the three guys an Uber back to Luke's apartment.

Ryan awoke to the mother of all hangovers. Never mind the fact that his jaw felt like it had been disconnected from its hinge and his ribs singed with pain every time he breathed. He lifted himself off of Luke's couch, gulped a large glass of cold water and then rooted around the kitchen cabinets looking for some sort of pain reliever.

Not finding any, Ryan wandered into Luke's bathroom. There on the floor, looking even worse than Ryan felt, was Diego, his head hanging over the toilet bowl. Ryan patted his back, and Diego glanced up, groaned, and then lowered his eyes back to the toilet seat.

"You look catastrophically hung over," Luke scoffed at Ryan as he walked down the hallway.

"Not really sure you can take the moral high ground right now," Ryan fired back with as much gusto as he could muster at the moment.

"True," conceded Luke with a chuckle. He seemed to be in about the same shape as his buddies.

Two hours later, Ryan, Diego and Luke had managed to brush their teeth (Luke stockpiled extra toothbrushes for the overnight guests who frequented his apartment), finger-comb their hair (except for Diego, who again extolled the virtues of the buzz cut) and throw on some clean t-shirts from Luke's freshly laundered pile of clothes.

They gingerly walked a few blocks to a family-owned diner to order a greasy breakfast that could soak up all the alcohol sloshing around their bellies. They were quiet aside from placing their orders, merely heaving a small grunt or groan as they downed glasses of orange juice and sips of black coffee. Once they'd each got a few bites of bacon, eggs and hashed browns down, Luke broke the silence.

"So, are we going to talk about the elephant in the room, or what?"

"And by elephant, do you mean the stalemate between Ryan and Angie, the fact you like a woman so much you didn't want to have sex with her, or that Ryan here got in a bar fight?" said Diego.

"Shit," said Luke. "When you say it like that, we have a goddam menagerie here." He looked up to find Ryan's brow furrowed in confusion and Diego's appearance aghast. "Not ménage, you pervert," Luke said. "*Menagerie.*" After a flash of relief from Diego, Luke was met with more blank stares. "Menagerie. A collection of animals. You know. Made famous in the Tennessee Williams play, *The Glass Menagerie*," he explained with an exasperated tone.

Diego snorted. "I've said it before and I'll say it again. Who are you?"

"Sometimes, I wonder just how well I really know you," Ryan said.

"I'm an enigma." Luke shrugged.

"That is true," said Ryan.

Diego quietly chuckled to himself.

Luke scowled. "I said enigma, not enema."

"Yeah, I know," Diego said defensively, but the humor in his eyes was evident.

"Okay, here's the plan. We're gonna spend five minutes sharing our feelings like a bunch of teenage girls, and then we're gonna go do a bunch of manly shit like chop down a tree with a crosscut saw," said Luke.

"Works for me," agreed Ryan. "So who's going to start this sewing circle?"

With a deep sigh and a sag of his shoulders, Luke piped up. "I'll begin. I, Luke Beauregard Devine, like a woman. A lot."

"Yeah, we got that last night," Diego said dismissively. "I thought we were clearing the air."

Luke looked up at the ceiling. "She makes me feel solid and liquid at the same time." Ryan and Diego stared back in shock. "She made it clear up front it would just be a one-night thing, but I knew instantly I wanted more. So, we just talked until we fell asleep on the couch. We talked about everything and nothing. She was gone when I woke up. We've hung out a few more times just as friends. I'm trying to show her what more with me would be like," he rushed out. "Damn! Feels good to get that off my chest."

"Wow, brother. That is quite a story. I'm really glad to see you finally maturing." Ryan placed one hand on Luke's chest and used the other to pat his back.

"Where are things now?" Diego asked.

"I'm not sure. Like I said, we've seen each other a few times, and we talk on the phone almost every night."

"Every night?" asked a shocked Ryan.

"Almost, yeah. I just need to get the balls to tell her how I feel . . . if she doesn't already know."

"Keep us posted, man," said Diego, and by the warmth in his voice, Ryan could tell that Diego cared about Luke's happiness just as much as he did. A seemingly choked-up Luke cleared his throat and looked at Ryan, indicating for him to go next.

Ryan lowered his head and squeezed his eyes shut. He inhaled deeply and nodded his head, finally ready to talk this through. "As you know, Angie and I had been spending a lot of time together. And I was starting to think that maybe *she* was who I was meant to meet. Maybe this whole fool's errand was about *us*. We ended up sleeping together the night you guys met her, and it was perfect. She was perfect. That is, until she kicked me out of her bed the next morning and told me things didn't need to get awkward. That we could just call it a stress reliever."

"I do find sex relaxing," Diego said with a thoughtful nod.

"Since when do you have sex?" said Luke. Diego scowled at him, but Luke ignored it and turned back to Ryan. "Continue."

"Things with Misty always seemed kind of off, and I know you guys tried your best to tell me that she wasn't the right fit. I guess I just wanted so badly to capture that feeling I see from other happy couples that I was willing to ignore the warning signs." Ryan hung his head and exhaled loudly. Diego rubbed his back. "And the thought of another failed relationship—and a public one at that . . ."

"It's okay, brother. Take your time," Diego said.

"And then Frankie came over and, as I explained to you, things didn't go down the way they appeared on *Celebrity*

Monger. And to be honest, that didn't surprise me either. She just isn't the girl that I knew back home." The waitress returned at that moment to refill their coffees. The guys each nodded a thanks and then took a silent moment to have a sip.

"It's this stuff with Angie that really gets to me. I can admit it now, that I had fallen in love with her, and she betrayed me in the worst possible way. She didn't just break my heart, she broke my spirit."

"Wow, man, that is deep," muttered Diego.

"Yeah, someone should put it on a Hallmark card," quipped Luke. "But seriously, don't give up on love. If anything, you've shown me it's worth the risk and will be worth the reward."

"When you came to her defense like that against her jackass ex, it makes me think you still *are* in love with her, though," said Diego. The three sat in tense silence. Diego rubbed the back of his neck as if he was unsure whether he should have voiced that out loud. Ryan searched his feelings, only to determine Diego was right. He nodded grimly, and the other two nodded back in understanding.

"Okay, Diego, you're up," said Luke, shifting the attention away from Ryan, who was obviously struggling with his emotions.

"I got nothing," Diego responded with a shrug.

"What do you mean, you got nothing?" scoffed Luke.

"I mean I got nothing. No one seems interested in me, so I'm just throwing myself into work."

"I think my little sister has a crush on you," offered Ryan.

"Oh, shit. Well, that just makes me feel even worse," Diego retorted in horror. The three of them laughed heartily and dug back into their breakfasts.

THIRTY-THREE

Angie sat in the nondescript lobby waiting for her interview. She replayed Josie's words in her mind: "The rearview mirror is a lot smaller than the windshield." *That's right. I need to stop looking back and focus on what's ahead.*

She couldn't believe that Harlan's cousin's landlady's aunt worked at the *New York Times*. While she'd heard a politician lambasting the prestigious newspaper as "fake news," she knew it didn't get more respectable than this. She wanted to yell at the Twitter-prone public servant that he should spend a week at *Celebrity Monger* and then he'd understand the meaning of "fake news."

Her heart raced and her palms were sweaty as she psyched herself up for her interview with an editor. Aside from landing a story in the *New Yorker*, writing for the *Times* was all she'd ever dreamed of. She'd been reading the respected newspaper since high school.

A middle-aged woman wearing a pair of black pants and a burgundy sweater set walked into the waiting area and motioned for Angie to follow her. She led her down several hallways and past a massive newsroom with rows of desks and banks of computers. Angie felt a thrill watching these respected journalists bustling to share the truth and shape the world's views. It was a place she desperately wanted to be a part of. The receptionist walked Angie into a windowed office where a thin and elegant African American woman in her late fifties sat behind a large desk.

"Ms. Prince to see you," said the receptionist. Angie held out her hand and tried to offer a firm and confident shake to the highly respected associate executive editor for the paper. She motioned for Angie to be seated. Angie dried her hands on her black suit pants and sat down.

The editor pulled a folder from a stack on her desk and opened it. She put her bifocal glasses on and glanced through the papers.

"So, these are all really well written and researched, Angie," she said, removing her bifocals and looking Angie in the eye.

"Thank you," said Angie, smiling a nervous smile. She took a moment to let the magnitude of that compliment wash over her.

"You have strong technical writing skills, but these stories lack an emotional element that will make the reader want to connect with them," she continued, waving her hand in the air. "Take this one here. You write about love and technology, but in a very . . ." She paused, apparently searching for the right words. ". . . sterile or clinical way."

"I . . ."

"Good writing isn't enough these days. With competition from online and broadcast sources, we need to find a way to bring people the news and connect it to them on an emotional level. And I just don't see that here. I want to encourage you to keep writing. Feel free to send me samples. I would be happy to look at them. But for now, I don't think you're ready for a position here. I'm sorry."

"Me, too," said a resigned Angie. "Well, thank you for your time and advice." She shook the editor's hand and walked out the door.

Say Anything. That was the film Ryan mentioned when they had grown frustrated with the search for the Subway Girl. Even Harlan claimed it was a classic romantic comedy. She had already made her way through the AFI top 100 movie list. Never mind that she'd had to watch *Psycho* with all the lights on while simultaneously balancing her checkbook, and sleep in bed with Josie after *A Clockwork Orange*. She'd done it. It was something to help her feel connected to Ryan, despite him not wanting anything to do with her.

So, *Say Anything*. She thought she should watch it. It would be a just punishment. She wouldn't be landing her dream job anytime soon, and she certainly wasn't going to get the guy. No, she deserved to see two souls overcome the odds and find love together. She deserved to watch their happiness bloom—their unabashed love. She deserved to wallow in the misery of knowing that would *never* be her.

Sitting alone on her living room couch, Angie pushed play and found herself entranced by the unlikely relationship between overachieving Diane Court and the directionless Lloyd Dobler. She found herself growing agitated when Diane broke things off with Lloyd because of her dad's influence and insistence he wasn't good enough for her. When Lloyd stood outside Diane's window and had his "boom box moment," as Ryan had called it, Angie's tears started to flow.

She sobbed through the remainder of the movie, mourning the love she would never have and feeling moved by the theme of forgiveness. Could Ryan forgive her? What would it take for her to prove to him she was worthy of his love? What would be her boom box moment?

After the movie ended, Angie clicked over from Netflix to regular television. Just as she was about to get up and throw away her dirty tissues, she heard a voice that stopped her in her tracks.

"Hi. I'm Misty Waites," Misty purred, standing in front of a cafeteria-style counter. "My romance with Ryan may not have worked out, but I'll always be a Subway girl," she said seductively. "Come in this month for specials on the Applewood Pulled Pork sandwich and choose from a range of fresh veggies to make your sandwich complete." She finished off by encouraging people to eat fresh. She cocked her hand on her hip and gave the camera a sultry smile.

Angie almost threw up in her mouth. Leave it to that schemer to exploit her "relationship" with Ryan into a commercial for a sandwich chain. How could Ryan have lumped Angie into the same category as Misty and, even worse, Frankie? *How could he not see I'm different? That what we shared was different?*

Fueled by frustration and despair, but enthused with a sense of resolve, Angie stopped crying, blew her nose and opened her laptop. She would do the only thing she knew how to do. It was time to stop being fragile like a bomb and start being fragile like a flower.

If it worked, would Ryan even see it? Would he jump to the conclusion it was all a career ploy? Would he take it for the grand gesture it was meant to be? Or would he just despise her more? She didn't know the answers, but she had to give it a try.

THIRTY-FOUR

THREE MONTHS LATER

Ryan ran his fingers through his hair as he waited for a graphic to render. He was thankful Luke had brought in some new accounts while he had been busy with the Subway Girl. Work was steady and providing a distraction from the thoughts of Frankie, Misty and Angie that still inevitably invaded his mind.

He conceded that he'd lost Frankie a long time ago to a life that wasn't for him. He never really even knew Misty, and what he did know wasn't all that interesting. But he *knew* Angie. Her cynicism toward love, her sarcastic quips, and her persistent eye-rolls were just ways to firm up that tough exterior. Through their time together and her writing, he knew the passions, interests and dreams beneath that harsh veneer. So much so that, even now, months after he stormed away from her apartment, he felt a pang in his chest—a combination of hurt over her betrayal and sorrow for what was lost.

Looking out his office window, rubbing his heart with his hand, he caught movement in the reflection. He turned to see Harlan in the doorway.

He stood and turned to face the camera operator. "I don't have anything more to say to you. Any of you," he said, a rare spiritedness in his voice, which only made him think of Angie more.

"You don't have to say anything. I just thought there was something you should see." Harlan gently placed a flash drive and copy of the *New Yorker* on Ryan's desk. "Listen, man, I–"

With growing anger in his voice, Ryan said, "Just stop."

"Just watch it," said Harlan, pointing to the drive.

"Why can't you just leave me alone?" Ryan lashed out. Yes, he was still reeling over the betrayal, even months later. Time had done little to heal his broken heart, but Harlan didn't know that. Why couldn't he just let this whole disaster fade into oblivion like the sinking ship it was?

"And read the article." Harlan shuffled through the magazine until he reached the desired page. Ryan glanced over to see Angie's name in the byline. *Seriously? Did Angie really just bring all of this back up to get herself a story in* the New Yorker? Ryan must have snorted aloud, because Harlan added, "It's not what it seems. None of it was."

Ryan's shoulders sagged and he slumped into his seat. "Why are you doing this?"

"Because I'm not a complete asshole. And Angie's my friend. I'm sick of watching her suffer when maybe she doesn't need to anymore." With that, Harlan walked out of the office.

Ryan placed a hand on the flash drive and pulled it toward him. With trepidation, he inserted it into his computer. The hum of the drive loading was eclipsed by the churning sounds in his belly. After a moment, clips of Angie throughout the Subway Girl journey played on his screen.

> *"It's okay. She just wasn't the right girl for you. You deserve someone who's going to appreciate your sense of humor and all your movie references . . . and how kind-hearted you are."*

He immediately recognized this one from the night Misty confessed her infidelity to him. He hadn't noticed before the intensity of Angie's embrace or how her head tilted to the side with a hint of sincerity. The clip abruptly ended and cut to Angie with Frankie in what appeared to be an office at *Celebrity Monger*.

> *"He is a great guy. He's sweet and romantic and wants to believe in the very best of people."*

> *"You may think you're all tough and shit because you've lived here for a few years. But I'm a New Yorker. So don't mess with me. The exit is that way. And if I need to call security, I will."*

Angie had kicked Frankie out? She hadn't sent her to his apartment with instructions to seduce him?

> *"It's bigger than your ambition, Barry. You're screwing with this man's life. Ryan's been through enough. He didn't sign up to be used by you. All he wanted was to find happiness. I can't be a part of this anymore . . . I quit."*

She quit her job? Over me? Ryan scrubbed his fingers over his jaw. How could he have not given her the chance to explain?

> *"He won't talk to me, Harlan. He thinks I brought that shrew back into his life for the sake of ratings*

and manipulated the footage to make him look bad. But I would never hurt him like that. Never."

Of course she wouldn't hurt him. That wasn't Angie. He was such an ass for thinking otherwise.

"Can't he see that he's the love of my life and anyone that comes after him will only be there because they are willing to have me? I love him. And he hates me."

The tightness in Ryan's chest returned. After closing the files, Ryan dragged the magazine closer. He took a deep breath.

Over the next fifteen minutes, he read Angie's personal essay–the very *public* essay–that put him and the Subway Girl story back in the spotlight. Somewhere he most definitely did not want to be. Once done, he closed the magazine and gently placed it on his desk, running his fingers across the cover. He leaned back in his chair, his hands clasped behind his neck, pondering his next move.

THIRTY-FIVE

Angie sat in the velvet-backed bar seat at the King Cole Bar waiting for Harlan to arrive. She took another sip of her Bloody Mary. The drink reminded her of Ryan, and she felt a pang of sadness. Despite months having passed since she last saw him, the wound was still fresh. She often found herself overanalyzing conversations and choices, fantasizing about alternate realities, depressing herself with thoughts of "what if," and making herself plain crazy with grief over missing him so much. At least the article had been cathartic, helping her atone to some degree.

She felt a tap on her shoulder. Harlan was standing next to her. He picked up the drink she had ordered for him, tossed the straw aside and took a large gulp before placing a copy of the current issue of the *New Yorker* on the counter. He flipped through the pages until landing on her article and handed Angie a black Sharpie.

"Sign it, please."

"My first autograph," she replied, a slight smile crossing her face.

"Well done, young lady. Now a toast." He lifted his half-empty Bloody Mary glass in the air. "To Angie and her first of many published pieces in the *New Yorker.*" Harlan leaned forward and clinked Angie's glass. "And, to her new job as a legit reporter—albeit a very broke reporter—for the *Standard.*"

Feeling a combination of pride and misery, she took a long slow sip and lowered her glass to the smooth dark wood bar top.

"Why do you look so depressed? For nearly four years, all you've talked about is getting a story published in the *New Yorker*. Now you have," he said.

"Well, if you read the story . . ." *If Harlan had read it, he would know this is a bittersweet victory.* She didn't want to see sympathy in Harlan's eyes. That would just depress her more. While avoiding eye contact with him, she glanced across the room. Her jaw dropped at the sight of Ryan in the bar's doorway. His blank expression accessorized his faded jeans and shiny nylon bomber jacket.

Angie's heart raced with a mixture of panic and hope. Had he read the story? Was he here to forgive her? To berate her? Her mouth dried, and she slowly swallowed as Ryan approached. Harlan reached out his hand, and Ryan shook it.

"I brought a friend," said Harlan.

Angie turned to face Ryan. It had been months since she had seen his caramel-colored eyes. Months since he had called her a liar and manipulator. Months since she had known she was undeniably in love with him.

"Hey," she said, her voice shaking slightly.

"Hey," he said back, with no emotion in his voice.

A thick cloud of tension hung in the air.

"I'll let the two of you talk, and before you ask, no, I'm not recording this," said Harlan. Angie let out a small chuckle, equal parts relief and fear.

"So, I saw the *New Yorker* story. Congratulations," said Ryan with a shrug. "It seemed like . . ."

"A boom box moment?" She lifted the magazine and held it over her head, in an impersonation of Lloyd Dobler.

"Yeah." He nodded.

"Thanks." *Okay, so he saw the story. But is he angry?* With his features passive, she couldn't tell.

"It was really well written and heartfelt."

"Thanks," she replied yet again before swallowing hard. Unsure of what to say or how to respond to this overture, Angie stood motionless. If breathing weren't an autonomic nervous system response, she'd surely be dead. She was paralyzed by fear. But fear had got her into this mess. Fear of losing what she thought was important. Fear of getting hurt. Fear of letting herself love again. After a brief moment of silence, she said, "I was terrified you'd see your name in print again and just shut down immediately. I was so afraid you would hate the renewed attention and I would drive you away for good. That we would never be able to recover."

"I will say that was my initial reaction. But Harlan showed me some video clips he pulled. Things I hadn't seen before. I wanted to give you the benefit of the doubt, so I read it."

"You're not angry?" She held her breath, waiting for his response.

"No," said Ryan, shaking his head subtly. "No, I'm not angry."

Relief washed over her, and Angie smiled her first genuine smile of the morning. "Good. I've never wanted to hurt you, and I certainly wouldn't want to take advantage of you. Despite this being a big career win for me, my priority was making sure you knew how I felt. How I've changed. How I—"

"I just want to know if it's all true?" interrupted Ryan.

"Yes," said Angie. "Everything I wrote is true."

"You . . . believe in fate?"

"I do. You were meant to search for the Subway Girl so we could meet," she replied, staring into his eyes. "*I'm* your Subway Girl."

"And . . . you love me?"

"I do. With my whole heart. You're all I think about. Like, a *total* distraction. I would pretty much do anything to make you happy. Seeing you smile feels like a punch to the gut—in the best possible way. And I want to kiss you more than I want to breathe. I never expected to feel this way about anyone, but here we are."

A small smile crossed Ryan's face, pulling on Angie's heartstrings.

"You really gave all that money to charity?"

"After repaying the money for Mom's mortgage, I donated the rest. I selected the Film Institute for their work in preserving classic films . . . because of you," she said. Ryan rocked back on his heels and grinned. "Can you ever forgive me?"

"I can. I do."

"Can you ever . . . love me?" She pressed her lips together in fear. At least before she'd asked the question, there was a chance he could love her. Now, she'd know for sure, and she wasn't certain she could handle it.

"I can. I do," he repeated, but this time with a broad smile. Angie let out the breath she didn't realize she'd been holding. She bit her lip, lowered her head and squeezed her eyes shut, overwhelmed with relief and joy. Ryan gently grasped her jaw and lifted her head to look at him. "I know I fell for Misty based on all of this superficial stuff upon first seeing her, and I stayed longer than I should have because, foolishly, I thought we were meant to be. But I fell in love with *you*."

"Ryan . . ." She wanted to tell him he had her at "hello," that he didn't need to go on. That just knowing he loved her was enough. That the explanation was too much for her fragile heart to handle.

"I can't pinpoint when it happened. It wasn't when you refilled my popcorn bowl without me even asking. It wasn't when you asked about my day even when you'd had a bad one yourself. It wasn't when you rolled your eyes at my lame puns. It was sometime when all of those little things added up, like tiny drops of water causing a bucket to overflow."

"Ryan—" She held her hand up in an attempt to stop him from talking. She'd never been here before. In a place so honest and pure and raw. She wasn't sure she *deserved* to be here.

"And it isn't how passionately you express yourself in writing . . . or in person . . . or in bed. Although that last one's my favorite." He chuckled.

Angie slowly reached up and caressed Ryan's jaw. He moved forward and pressed his lips against hers. Angie choked on a sob.

"I wasn't sure you would ever be able to forgive me. I wasn't sure I'd ever be able to forgive myself."

"I'm sorry, too. Sorry that I didn't let you explain. Sorry that I jumped to conclusions. Sorry that I made you bear witness to that charade with Misty. I'm sorry you died a thousand times over the images of me kissing her. I'm sorry that I ever kissed her at all."

"You're forgiven."

Ryan ran his thumb across Angie's cheek, wiping away tears, before rubbing it across her lower lip. "It's been a long and lonely four months," he groaned.

"Four months and two days."

"Sassy mouth," he murmured, shaking his head.

"Still want to kiss it?" she asked, thinking back to that first night they got together.

"Now more than ever."

Angie felt that four-month gap close in an instant as his lips sealed around her own.

It was too much.

It was not enough.

And it was just what she needed.

All at the same time.

She glanced up just in time to see Harlan duck out of the doorway of the bar, but not before lifting his fingers to his forehead in salute.

THIRTY-SIX

ONE YEAR LATER

"Don't worry. They're going to love you," Ryan said, stroking Angie's cheek as they settled into their seats on the flight to Des Moines, Iowa, the closest airport to Ryan's hometown.

"I'm not worried," Angie told him. But she knew he could see the hesitation in her eyes. He'd voiced the same concerns when he met Angie's mom a few months earlier, despite Angie trying to convince him there was nothing to worry about.

"They really are the nicest people you'll ever meet," he stated matter-of-factly.

She snorted. "One look at you, and I have no doubt about that." *Yup, defuse with sarcasm. Being in love certainly hasn't changed my* MO.

"So, what has you worried? And don't try denying that you're worried, because you didn't even roll your eyes when you huffed just now, and that's got me concerned," he teased.

"Ha ha," she said. "It's just . . . they are these amazing relationship role models, and I know you want what they managed to capture . . . and I just . . ." Ryan's belief in love and fate was so deeply rooted in his background that she longed for his family and friends' approval. She wanted them to agree with what she knew in her own heart—that she and Ryan were destined to be together.

"Shh." He shut Angie up with a kiss. "Listen, I get where you're coming from, but you don't need to be intimidated by what they have. Let's focus on what *we* have. You're everything I never knew I wanted but absolutely need."

"You're just saying that to make me feel better," she huffed out of nervousness.

"No, I'm not. You own me, and I'm pretty sure I've cornered the market on your heart. And anyway, their marriage is not all rainbows and unicorns and shit. They have their issues. My parents have been married so long that Mom finishes most of Dad's sentences. She also starts most of them and fills in the middle, too." He chuckled. "One time she was so mad at him, but instead of the silent treatment, she gave him the *speaking* treatment." He nodded as if to emphasize this was a fact. Angie leaned forward to kiss him. *God, he kisses like he has days until he needs to get to the good stuff. Like kissing* is *the good stuff.*

After the long flight and drive to Ryan's hometown, Angie and Ryan walked into his childhood home. Angie handed Ryan's mom the packages of cinnamon and chocolate babka from Zabar's, the famous New York bakery.

"I would have brought flowers, but they don't travel as well as pastry," Angie offered with a wavering voice and a nervous laugh. She scolded herself for sounding so wishy-washy.

"Well, these look just delicious, Angie. Thank you for your thoughtfulness," Ryan's mom replied.

"My pleasure, Mrs. Carlson."

"Please, call me Susan."

Angie bloomed at the invitation.

"Let's open these up. Dad won't mind. Why wait until after dinner to have dessert? Better to start with it, so you know you have room," Susan said with a wink. Angie sighed in relief.

This was much easier than she'd expected. Angie helped Susan put slices of the layered, loaf-shaped coffee cakes on plates and pour coffee. Ryan sat silently and watched with a lovelorn grin on his face. Over babka and coffee, Susan insisted Angie share celebrity stories with her.

"It was probably my favorite *Celebrity Monger* piece. Here was this actor who played some of the most iconic and stereotypical macho roles out there—cowboy, mob boss, astronaut, boxer—and he was wearing a tiara and drinking tea with his granddaughter. Pinky extended and everything."

"Oh, I would have loved to see that," gushed Susan. "After I saw him in *Over the Moon*, I added him to my 'Hall Pass' list."

Ryan choked on his pastry. "Wha—" he spluttered between coughs, while Angie covered a gasp with a giggle.

"What? You think just because I'm your mother, I'm not a woman?"

Ryan put his hands up in a silent plea for his mother to stop all manner of discussion on this topic. He turned to Angie, and she recognized the look as begging her to say something.

"He insisted I join them for finger sandwiches and mini cupcakes, which I later learned the two of them had baked earlier in the day. It was just the sweetest. He died less than two weeks later. And while everyone mourned the loss of an acting legend with all of his awards and box office records, I just kept thinking about the sweet grandpa."

"Oh, that man," Susan said dreamily.

"You never told me that story." Ryan stared at Angie in wonder. "What about your anecdote of a famous actor didn't you think I would appreciate?" he teased.

"You never asked," she said with humor. *There's still so much for us to share with one another.* She looked forward to what revelations, laughter and love each new day would bring.

Just then, the front door opened and in bounded Ryan's sister, Finlay, a spunky brunette wearing a collegiate sweatshirt, denim cut-off shorts and pink flip-flops. Ryan rose from the table in time to catch her as she leaped up and hugged him.

Ryan responded by wrapping his arms around his sister and squeezing her.

"You're home!"

Ryan covered his ears at the sound of Finlay's scream, although she continued to cling to him. He twisted his body side to side, trying to shake her off. Finlay eventually landed on her own feet and turned to find Angie smiling brightly at her.

"Angie!" Finlay squealed, enveloping Angie in an almost painfully tight hug. "Skype does not do you justice!" Over the past few months, Angie had established a solid friendship with Finlay, with the two usually mocking Ryan for his various offenses, from terrible puns to movie quotes.

"Or my nose?" Angie teased.

Finlay whipped her head around to Ryan, who wouldn't meet her eyes. "He told you about my wanting your nose?" Finlay asked. "Such a jerk," she muttered. She swatted Ryan's arm and then reached up to kiss his cheek. "Come sit." She pulled Ryan and Angie into the living room and onto the couch.

"I'll take care of this." Susan gestured to the dishes.

"Let me run upstairs. I have something in my bag for you," said Angie as she stood and walked out the room.

"How's school?" Ryan asked Finlay.

"Oh my god," Finlay said, watching Angie walk away. "Quick, before she gets back. Tell me everything." Ryan shook his head, enjoying Finlay's teenage exuberance. "She is so awesome, right?"

"Yeah, she's pretty awesome," Ryan agreed.

"And you're happy?" Finlay looked past him to make sure Angie wasn't back.

"Very. But really. How's school?"

"Good. I love my roommate, and my dorm is fun but not out of control. Classes suck. I'm taking a bunch of intro science classes as prerequisites right now for my major, so it's pretty boring. And the labs are going to be the death of me."

"Death by Bunsen burner, huh?" said Angie, who had returned to the living room.

"And she's so funny," Finlay enthused. Ryan squeezed Angie's hand as she absorbed the compliment.

"Why can't you trust an atom?" Ryan asked Finlay.

"Uh . . . Why?" Finlay asked with suspicion in her voice.

"They make up everything."

Angie grinned and Finlay groaned.

"Ugh. I thought maybe the big city might change him for the better. No such luck," Finlay grumbled.

"I'm from the big city. Believe me, it doesn't get any better than Ryan," Angie said. It was true. He really was the perfect complement to her. He helped smooth out her rough edges. Made her think about things in new ways. Motivated her to be a better person.

"Thanks, babe." Ryan beamed.

"Speaking of big cities, I was working on a story about community farming in urban areas and interviewed Dr. Haven Abromowitz," said Angie, hiding Finlay's gift behind her back.

"Get out! She's amazing. She's one of the pioneers of the Fineman method," Finlay exclaimed.

"That's right. And I actually know what that is now. I was telling her about you—"

"What? Oh my god. Are you serious?" squealed Finlay. Ryan glanced at Angie, and she didn't mistake the adoration in his eyes. She not only saw it, she felt it deep in her heart. To collect herself, Angie lowered her eyes to the ground before resuming her conversation with the young farming enthusiast.

"I told her all about you and your passion for agriculture. So she autographed a copy of her book for you." Angie pulled the book out from behind her and handed it to Finlay, whose mouth gaped open in shock. Finlay opened the cover and quietly read the inscription inside.

"'To Finlay. Keep growing your passion. Wishing you the best, Dr. Haven.' Dr. Haven?" Finlay practically screamed. "We're on a first-name basis." Finlay jumped off the couch and encased Angie in a tremendous hug. "This is the most thoughtful gift anyone has ever given me." Angie bit her lip in relief.

"There's a little something extra in there for you," she whispered in Finlay's ear. Finlay's brow furrowed. She flipped through the book until it opened to a page with a bookmark. Though it wasn't a bookmark. It was a photo of Diego at the beach wearing nothing but board shorts. Finlay's eyebrows shot up. Angie winked in response. Finlay slammed the book shut and pulled Angie into another embrace. She pulled back and grabbed onto Angie's shoulders, looking her square in the eyes.

"If he ever hurts you," she said, gesturing to her brother, "tell me, so I can kick him in the balls." Ryan winced and shook his head.

"No worry," said Angie. Ryan sagged in relief. "I'll cut them off well before you would ever get the chance."

Angie snuggled up under the cozy down comforter, relishing how comfortable she felt. She was sleeping on the spare twin bed in Finlay's room. Ryan's parents may have been progressive enough to have "Hall Pass" lists, but they certainly weren't going to let their unmarried son sleep in the same room as his big-city girlfriend. Angie was okay with that. In fact, she and Finlay had stayed up well past midnight swapping embarrassing stories about Ryan, like how, at twelve, he'd dreamed of being a famous rapper—RC Cola—or the time he'd bawled like a baby when Angie took him to see *Les Misérables* on Broadway for his birthday.

Finlay had left early that morning to get back to campus. After she and Angie said their goodbyes, Angie crawled back under the heavy comforter and drifted off to sleep. Without the noises of the city to keep her awake, it was easy to fall back into a restful snooze. She awoke to sweet kisses being pressed against her shoulder and neck.

"Hmm," she hummed in pleasure. "Keep going."

"Morning, beautiful," Ryan murmured into her ear. He crawled under the covers with her and wrapped his hand around her breast.

"Where's your dad?"

"Not really interested in thinking about my dad right now," he mumbled. "But he's at work." The pinch of her nipple was enough to dampen Angie's underwear. "Everywhere my fingers go, my tongue's gonna follow." *Mmm.* He'd made that threat before and, thank goodness, always followed through. For someone who prided himself on being such a nice guy, Ryan sure had the dirty talk down pat.

"And your mom?" she moaned as Ryan's skillful hands continued to work her body into a frenzy.

"Downstairs making you waffles before we head out to explore the town," he whispered as his hands dipped into her panties and he pushed a finger inside her. Angie's back arched and she moaned a "yes," but then she gently pulled Ryan's arm away and rolled over to face him.

"We can't do this here with your mom downstairs."

"But you just moaned yes." Ryan had a lustful look in his eyes—a look Angie was all too familiar with.

"That was for the waffles," she quipped. Ryan tickled her until she begged him to stop. Breathless from both exertion and unquenched desire, he acquiesced and helped her up, but not before sticking his finger in his mouth—the one that had been taunting Angie—and licking it clean.

"Damn, that's hot," she panted. Ryan chuckled and winked.

Angie loved the feeling of the wind whipping through her hair. It was a perfect seventy-five degrees, but without the humidity she might find in New York at this time of year. The open road stretched out in front of her, and cornfields filled her vision on both the left and right. Ryan clutched the grab handle near the roof of the car with one hand and white-knuckled the seat with his other.

"You might want to slow down there, Speed Racer. You're going a bit fast," he suggested.

"No way. I'm going just right," Angie retorted, turning to him and flashing a smile.

"Eyes on the road," he warned, pointing her toward the windshield. The car swerved as she returned her vision forward and pushed down on the accelerator.

"Hey, hey. Please don't get all Danika Patrick on me."

"Ha! I thought you were going to say Thelma and Louise, Movie Boy." Having long since finished watching the Film Institute's top 100 films, she had moved on to their greatest heroes and villains list, where she'd discovered the poignant female buddy flick.

"Well, that too. Don't want to die today." Angie's foot pressed harder on the gas pedal. "Jeez, you're a menace," he huffed, his body pressed back into the seat with the force of her acceleration.

"I'm your menace," she replied sweetly.

"Yeah," he said. "You're my menace."

I'll never tire of hearing him say "mine."

"Oh, please. There's no one arou—" She was interrupted by the sound of a police siren. Angie looked around, trying to figure out where the noise was coming from, and spied a police cruiser coming up fast behind her. "Aww, shit."

Ryan clenched his fists in frustration as Angie eased onto the shoulder of the two-lane highway. She rolled her window down and looked in the rearview mirror as the officer approached the driver's side of the car. Ryan shook his head in frustration.

"License and registration," said the officer in an authoritative voice as he removed his mirrored sunglasses. Ryan opened the glove box and grabbed the rental car agreement.

Angie smiled brightly at the officer. "Is there a problem, officer?" she cooed. She'd never been pulled over by the police before. Heck, she'd just gotten her driver's license a few weeks ago. But she'd seen enough movies and television shows to know the drill: flirt, flirt, flirt. She batted her eyelashes and grinned up at the police officer.

"License . . . and registration," he repeated, and it was evident he wasn't falling for her charms. Angie's confidence faltered, the realization hitting her that she probably just set a record for getting a speeding ticket so soon after becoming officially licensed to drive. She reached into her purse for her wallet while Ryan handed her the registration papers. The officer leaned down to peer into the passenger side, and Ryan looked into his face.

"Is that Douchebag Dooberman?" Ryan asked.

"It's Officer Dooberman now," the policeman responded coolly.

"Ryan," she hissed through gritted teeth. Handcuffs flashed through Angie's mind. And not the fur-lined fetish kind. *What is Ryan doing, ratcheting the tension up further?*

"Well, well," the officer said. "The prodigal son returns."

Ryan lunged toward the car door. Panicked, Angie reached her sweaty palms out to stop him, but he was too quick and exited the car.

"Doobie!" Ryan shouted.

Officer Dooberman's demeanor changed immediately. "RC!" He and Ryan shared a bro hug complete with a few forceful pats on the back. Angie rolled her eyes at the realization that, of course, Ryan knew the police officer. The town was so small, he knew *everyone*. Perhaps their friendship would come in handy and help her avoid a hefty fine.

"I heard you were home for a visit," Doobie said.

"Yeah. Angie and I just got in yesterday and are staying through the weekend. Angie"—he gestured for Angie to get out of the car—"come meet Doobie."

"Officer Dooberman," the officer corrected.

"Really?" Ryan scoffed.

"Nah, just messing with you." Doobie snickered.

"Nice to meet you, Doobie," Angie said, extending her hand for a shake.

"So you're the New York girlfriend?"

Angie looked back and forth between Ryan and Doobie, wondering how he would know that a) she was from New York and b) she was Ryan's girlfriend. And the way he said "New York girlfriend," like she was an oddity, made her feel like she had her work cut out for her in winning over his friends.

"I'm guessing you heard that from Edna. Am I right?" Ryan chuckled.

"Yeah." Doobie shrugged as if to say Ryan's question was unnecessary.

"Here in town we don't need texting, Instagram, Twitter or WhatsApp. As you know, we've got Edna," Ryan explained to Angie.

"Yes, ma'am," confirmed Doobie. "So, we meeting up for beers Saturday at the bar?"

Ryan glanced at Angie. She nodded.

"Yeah, man. Sounds great," Ryan said.

"Cool," said Doobie.

"Be sure to bring Jessica," Ryan said. "Doobie's wife," he clarified to Angie.

Doobie, heading back to his patrol car, called out, "She wouldn't miss it." He got into his car as Ryan walked back around to the passenger side of theirs. Angie stood rooted to the spot—somewhat dumbfounded—wondering what had just happened.

Ryan leaned against the car door and tapped on the hood. "You okay there?"

"You didn't plan this whole thing, did you? To teach me a lesson?" Angie asked as she got back into the driver's seat.

"No." He laughed. "But you deserve to be taught a lesson, Lightning McQueen."

"Ka-chow!" she called, in homage to the movie, as she peeled away from the shoulder and continued to race down the highway.

"We're heading over to the bar," Ryan called to his parents, who were in the living room watching a documentary. It was the night before they were set to head back to New York, and the plan was to introduce Angie to his friends, followed by some alone time together. "I'm taking the truck."

"Have fun," his mom shouted back. Ryan grabbed Angie's hand and guided her out the front door to a worn pickup truck that looked more like a movie prop than a working vehicle.

When they arrived, the bar was crowded, and everyone there seemed excited to see Ryan return home for a visit. Sitting around a wood table with ten of his closest childhood friends, Angie went on a charm offensive, eager to impress and convince them she was worthy of the wonderful man who'd brought her. She regaled them with stories of celebrities behaving badly and Ryan behaving goofily, which earned her acceptance, adoration and a round of brews on the house.

"I need to get you alone," Ryan whispered in her ear. He ran his tongue along the outer shell, and Angie's body shuddered deliciously in response. He leaned back to assess her interest, and she nodded in agreement. After goodbyes and promises to talk soon, Ryan and Angie hopped in the beat-up truck and hit the highway toward Sutter Creek. They drove without saying a word, neither of them feeling the need to replace the comfortable silence. When they reached the riverbank, Ryan walked around the side of the truck and helped

Angie out. She looked up into the sky, astounded by how clearly she could see the stars.

"Wow," she breathed out.

"Yeah," Ryan said. "Without all of the light pollution, you can really see nature's beauty." Ryan leaned down and gently stroked Angie's cheek. She lifted her head and reached up on tiptoe to kiss him. When he sucked her bottom lip into his mouth and slowly grazed it with his teeth, a cross between a groan and a growl bubbled up from her.

Ryan grasped Angie's hand and guided her toward the back of the truck. He laid out several blankets and pillows, which she hadn't noticed had been stacked up in the back.

"Ever have sex outside, in the back of a pickup truck?" he asked her.

"No." She shook her head as he climbed into the truck bed and reached out a hand to help her up. She climbed in, a thrill running through her. He pressed his body against hers.

"Ever have someone take you so hard you see stars, while you look up and literally see stars?" He leaned forward, and she instinctively lay down so his body could cover hers.

"No," she whispered, running her fingers through his hair.

"Ever have a tongue buried deep inside you and no one was around to hear you cry out in pleasure?" He groaned, his face pushed into her neck as he breathed her in.

"No," she gasped. Ryan pulled back to stare into Angie's eyes.

"Want to?"

"Oh god, yes. Yes and yes!" She wanted all of it. All of him.

They crawled under a blanket and made love, with Ryan maintaining a slow and luxurious pace that brought Angie right to the brink. She rolled over so she could straddle him, taking control for the first time that night.

"Yes. Take what you need," he panted.

"I need you. I need everything."

"I love watching you ride me. So beautiful," he moaned while he guided her hips with his hands.

The slide of his body awakened every nerve ending in Angie's body. She was all tingling sensations, building and building with a tension she couldn't control or alleviate. The anticipation of the intense clenching was so great, she was unsure if she'd be able to handle the release.

"Feels so good." Ryan sat up and ran his hands through Angie's hair.

"Yes. I love you so much." Ever since that day at the bar, where she'd confessed her love for him, the words tumbled out easily. Walking through Central Park. "I love you." Eating cupcakes in Greenwich Village. "I love you." Arguing over which was better, the original *Ghostbusters* or the remake. "I love you."

"I'll never tire of hearing that."

"I'll never stop. Ryan. It—feels—so—g—" she started, "good" turning into "god" as the coil tightened and tightened until she quaked around him and was nothing but sparks and warmth and bliss.

After she'd ridden him to her shattering release, Ryan gently flipped Angie onto her back and eased inside. He pounded into her, chasing his own relief in earnest, triggering Angie to let go one more time. Ryan collapsed, his chest heaving from exertion. As he caught his breath, he rolled onto his back and groaned in satisfaction. Angie scooted over to lay her head on his chest. He stroked her back and pulled the blanket up higher so she wouldn't shiver from the cool night air combined with the sheen of sweat that covered her skin.

"This is my favorite place," Ryan said wistfully.

Angie glanced up at the stars. "It really is beautiful."

"No," he said. "I mean being here with you in my arms."

Angie sighed. She couldn't imagine anything better either.

"What do you say we do this together . . . forever?"

"What?" Angie gasped. She lifted up from his chest. "Are you saying what I think you're saying?" She couldn't believe her ears. Ryan shifted from underneath her and rolled her onto her back. He looked down at her with so much love in his eyes, it was almost more than Angie could bear.

"I know this isn't the traditional way—since I'm not on bended knee—but I figured how we got together wasn't all that traditional to begin with."

"That's true," she agreed, her heart racing.

"And I know you aren't into grand romantic gestures," he said with a raised brow.

"That's true, too." Although he had certainly worn her down, and she was loving the romance in this moment. Ryan reached into his pants, which were half hanging off the truck bed, and grabbed something from the pocket. He held it up to Angie.

"This was my great-grandmother's." It was an Asscher-cut diamond with a ruby flanking each side.

"It's stunning," she replied with reverence, reaching out to gently finger the band. While she was certainly no expert on diamonds, Angie had worked on enough engagement stories at *Celebrity Monger* to know what she was talking about.

"This morning, I told Mom I was going to propose soon, and she pulled the ring from her apron pocket. Said she knew the minute she met you, you were the one for me." Tears welled in Angie's eyes. "My great-grandmother wore this ring for most of her life. She and my great-grandpappy were married at the All Saints Church here in town and were happy together for sixty-three years."

"That's beyond beautiful."

"So, Angie Prince, will you spend the next sixty-three years with me? Will you marry me?" Ryan moved the ring toward Angie's left hand.

"Only the next sixty-three, huh?"

"Well, my belief in fate has recently gotten shaken a bit, and I'm not convinced you're the right girl for me. So sixty-three years is the longest commitment I can give you at this time. If it makes you feel any better, we can always play it by ear and add a few years on if it's working," he teased.

"Hmm. I suppose that makes sense. I'm not really a big believer in fate and love either," she tossed back, though she knew that was no longer true. Ryan knew it, too.

"So, what do you say? Will you marry me?"

"For sixty-three years?"

"Yes. A minimum of sixty-three years."

"Yes. Yes, I will marry you," she cried, pulling him down to her for a kiss. As he pulled back, he slid the ring onto her finger.

"We'll have to get it sized. If you want it."

"I do."

"Practicing for the wedding already?" He chuckled.

"Yes."

And they lived happily—and sappily—ever after. Angie, surprisingly, didn't want it any other way.

THE END

Keep reading for a sample of

Links

A second chance romance from Lisa Becker

Now Available

PROLOGUE

1 9 9 9

Charlotte Windham did a quick check of her teeth in the small compact mirror hanging from her key ring before knocking on the oversized wooden door. She undoubtedly had some remnants from lunch trapped within the metal wires of her braces. She pulled out a piece of apple peel from her right incisor and patted down her dark brown hair which, despite seeming an impossibility, was both simultaneously stringy and frizzy. She let out a loud exhale and knocked on the door.

A housekeeper, wearing a grey uniform, opened the door and welcomed her in. She led her past a formal entry and proper living room into the kitchen –a large, modern space with granite countertops, light wooden cabinets and enough kitchen gadgets to stock an upscale home goods store. Despite coming here twice a week for the past three months to tutor the Stephens brothers, Charlotte always stared in awe at the amazing home which was such a far contrast from the small two bedroom apartment she shared with her mom.

"The boys will be right down," said Norma kindly, gesturing to the kitchen counter which housed an array of soft drinks and snacks. Charlotte fidgeted with the silver locket around her neck –a gift from her father who died in Somalia when she was a young girl while serving in the Marines. Before she could dwell on it further, Garrett and Marcus bounded down the stairs and into the kitchen.

"You're such a wuss." Garrett punched Marcus in the arm.

"Dude!" Marcus countered, reaching out to swat his twin brother, but finding him already out of reach. "Oh, hey Charlotte."

"Hi, Marcus." Walking up, Charlotte gave him a little wave. "Hi Garrett," she breathed, looking at him for a nanosecond, before shifting her eyes to the floor.

"Oh hey, Glasses," Garrett casually tossed out. Charlotte instinctively adjusted the oversized black frames perched atop her nose. The glasses were a necessity since she was eight. While she would have loved to get contact lenses, they were a luxury her mother couldn't afford. She looked through the slightly smudged lenses and took in the image before her.

Marcus and Garrett Stephens were identical twins but couldn't have been more different in Charlotte's eyes.

At age sixteen, both Stephens brothers were already five foot nine and if their growth patterns and genetics were on track, they were well on their way to being more than six feet tall. Hazel eyes were offset by dark eyelashes, the kind women yearn for. Straight white teeth were the centerpiece of a dazzling smile punctuated by a large dimple on the left cheek.

To the untrained eye, it was difficult to tell them apart save for the small cleft in Garrett's chin, which she mused must be a mark left by the gods to name him as one of their own. To Charlotte, he was a god of perfection (unless you counted his lackluster academic performance.)

The personality differences between the twins were a bit starker than the physical ones. Both boys were exceptionally ambitious about their future goals. Garrett was determined to be a professional golfer. As a junior, he was already the star player of his high school team. The intense schedule of practice, private lessons, matches and rigorous weight training sessions coupled with his disinterest in school left him teetering precariously between a pass and fail in several classes, most notably, English. Without keeping his grade to at least a C, he would be forced off the team, on the bench and out of the sightline of those who could make his dreams of playing college and, one day, professional golf, a reality. Hence his need for a tutor -Charlotte.

Mr. and Mrs. Stephens had originally hired a local teacher to assist Garrett, but found the attractive young woman to be too much of a distraction. When Lindsay, their daughter, brought Charlotte over to work on a school newspaper project, they quickly realized the mousy teenager would pose no distraction to Garrett and would serve as the perfect tutor because the two were in the same English class.

Marcus, on the other hand, was determined to go to a top college and medical school. Though he earned high marks in all his classes, he wouldn't be guaranteed acceptance without a higher score on the reading and writing portion of the SATs. Charlotte would serve a dual purpose in helping both brothers, as she had earned one of the top scores in the state on her SATs and was recently honored at a school assembly.

So twice a week, Charlotte would spend an hour helping Garrett with class assignments and an hour with Marcus working on SAT prep.

"Dude. Just ask her to prom. What's the worst that can happen?" Garrett grabbed a handful of chips from a bowl and shoved them in his mouth.

"Uh, she could say no and humiliate me in front of everyone," Marcus replied. "Enough about me. You going to take Gabriella?"

"Nah. Already tapped that."

"One and done, huh?" Marcus smiled wryly.

"Yeah. You know me. Love the chase; hate the commitment."

Charlotte cleared her throat, reminding them she was indeed neither invisible nor deaf. They both looked at her and she grinned at them, gesturing with her head to the table.

"You go first. I got a call to make," said Garrett. "Let me show you how it's done." Marcus sat at the table and pulled out his SAT prep workbook. Charlotte sat next to him and smiled.

"Let's get started with page sixty-two today," she began as Norma continued to tidy up the kitchen. Marcus looked at the question and studied the multiple choice responses. Meanwhile, Charlotte glanced at Garrett, who pulled out his cell phone while cracking open a diet soda.

"Hey Christy. It's Garrett." Marcus turned the page to Charlotte, who nodded in acknowledgment as he selected the correct answer.

"Nothing. Just hanging out. What about you?" continued Garrett.

"Remember the root words we talked about last week," Charlotte advised Marcus, while maintaining an ear to Garrett's conversation. Marcus continued to go through the options.

"Listen, I really liked the way your hair looked, all pulled up in a bun today. I was wondering if you'd wear it like that when we go to the prom together. Whadaya say? Wanna go with me?" Garrett crooned smoothly into the phone. Charlotte sighed and looked at Garrett longingly, not wishing he would notice her hair as it was a mess most of the time, but that he would at least notice *her*.

"Yeah? Cool," said Garrett. Marcus tilted his head to the side in a few quick bursts, ushering Garrett out of the room

"Perfunctory. Is that the right answer?" Marcus said to Charlotte, whose eyes had followed Garrett to the living room. His question snapped her back to the task at hand.

"Yes. That's correct," she said, faking a smile. The hour dragged on as Charlotte wrapped her head around the fact there was no chance -ever -she would go to the prom with Garrett, let alone have him notice her. Once her time with Marcus was done, he shut his practice book and grabbed his soda from the table.

"Thanks, Charlotte. See you at school tomorrow," he said before walking out of the kitchen and shouting, "You're up, loser!"

"No, no, no. Watch your language, Mr. Marcus," chastised Norma, who was in the kitchen preparing stir fry vegetables for dinner. She had started working as a nanny for the Stephens when Garrett and Marcus were babies and stayed on as a housekeeper as they grew. Marcus rolled his eyes, but with his back turned to Norma so she didn't see.

Garrett came into the kitchen a few minutes later -late as usual. Charlotte straightened herself up and pushed her hair back off her face and her glasses up higher on her nose. She smiled at him. He reluctantly sat down and took out a spiral notebook and his copy of *A Tree Grows in Brooklyn.*

"Can we only do a half hour today? I've got plans to meet the guys at the gym." Before she could answer, Norma chimed in.

"No, no, Mr. Garrett. You know the rules. One hour." Norma shook her head. Garrett scowled at her as he was now on the receiving end of a finger wag from Norma. "You know your parents say school is very important."

"Yeah, yeah." He turned to Charlotte. "So, where do we start, Glasses?"

"Well, what Norma just said is a perfect segue into talking about the themes of the book, one of which is the important role education plays in Francie's life."

"Uh huh," he said, walking over to the bowl of chips and bringing it to the table.

"Why don't you find three places in the book illustrating why or how education is important to Francie."

Garrett exhaled loudly, stuck his pencil in his mouth, and flopped open his notebook, noisily shuffling the papers until finding a blank sheet.

While he poured through the text, slightly huffing with annoyance, Lindsay walked into the kitchen. In strong contrast to her brothers, Lindsay was a petite and bubbly girl who favored her mother's looks –a perfect blonde bob and bright green eyes.

"Hi Charlotte," she said, making eyes at her like she knew Charlotte was enjoying her proximity to Garrett. Charlotte's eyes bugged out and she shook her head, warning Lindsay from saying anything. Lindsay just grinned at her and giggled. "Come up to my room when you're done."

"Okay," replied Charlotte as Lindsay walked away. Garrett continued to write on his paper and let out a loud huff, realizing he had made an error. He grabbed for an eraser and grazed Charlotte's hand as he did.

Every stringy and frizzy hair on the back of Charlotte's neck stood up on end. She let out a shaky exhale and tried to calm her emotions. Just his slightest touch –accidental though it was –set her heart afire. If only he would see her as anything but a brain in oversized black frames.

ONE

GARRETT
PRESENT DAY

Damn! I'm late...again. You'd think with nothing to do, I'd get my act together enough to be on time for a family lunch. I fell asleep on the couch after my rigorous night's activities with Dani, spelled with a heart over the "i."

She's a Laker girl. It took me three weeks, and a dinner reservation at Genevieve, to convince her to go out with me, but it was worth the effort. She was insatiable in bed and her flexibility was a total turn on. Without much sleep last night, it's no wonder I passed out on the couch after my morning workout.

I rush past the valet and glance at the incoming call on my cell phone thinking it's Mom checking on my arrival status. It's not Mom. It's only been a few hours since I slipped out of Dani's bed before she woke up this morning and she's already calling me for the second time today. I let it go to voicemail again and figure she'll get the hint. Then again, she likely won't.

Dani with a heart over the "i" isn't the brightest bulb in the marquee.

As I race to the restaurant, I scowl knowing Mom's going to have my head. Actually, she's probably used to it by now. I'm surprised they don't give me fake arrival times knowing I'm always ten minutes behind.

I rush through the revolving door of the restaurant, through the bar, and smack into a woman. She brushes against my bum shoulder and the pain burns right through me. Minding the manners Mom hammered into me from a young age, I mutter, "Sorry," when I'm honestly not. I look down and notice something familiar about her.

"Hi, Garrett," she says, sharing a small smile. "It's been a long time. How are you?"

"Um. I'm fine." My brows furrow as I wrack my brain trying to figure out who the hell this woman is. She's short, about five two and roughly my age. I glance down and notice full, round breasts, slightly wide hips and thick thighs. Not my usual type, so I'm pretty sure I haven't slept with her. At least I don't have to worry about that embarrassing scene. She's got chocolate brown eyes, looking at me with warmth. "And...how are you?" Shaking my head I am still trying to place her.

"I'm doing well," she replies, her smile growing.

"I'm glad to hear that," I say, trying to be polite and end this awkward reunion that clearly has me clueless.

"Well...I guess I should go." She turns back and waves to a woman sitting in a far booth of the restaurant. On further inspection, she's waved to Lindsay, my sister, who of course made it to our family lunch on time. Seated with her are my parents, with Mom frowning at me and shaking her head. Like she didn't expect I would be late. Marcus isn't here yet either. Guess the twin thing really does run deep.

"You know Lindsay?" I ask her.

"Uh, yeah," she says, with a small chuckle and a noticeable hint of sarcasm.

"My parents?"

"Of course." She shakes her head slightly like it's hitting her I have no damn clue who she is. Then she confirms my suspicions and just lays it on the line. "You don't know who I am, do you?" Her eyes are alight with humor.

"Umm. I'm afraid you have me at a disadvantage," I splutter, rubbing my hand behind my neck –my tell –before flashing her my most charming, dimpled smile. Before she can respond, a lady in her mid-sixties with salt and pepper hair wearing an outfit appropriate for someone twenty years younger –but this is LA after all –walks over.

"Pardon the interruption," she begins. "I would just be kicking myself if I got home and didn't take advantage of telling you what a big fan I am."

"Oh, thank you," I say, turning on the faux charm I reserve for situations such as this.

"My husband and I loved your book." The lady turns fully toward this mystery woman. "I wish I had it with me for you to sign. Maybe I could get your autograph on something else?" I cock my head to the side and watch Mystery Woman. She turns back toward the elderly lady and smiles sincerely.

"Sure. I'd be happy to sign something."

The lady reaches into her oversized zebra-print bag and produces a pen and small notepad. She hands them to Mystery Woman and turns to me, smiling.

"Who should I make this out to?" asks Mystery Woman.

"Donna and Frank. Your *dear friends*, Donna and Frank."

"My... dear... friends... Donna... and... Frank," Mystery Woman murmurs aloud as she writes a note. Watching her autograph the note, I can't help the grin spreading across my face. Once she finishes, Donna reads through the note, her eyes widening with delight.

"Thank you, Charley," she says.

"My pleasure," replies Charley –Charley? –who looks tickled.

"Charley?" I rack my brain to no avail.

"Yes," replies Donna with pride. "You are standing with the brilliant novelist Charley Windham." She turns back to Charley before walking away. "Thank you again, dear."

"Charley Windham?"

"Uh-huh," responds Charley, giving me a look like I should piece it together.

"Charley Windham. Why does that name sound so familiar?" I rub my hand on the back of my neck while Charley looks at me with amusement. "Wait, you're Charley Windham. Who wrote *The Crossing Guard?*" Charley shakes her head and laughs.

"That's me." Charley giggles, unable to control the wide smile spreading across her face.

"Yes. Now I know. I read your book. In fact, everyone on the tour read it. You couldn't walk around a locker room or airport terminal without seeing someone with it in their hands."

"That's nice to hear." She grins at me with her head tilted and nodding her head slightly up and down, giving me the impression she's waiting for me to say more.

"That explains who you are, and I get you would know who I am, but how do you know my family?"

"That is the question of the moment, isn't it?" She smiles smugly.

"You're enjoying this, aren't you?"

"Immensely." She is grinning unabashedly.

I look back over at my parents and sister and see my brother Marcus walk in through the restaurant's back entrance. After a quick exchange, Lindsay points to where Charley and I are standing. Marcus waves to Charley and she waves back.

"Oh, you know my ugly as shit brother too?"

"Ugly as shit? You're identical twins," she laughs.

"Nah." I shake my head with a playful sneer. "I got the looks. He got the brains."

"You got the looks?" She watches me with a raised brow.

"Yep. All of 'em."

"I suppose you got all of the humility too?" I can hear the humor in her voice.

"Seems more like humiliation these days." I rub the back of my neck and look down at my shoes. I really messed things up and now I don't know if my career is over.

"Hey, don't knock yourself. Not your fault you have shoulder issues." She places a hand on my arm and her slight touch causes all my blood to rush south.

"You follow my career?" I ask, my spirits surprisingly improving. There's something about this woman that's got me intrigued and I don't just mean 'cause I can't place how I know her.

"I've been known to glance at the sports page now and then," she says with smiling eyes.

"So, how did you say you know my brother again?" Marcus, his wife Abbey, and Lindsay start to walk over to us.

"I didn't."

"You're not going to tell me."

"I'm finding it quite entertaining you don't know who I am," she says again.

"Of course I know who you are," I scoff.

"You do?"

"Yes. You're the charming and talented writer having dinner with me on Saturday night." Charley lets out a nervous giggle and glances down at the floor and damn, if that's not the cutest thing I've ever seen.

"You want to have dinner with me on Saturday?" she says on a breath and I wonder how she would breathe my name as she's coming undone beneath me. Before I can respond, Marcus places his hand on her shoulder.

"Well aren't you a sight for sore eyes." Charley turns toward him and Marcus scoops her up into a big hug.

"Good to see you, Marcus. This must be your wife." She turns to the short red head with wide green eyes and a full smile standing between Marcus and Lindsay.

"Yeah, this is Abbey," says Marcus, turning to the side, allowing the small woman to shake Charley's hand.

"Wow. I'm a huge fan," she begins, grasping Charley's hand and pumping it furiously. "The *Crossing Guard* was my favorite book of last year. My book club spent hours discussing it."

"Oh, thank you," says Charley, with the same genuine appreciation she showed to Donna a few minutes ago.

"I didn't realize Marcus knew you. I probably would have begged him to ask you to come meet with us," Abbey continues, still holding onto Charley's hand.

"Oh, believe me, she doesn't owe me any favors. It's the other way around. If it weren't for Charlotte here, I probably wouldn't have gotten into a good college," he says to Abbey.

"Charlotte?" I repeat.

"Of course. Charlotte Windham. You know, our high school English tutor," he says, looking at me like I'm a dumbass.

Charlotte Windham. Charlotte Windham. Then it hits me. "Oh, Glasses. You're Glasses." I smile widely, proud of myself for finally putting it together.

"Yep. I'm *Glasses*," Charlotte sighs loudly. "Well, I need to get going. Great catching up with you all again and nice to meet you Abbey."

"I'm sorry, Charlotte," says Lindsay, shooting daggers at me with her eyes. *What is that death stare for*, I wonder.

"It's okay. Um...give me a call if you want to grab lunch. I'm waiting for a manuscript back from my editor, so I've got a ton of free time." With that, she turns and walks away.

"You're an idiot." Lindsay shakes her head and scowls at me.

"What? What did I do?" I'm flummoxed.